T0130075

# SHOOT
# THE DOG

A NOVEL

## BRAD SMITH

SCRIBNER

New York   London   Toronto   Sydney   New Delhi

SCRIBNER
A Division of Simon & Schuster, Inc.
1230 Avenue of the Americas
New York, NY 10020

First Scribner hardcover edition August 2013

SCRIBNER and design are registered trademarks of The Gale Group, Inc.,
used under license by Simon & Schuster, Inc., the publisher of this work.

For information about special discounts for bulk purchases, please contact
Simon & Schuster Special Sales at 1-866-506-1949 or business@simonandschuster.com.

The Simon & Schuster Speakers Bureau can bring authors to your live event.
For more information or to book an event contact the Simon & Schuster Speakers Bureau
at 1-866-248-3049 or visit our website at www.simonspeakers.com.

Manufactured in the United States of America

1   3   5   7   9   10   8   6   4   2

Library of Congress Control Number: 2013017221

ISBN: 978-1-5011-3788-4
ISBN: 978-1-4391-9758-5 (ebook)

*Again, for Bob and Jean*

"You can't run away from trouble. There ain't no place that far."

*Uncle Remus*

# ONE

When Virgil Cain came in from baling hay it was three minutes past noon and the phone in the kitchen was ringing. Jake Norsworthy from Woodstock Saddlery was on the line, saying that Virgil's harness was ready for pickup. Jake couldn't know it, but with the ten-acre hayfield behind the barn baled and ready to be loaded onto the wagons, his timing couldn't have been better. Virgil cut a thick slice of roast beef from the night before and laid it between two pieces of bread, slapped on some mustard, and ate in the truck on his way to the saddle shop. The day was hot and growing hotter, a carbon copy to the day before and the day before that. There'd been no rain for nearly a month. The truck had air-conditioning that had undoubtedly worked at one time but not in the years that Virgil had owned the vehicle. He drove with the windows down, his left hand idly keeping beat on the outside mirror to a Kristofferson song from the country radio station.

He'd picked up the old harness at an auction near Rhinebeck a couple of months earlier. He had reluctantly inherited two Percheron draft horses from area vet Mary Nelson last year, and since then he'd been waiting for Mary to find a home for them. In truth, he had pretty much given up on the notion of Mary finding a home for them. The animals had arrived at Virgil's farm emaciated and sickly, like most of the horses Mary had shown up with over the past several years, and Virgil—with the vet's help—had nursed them back to

1

health, at which point Mary had confidently predicted that someone would adopt the two, taking them off Virgil's hands. The two draft horses, a mare and a gelding, each weighed over twelve hundred pounds now, and they were impressive to look at—their coats a gleaming reddish brown, their manes and tails a strawberry blond. They passed their days picking at the grass in Virgil's pasture field in front of the barn or standing lazily beneath the large sugar maple in the corner, alongside the dozen or so other horses Mary had delivered over the years.

Virgil had recently named the two Bob and Nelly after a team of mules he'd seen Gabby Hayes driving in a movie. He had never bestowed a name on a single animal on the farm in the past—none of the other horses, none of his beef cattle, not even the half-feral barn cats who kept the granary free of rats and mice. But he named the Percherons because he intended to put them to work, and—in Virgil's mind— the hired help needed to be called something.

He'd found a book at the library in Saugerties that described in considerable detail how to break draft horses to harness. When first dropping the Percherons off, Mary had mentioned that the previous owner had used them in country plowing competitions, when he wasn't starving them or mistreating them in general. If that was true, then the two animals had forgotten most of what they'd learned. Maybe they had mental blocks regarding that part of their history. Virgil couldn't blame them if they did.

The book, *How to Break Your Horse to Harness,* was written by a man named Robert Leroy Smythe and published in 1927. The librarian had offered to do a computer search of the neighboring library branches for Virgil, in the hope of turning up a more modern volume on the subject, but Virgil had declined, reasoning that whatever methods had worked in 1927 were likely to still be effective today. Unless, of course, a person was dealing with some newly developed computerized horse, and there was nothing about Bob or Nelly that suggested this was the case.

The harness he'd bought at the auction was dried out and brittle but mostly salvageable. Virgil had cleaned the leather with saddle soap and then lubricated it with mink oil. The hardware was brass and had shined up nicely. He'd first hitched the animals up singly, walking them around the barnyard, getting them used to stopping and going, and turning one way or the other. Neither seemed at all accustomed to the harness, which may have been different from the setup they were used to, but they did appear to recognize the prompts—"whoa" to stop, "giddyup" to go, and "haw" and "gee" to turn left and right. The author Smythe made note of the fact that in England the commands for turning were reversed. Intending to keep to Ulster County, or at the very least to the confines of North America, Virgil saw no reason to burden Bob and Nelly with that information.

The first time he'd put the horses in tandem, a week ago, Bob had headed left for the water trough just as Nelly was turning right, and Bob's pole strap snapped in half. Virgil took the complete harness in to Jake Norsworthy that day and told him to replace whatever was needed.

The leather shop was on the west edge of town, a half mile off 212. Virgil walked in to find Jake talking to a young blonde woman who was holding a western saddle in both arms as if it were a newborn lamb. The woman's long hair was pulled back in a ponytail and she wore tight jeans and cowboy boots and a T-shirt with a silk screen of Dwight Yoakam across the front.

"Merle Sanders said she came into Kettle & Crock for breakfast this morning and was just as nice as could be," the woman was saying.

Virgil nodded past the woman to Jake.

"I've heard that about her," Jake said, returning Virgil's nod.

The young woman hadn't heard Virgil come in and she turned to see him now, the ponytail whipping around her neck. "Olivia Burns is in town," she announced.

"I see," Virgil said.

"The movie actress," Jake elaborated.

Virgil nodded again, trying to think of something to say that might suggest some interest in the subject on his part. He couldn't come up with a damn thing. "So my harness is ready?" he asked.

From the saddlery he drove to the co-op, where he bought a couple rolls of binder twine, enough to finish the season. The girl working the cash register was maybe sixteen, a high school student no doubt. When she gave Virgil his change she told him that Olivia Burns was in town.

Back at the farm Virgil pulled the hay wagon from the drive shed. Earlier that month he'd removed the steel tongue from the wagon and replaced it with a double whippletree of chain and oak. Taking a couple of nylon leads from a peg on the wall, he walked into the front field to retrieve the two draft horses, and then he led them to the wagon, where he fitted them both with Sweeney collars and the double harness. He hooked them to the hay wagon and when he said giddyup, Bob and Nelly did just that.

Once they were in the hayfield, it took a while to get the timing down, although that was Virgil's fault as much as the horses'. He was every bit as green at this as they were, and maybe more so. The pace was the tricky thing. The team needed to walk slowly enough that Virgil had time to toss the hay bales onto the wagon without falling behind. The problem came at the end of the field, when the horses turned back toward the barn. Heading for home, they immediately sped up, at one point breaking into a trot. Virgil had to grab the reins and slow them to a walk. Every few minutes he whoa-ed the team and jumped up onto the wagon to build the load. After an hour or so, things fell into a rhythm; by the time the first wagon was full, Bob and Nelly were working fairly well, as if there existed in them some sort of muscle memory from their plowing days. Virgil left that load by the barn, shifted horses and harness to an empty wagon, and went back into the field. The heat was oppressive but there was a breeze from the east that made working tolerable. When the third wagon was loaded, it was nearly suppertime.

As Virgil led the wagon and team around the barn and into the yard, he saw Claire sitting on the side porch of the house, drinking a bottle of beer and watching him with an amused expression on her face, as if Virgil were an eight-year-old who had managed to cobble together a go-cart that actually rolled.

Virgil unhooked the team and led them into the pasture field, where he rubbed them down quickly with a gunnysack and then rewarded them both with a bucket of grain. Claire's expression remained virtually unchanged as he made his way to the house. She was wearing khaki pants and a white cotton shirt, the sleeves rolled to her elbows. Her dark hair fell loosely to her shoulders. She was tanned and relaxed and looked beautiful. She had a job that could be stressful at times, but Virgil always swore that the tension drained from her the moment she pulled in the driveway.

"What are you smiling at?" he asked.

"You."

"Did I do something funny?"

She took a drink of beer. "You and your horses."

She must have gone into the house and retrieved a beer for him when she saw him coming. She handed it over.

"Diesel fuel for the tractor is expensive," he said when he'd had a drink. "And it's about time those nags earned their keep."

"You forgot to mention your carbon footprint."

"That too."

"Or maybe you're just stuck in the nineteenth century," Claire said.

"I've been stuck in worse places."

"You certainly have."

They sat quietly for a time. The sun had reached the tree-tops to the west but there were still a couple hours of day-light left. Bob and Nelly walked along the fence line to the far corner of the field, where the rest of the orphan herd was grazing. It seemed to Virgil that the two draft horses moved differently now, with an element of pride, now that there was a change in their status on the farm. It had to be his imagina-tion. What would horses know of the dignity of work?

He looked toward the barn, where the three wagonloads of hay were parked. Earlier he'd backed the elevator up to the mow window and mounted the electric motor to the base.

"You feel like a workout?"

She followed his eyes to the wagons. She'd helped him mow bales in the past. "Sure."

"I'll cook you a steak afterwards," he said.

"You got a deal."

"You want the mow or the wagon?" he asked.

"Nice try," she said, smiling. "It's a hundred degrees up there. I'm staying on the wagon."

It took them an hour and a half to unload the hay. When Virgil came down out of the mow, he was shirtless, his torso drenched, the sweat mixed with dust and chaff. Claire had pulled her hair back in a ponytail before they'd started and her face and neck were streaked with dirt and sweat. She removed the gloves Virgil had given her and laid them on the wagon.

"You hungry?" he asked.

"I could use a shower first. So could you."

"You want to save some water?"

The shared shower led to the bedroom, and then back to the shower. It was full dark when Virgil grilled the steaks on the porch. Claire found enough stuff in the fridge to make a salad and she cut thick slices of zucchini to cook on the grill with the beef. She opened a bottle of red wine she'd brought with her and they ate outside at the picnic table. The drought had knocked the mosquito population down and the heat had relented slightly when the sun disappeared, so it was nice sitting out on the lawn.

"So how much money did you save today?" Claire asked. "You know—leaving the tractor in the shed?"

"Hell, I don't know," Virgil replied. "Not much." He glanced at her, then looked away.

Claire studied his profile in the dim light from the porch lamp. He was aware of her scrutiny, and as always it made him uncomfortable. He didn't like to be the center of attention, even here, on his own property, alone with a woman he'd been in the shower with an hour ago.

"When are your taxes due?"

"Middle of the month," he said.

"I can help you with some money."

"No," he said.

"Why not?" she asked, even though she'd known the answer before asking.

"Because that's not the way this works."

Claire had a drink of wine. "Is everybody from the eighteen hundreds as stubborn as you?"

He smiled at that. "Hand that bottle over, will you?"

She did and watched as he poured. The conversation about money was finished, she knew, whether she liked it or not.

"You weren't in Woodstock today by chance," she said.

"I was, actually."

"Olivia Burns is in town."

"So I hear," Virgil said.

# TWO

Sam Sawchuk had arranged to meet with Olivia Burns at noon at Bernie's, a bistro on Main Street in Woodstock. The actress was already there when Sam walked in, sitting alone at a table by the windows while the waitstaff gathered by the counter and stared at her. Olivia wore loose cotton pants and a plain white T-shirt, and she had a well-thumbed copy of the novel *Frontier Woman* in front of her.

Sam had put on a few pounds of late and it bothered her when she allowed herself a moment to think about it, and particularly on days like this, when she was required to meet with a quite beautiful and slender actress nearly ten years her junior. So, in spite of the heat, she dressed that morning in black leggings and a large black sweater that nearly reached her thighs. She told herself she would begin working out once filming began but knew goddamn well it would never happen. Maybe during post. She'd had her hair cut the day before and had some auburn highlights added to the chestnut brown. She still looked good, and though she was obviously not as fetching as the woman she was meeting for lunch, Sam had always considered herself voluptuous—and that was something Olivia Burns couldn't lay claim to. Sam knew, from considerable experience, that men dug women with a little flesh on their bones.

She walked across the restaurant now and the two women embraced. Sam removed her baseball cap, also black, with

*Monkey Sex* scripted in red across the front, and placed it on the table. She had a leather carryall, which she put on the floor.

"What's Monkey Sex?" Olivia asked when they were seated.

"A film Robb and I did last year," Sam said. "Super cool. About the games people play, in relationships, you know? We're just finishing it. Trying to get it into Sundance."

"I'd like to see it."

"Well, it's still pretty rough."

A waitress, no more than twenty-one, approached with menus and a pitcher of water. She poured for them both.

"I'll give you a couple of minutes," she said.

"Thank you," Olivia said.

"I love your movies," the waitress said.

Olivia thanked her again and she left. Sam picked her menu up, glanced through it without really looking at it. She put it aside and looked around the nearly empty restaurant. A blackboard on the far wall listed the daily specials. Sam read the board, then turned back to Olivia, her eyes finally settling on the book.

"How many times have you read it?"

"I guess twice all the way through," Olivia said. "Now I just jump around, here and there."

Sam nodded. "Robb and I were talking last night about how inspired we are just being here. We love the country! We just love it. The trees and . . . everything. It brings the world of the book so close. You can almost taste it. This is going to be great. This is going to be . . . fucking great."

"I'm looking forward to it."

Sam opened the menu again, and then closed it once more. She exhaled. "Here's the thing," she said. "Peter Dunmore is out."

The announcement caught Olivia completely off guard.

"He quit?" she asked.

"Well . . . not exactly."

"What happened, then? He was one of the reasons I signed on for this. He seemed so into it when we met in LA. And the guy's an amazing director."

"I totally agree," Sam said. "Totally. The problem is . . . well, it's USN. They've got a problem with him. I don't know what it is, and as usual they're not saying. It could be political, it could be personal . . . you know how it is with these fuckers."

"It's a feature," Olivia said. "Why is USN calling the shots? What's a network have to do with it?"

"They have first-run rights for TV," Sam said. "They're putting up a big chunk of the budget."

Olivia fell silent as the waitress returned.

"Um," Olivia said. "I'm just going to have tea, okay?"

"We have herbal."

"That's fine."

The waitress looked at Sam.

"I'll have the chicken wrap," Sam said, indicating the specials listed on the wall. "And coffee."

Olivia picked up her copy of *Frontier Woman* and turned it over in her hands. "Shit. This isn't good."

"I know," Sam said. "It sucks. I feel so bad for Peter."

"There's no chance—"

"No. It's done."

Olivia sighed and placed the book on the table. "So we don't have a director," she said. "And we start shooting in a week."

"Well, we lucked out there," Sam said at once. "Robb has agreed to take it on."

"Who is Robb again?"

Now it was Sam who was surprised. "Robb is my husband. We had dinner in New York last week. He . . . um . . . sat beside you."

"Right," Olivia said. "Of course. And he . . . he's a director?"

"He's a very good director," Sam assured her. "He actually directed *Monkey Sex* last fall. The film I told you about, that's going to Sundance."

"You said you were trying for Sundance."

"Well, yeah. But it looks promising."

"What else has he directed?"

"Well, he did a very personal little film . . . um, that he wrote *and* directed, in fact . . . about his experiences going to a private school. Sort of a coming-of-age thing, about this young man who didn't quite fit in. You know, he wasn't a jock or a great student, but he was very sensitive and artistic and—"

"What was it called?"

"It was called *Days at Dundurn.*"

Olivia shrugged. "I don't remember it."

"It never actually had a theatrical release," Sam said. "But it was at the Minneapolis Film Festival. And it was at Charlotte too. You know, North Carolina."

The waitress brought Olivia's tea then, setting the ceramic pot on the table along with a cup.

"Do you need lemon or anything?" she asked.

"This is fine," Olivia said.

"Would it be, like, totally uncool if I asked for your autograph?"

"Not at all."

The waitress had a piece of paper ready, in the event that it wasn't, like, totally uncool to ask. Olivia got the woman's name and signed the paper. Sam waited impatiently, fingering the black ball cap.

"Robb loves the book," she said when the waitress had gone. "Loves it. And the truth is, he's helped out a lot with the script. You know, story editing. Shaping it."

"Stuart never mentioned that," Olivia said.

"He wouldn't," Sam said. She shook her head, rolling her eyes toward the ceiling. "Writers, you know?"

Olivia looked out the window, to the busy sidewalk. It was tourist season and the streets were full.

"Robb's spent a lot of time in the country," Sam said. "His family had a place in the Poconos growing up and he used to canoe . . . and all that. I think we're really lucky to have him." She hesitated. "He absolutely loves the book."

"You mentioned that," Olivia said, turning back to Sam now.

"And Levi's totally behind Robb too," Sam hurried to add. "I heard you guys had dinner in New York?"

"We did," Olivia said. Her tone grew flat.

"What?" Sam asked.

"Nothing," Olivia said. "Actually, I was wondering—did Levi really go to Yale?"

"Yale?" Sam repeated, then recovered quickly. "You know, I think maybe he did. I seem to recall something like that. Smart guy, Levi Brown."

Olivia nodded. She didn't seem eager to pursue the subject and Sam was glad to let it pass.

"Robb's really eager to talk to you about the role of Martha. He wants to know how you see her." Sam took a drink of water. "He has a reputation as an actor's director."

She waited for some sort of response. Olivia poured tea into the cup and took a sip.

"I hope you're okay with this," Sam said. "Bottom line, we have to play the hand that USN dealt us. Those fuckers."

"I guess we have to."

"And you're good with it? Right?"

"I guess I have to be."

When she left the bistro, and her uneaten chicken wrap, in downtown Woodstock, Sam got into her car and headed back to New York City. Once on the thruway, she called Robb. He and Levi were scouting locations in the mountains west of Bearsville.

"Hey," he said. "How'd it go?"

"Good."

"She didn't freak?"

"No, she was fine," Sam said. "She, uh . . . she couldn't come right out and say it, obviously, but I don't think she was all that convinced that Dunmore was the right guy for this in the first place."

"And she's okay with me?"

"Oh yeah. She mentioned that she thought you were really smart when we had dinner in New York. She said . . . and I'm quoting here . . . she said, 'Robb really gets the book, doesn't he?' So there you go."

"That's cool."

"It is," Sam said. "So where are you, honey?"

"Some back road somewhere. Levi found a place on the web where they do Civil War reenactments, so we're heading there now. They have log cabins and a blacksmith shop and all that."

"Levi the Yale graduate?"

"What?"

"Nothing," Sam said. "Just Levi embellishing again. I'll tell you later."

"Where are you?" Robb asked.

"On my way to the city. I have USN at four. I'll keep you updated."

"Later, babe."


The United States Network had its east coast offices on Madison Avenue. When Sam was ushered in to the boardroom, Alan Hammond and Justine Warner were already there, sitting at a long glass table. Sam had arranged the meeting over the phone that morning from Woodstock. Alan Hammond was his usual jovial self, but Justine seemed a little miffed at being summoned on short notice.

"Peter Dunmore is out," Sam told them.

"What do you mean—out?" Justine said.

"He's no longer on the film," Sam said.

"Why not?"

"That's a good question," Sam said. "The short answer is that Olivia Burns doesn't want him."

Sam watched as the two producers exchanged glances. There was a bowl of fruit on the table and she leaned forward to take an apple.

"At dinner the other night she said she was thrilled to be working with him," Alan said. "This is a bit of a turnaround, isn't it?"

"I would say so," Sam agreed. "Actors, you know?"

With that, Justine got up and left. Sam wasn't surprised, although she'd been hoping she would stay, that they could keep the discussion within the confines of the room. She watched the door close and then turned to Alan, determined to keep the conversation moving, with or without Justine.

"I know this is a shock but overall it's a good thing. If we have a clash of egos, it's best to figure that out *before* we start shooting, not in the middle."

"Is that what this is—a clash of egos?" Alan asked.

"Shit, I don't know. I'm as confused by it as you are."

Alan nodded, then got to his feet and moved to a sideboard, where a carafe of coffee sat. He was a big man, pushing three hundred pounds, and had a lumbering gait like a cartoon bear. He poured a cup for himself before turning to Sam.

"Coffee?"

"No, thank you," she said and took a bite of the apple.

Alan returned and sat down opposite her. He asked what the weather was like in the Woodstock area, even though it was only a ninety-minute drive away. Sam had always felt comfortable with Alan. He was a kind man, she thought, and she considered him an ally. He'd been very positive about *Frontier Woman* from the start. It was Justine who had played devil's advocate, suggesting that the film would have a tough time finding an audience in the eighteen to twenty-four demographic. Sam's response to that had been emphatic— Olivia Burns would deliver the audience.

Sam had finished her apple and was looking for somewhere to discard the core when Justine returned and sat down at the head of the table.

"Peter says you slashed his salary."

"That had nothing to do with this," Sam said. "That was a contractual thing that his agent fucked up royally. We had a preliminary agreement contingent upon the final budget. I have no idea what the agent told him, but in the end, the numbers didn't mesh with whatever the hell he promised Peter. Trust me, that is a separate issue from this."

"Not according to Peter," Justine said.

"What was I going to do?" Sam asked. "Tell the man that his lead actress didn't want him on the movie? Sorry, but I'm not that callous. Besides, he would have gone running to the press and all of a sudden we have all kinds of negative publicity on a film we haven't started shooting yet. No thank you."

Alan had a drink of coffee and carefully placed the cup on the table. It looked like a toy in his massive hands. "Is there something we can do?" he asked. "Run interference between Peter and Olivia, maybe sit them down together? And then find some extra money for the salary discrepancy?"

"Forget it," Justine said. "Peter won't come back. He's pissed and he's moved on."

Sam exhaled heavily and shook her head.

"So where do we go from here?" Justine asked.

"Well, we actually got lucky," Sam said. "I managed to talk Robb into directing it."

"Who?"

"Robb Fetterman."

"He's . . . your husband, right?" Justine asked.

"He is," Sam said. "And he's one of the producers, of course. He's been story-editing the script, so he knows it inside out. We really lucked out on that count. I mean—he can hit the ground running. We start shooting in a week."

"Has he directed anything?" Justine asked, her voice bordering on incredulous.

"Three features," Sam said. She continued quickly, "And some commercial stuff, some music videos. He has a great eye. Hey—he's an artist."

Alan was on his feet now, moving to the sideboard to place his empty coffee cup there. Justine had opened the laptop and was typing into it—checking out Robb, Sam surmised. Alan stepped over to Sam, picked up her discarded apple core, and turned to drop it into a wastebasket beneath the sideboard. Then he leaned across the table and gently closed Justine's laptop.

"USN is finished with this," he said. He smiled at Sam. "We wish you every success with the project."

# THREE

Virgil baled again the following morning once the heavy overnight dew had burned off the fields. By midafternoon, he had Bob and Nelly back in harness, drawing the wagons while he loaded the bales as he'd done the day before. An extra hand would have made the job much more efficient—one on the ground and the other on the wagon—but money was tight and Virgil couldn't afford to hire anybody, even for a couple of days.

As he had the night before, Virgil suspected that something had changed with the two draft horses. They took more willingly to the harness today and, once in the hayfield, they fell into the routine quickly and willingly. Maybe even eagerly. And Virgil could swear he caught Bob glancing with disdain over at the other horses left standing in the pasture in front of the barn, as if lording it over them that he was, quite literally, pulling his weight. There was a hierarchy in the herd that hadn't existed two days ago.

The hayfield ran from behind the barn to the side road that served as the southern boundary to the farm. Virgil and the team worked their way in that direction, gathering up the last of the hay at around five.

Making the turn for home, Virgil looked up to see two men standing on the gravel road, watching. There was a black Audi sedan parked behind them, the car idling, the windows up. Keeping the air going, Virgil surmised. One of the men, a stocky guy with streaked blond hair that fell artfully to his shoulders, was taking pictures of Virgil and the team with a digital camera. The other man was taller, dressed in black jeans and short Wellington boots and a faded plaid shirt. His dark hair was shorter but as carefully tousled, to Virgil's eyes, as his partner's leonine mane.

Virgil regarded them for a moment and then went back to work, whoa-ing the team so he could climb up and stack the bales. As he worked he heard one of the men shout hello, and he turned to see the pair attempting to climb the fence, looking like a couple of chimpanzees trying to ride a bicycle for the first time. They eventually found success, after the lion-hair freed the other's pant leg from the barbwire, and approached Virgil as he was jumping down from the wagon.

"These your horses?" the taller one asked.

Virgil turned to take a look at Bob and Nelly. "They're not my horses."

"Is your employer around?" the longhair asked, moving closer. Virgil saw now that he was heavily muscled, suggesting somebody who spent hours in the gym each day. His neck was thick and his shoulders knotted to a point that they seemed uncomfortable to carry around. He wore a snug T-shirt that showed off his biceps, and his walk was a rooster strut. Virgil had the immediate impression that when he wasn't in the gym, he was standing in front of a mirror.

"My employer?" Virgil repeated.

The longhair glanced at the taller one, shook his head slightly, presumably at Virgil's obtuseness. "Your employer. You know—your boss?"

"I haven't seen him," Virgil said. "Not in a long time."

The longhair fished a handful of business cards from his shirt pocket and offered one over. "I'm Levi Brown and this is

20

Robb Fetterman. We're making a movie in the area and we're out scouting locations. The film is a period piece. Um . . . do you know what that is?"

"You know, I think I do," Virgil said.

"The movie takes place in the 1840s," the man named Robb said. "I'm the director. What do you call those horses?"

"I call them Bob and Nelly," Virgil said.

The one calling himself Levi uttered a soft puff of exasperation. "What *kind* of horses are they?"

"Percherons."

"And they are considered . . . um . . . workhorses?" Robb asked.

"Today they are," Virgil said. "I wouldn't have called them that a week ago."

Levi glanced at Robb. "We need to talk to the owner. This guy isn't getting it."

Robb smiled at Virgil, then spoke slowly, as if explaining something to a child. "We might want to hire these horses for the film. You see, the movie takes place in the frontier days, when horses like these were commonly used for—" He stumbled then, searching for uses for bygone horses from bygone days.

"For what?" Virgil asked.

"Well, for work."

"You mean like pulling a plow, or yanking stumps, or hauling logs from the bush?" Virgil asked. "Or taking the family into town in a buckboard, or pulling a cutter in the winter, or bringing hay into the barn? You mean stuff like that?"

"Yeah," Robb said. "Stuff like that."

"I see what you're saying," Virgil said.

"If you could talk to your boss, we'd appreciate it," Levi said. "My cell number is on the card. We would pay, say, five hundred dollars a day for the use of the horses. Probably need them for a week or so."

"Five apiece?"

"For the two," Levi said.

Virgil shrugged. Robb was looking at the barn in the distance.

"How old is that barn?"

"Built in 1893," Virgil said. "According to the cornerstone."

Now Robb took a couple steps toward the building and held his palms forward at arm's length, thumbs touching. The classic director's pose.

"Look at that," he said to Levi. "Pull down those power lines and we got 1840, right there."

Levi stepped forward, crossed his beefy arms and had a studied look at the barn. His eyes narrowed as he presumably transported himself backward in time a hundred and seventy years. Finally he nodded, as if approving of whatever the hell his mind had conjured.

Still holding the pose, Robb looked toward Virgil. "I'm framing the shot."

"You're standing in horseshit."

Robb looked down and jumped back as if he'd stumbled into a nest of rattlesnakes rather than a little manure.

"For Chrissakes," he said, looking at his boots. "Do you have a towel or something?"

Virgil laughed. "I think I left my towel up at the barn."

"This fucking guy thinks he's funny," Levi said. He was finished with Virgil. "Have your boss call me, wise guy. You don't want me coming back and telling him that you cost him a chance to make some easy money."

"No, he might fire my ass," Virgil said. "That boss of mine."

"Right," Levi said.

The two of them turned and started for the fence.

"There's a gate over there," Virgil called after them. He pointed fifty yards along the fencerow. "As entertaining as it is watching you two try to climb that fence, you might be better off using it."

They did as he advised, heading off in the direction he'd indicated, without looking back or even acknowledging the suggestion. After Virgil had thrown the last of the bales on the wagon, he glanced over to see the two of them by the Audi, the longhair talking on a cell phone while the one named Robb sat in the grass by the shoulder of the road, cleaning his boots with a stick. Virgil walked to the front of the team and took hold of the harness to start for the barn.

"Looks like the circus is in town," he said to Nelly.

Nelly, of course, didn't say anything in reply, but she did jerk her head up and down. Whether she was agreeing with Virgil or just stretching her neck in the heavy collar was difficult to say.

"It's called *Frontier Woman*," Claire said. "I read it when it came out a couple years ago. It was a best seller. They were calling it the *Eat, Pray, Love* of the nineteenth century. Did you read *Eat, Pray, Love*?"

Virgil snorted.

"I can't believe I asked you that," Claire admitted.

He was sitting at the kitchen table, talking to her on the phone. She'd called from north of Albany, where she was working on a case. What case, he didn't know. She rarely offered information and Virgil, most of the time, didn't ask.

"The movie sounds like a pretty big deal," Claire said. "The budget is supposed to be around thirty million. And they have Olivia Burns in the lead."

"What's it about?"

"I can lend you the book."

"Or you could just tell me."

"It's about this woman, Martha Jones, back in the 1840s. She and her husband and daughter have this homestead on the frontier and her husband is killed by Indians. Instead of moving to town or marrying the farmer next door, she and the girl stick it out on their own. It's a backwoods feminist tale. Sure you don't want to read it?"

"Surer than ever."

"You're kind of a wiseass today, aren't you?"

"You're the second one to tell me that," Virgil said. "What happens in the book?"

"Well, she has a dalliance with Abner Doubleday."

"What?"

"She has a fling with Abner Doubleday. You know who he was, don't you? He invented baseball."

"He didn't actually. What the hell is he doing in the book?"

"Chasing Martha around the corncrib, if I remember correctly. And he catches her too. Or rather she lets him catch her. I think the author wanted to show us that women back then weren't averse to some good old-fashioned screwing, just for the joy of it."

"You can't just put a historical figure like that in a book," Virgil said. He got to his feet and walked to the sink, stretching the phone cord, and poured himself a glass of water.

"Says who?"

"Shit, I don't know." Virgil had a drink of water and stood looking out the window above the sink.

"So what did these guys say?" Claire asked.

"They want to use Bob and Nelly in their movie."

"What'd you tell them?"

"Once they decided I was the hired hand, and a dullard to boot, they really didn't want to deal with me. I'm supposed to have my boss call them."

"That's funny."

"What is?"

"The concept of you having a boss," Claire said. "So you going to do it?"

"I don't know if I want to get involved," Virgil said. "They seemed like a couple of posers. The guy who called himself the director was basically a half-wit."

"But they have money," Claire said. "And I know your taxes are due, and your soybean crop failed last fall, and you're not exactly flush. What are they offering?"

"Five hundred a day."

"Nothing to sneeze at," Claire said. "And how do you know this isn't the big break Bob and Nelly have been waiting for? This could open some doors for them. Maybe Broadway. Maybe they could get on Donald Trump's show. Bob's mane looks a little like Trump's. And you could ride their coattails. Well, horse tails."

"And you called me a wiseass?"

"Hey, it might be interesting to boot. You love movies, Virgil. This way you could watch them make one, and get paid to do it."

"I don't know." Virgil heard someone say something to Claire in the background. Another officer maybe.

"I have to go and uphold law and order," she said then. "Take the money, Virgil."

Hanging up the phone, Virgil went outside and sat down in a wooden chair on the side porch. The herd of orphans was standing around the water trough, Bob and Nelly towering over the others.

Claire was right about one thing. Virgil did like movies. In fact, if it weren't for old movies, he would never bother to turn on the forty-year-old Philco television in the corner of the farmhouse living room. Virgil didn't have cable on the farm, or a satellite either, but there was an ancient antenna bolted to the roof of the front porch and with it he could pick up stations from different places, depending on the weather and the time of day. There was a channel called Old Gold Movies out of New York City that ran films twenty-four hours a day, all of a certain vintage, nothing more recent than the 1970s. Often at night Virgil would tune in to see what the station was running. Sometimes he would turn the set off as quickly as he turned it on. Other times he would stay up too late, thinking he would just watch a half hour of something and then hanging in until the end.

As a kid in rural Quebec, Virgil had access to the CBC and a couple of small market stations from across the US border that ran a lot of old movies and defunct TV series. He remembered Saturday mornings, watching Johnny Weissmuller's stone-faced and athletic Tarzan, before moving on in the afternoons to the Gene Autry and Roy Rogers shorts. He watched Laurel & Hardy, the Marx Brothers, the great W. C. Fields. He liked Bogart and Cagney as good guys and bad, and he loved Peter Lorre in everything. He was drawn to westerns, and always had been. Claire Marchand once told him he was a cowboy, and she hadn't meant it in a particularly flattering way. But she'd bought him a book about western cinema, over a thousand pages with details of every western ever made, the great and not-so-great, with background stories from the directors, the cameramen, the actors, and the crew.

Virgil liked certain directors more than others—Hathaway,

Ford, Boetticher. Howard Hawks was a favorite. Like John Ford, he used secondary characters to great and often comedic effect. Virgil liked Victor McLaglen's swagger, John Carradine's sonorous voice, Walter Brennan's irascibility. He loved how Noah Beery Jr. rode his horse in *Red River,* hat pushed way up on his forehead, elbows flying as if he were about to take flight.

He wasn't interested in musicals, or fluff comedies where Rock Hudson pretended to be interested in Doris Day. He liked drama, but drama with style, films like Kubrick's *The Killing, The Hustler* with Newman, *The Men* with Brando.

Virgil didn't consider himself a film buff. He would never consider himself an anything buff. And he'd never been particularly interested in how movies were made. He had a feeling that finding out might disillusion him.

After a while he reached into his pocket and retrieved the card the longhair had given him. He looked at it for a moment before putting it on the arm of the chair. He got up and headed for the barn. He had one more load of hay to mow away before dark.

# FOUR

Sam and Robb had a room at the Hampton Inn in Kingston. The crew had been trickling in for the past few days and some of them were there as well. Adam Canfield, the cinematographer, was due in tomorrow. Some of the others—hair and makeup, grips and electrics—would be at the Econo Lodge across town. The production company wasn't paying for them to crash at the Hampton.

When Sam got back from the city, Robb was asleep on the bed, fully dressed, his left arm across his eyes. The smell of burnt hash was hanging in the air, along with something else, something heavy and pungent and acidic, an odor Sam didn't recognize.

She removed her boots and lay down beside him on the bed. She closed her eyes, thinking she'd love to have a nap before dinner, but her mind was working overtime and she knew she wasn't going to fall off.

She lay there silently for a half hour, mentally checking off the places she could go for money. The problem was that she'd already exhausted all the possibilities in getting the financing to begin with. The budget was around thirty million, and even before USN pulled their commitment of six million, she'd been almost five short. She hadn't told anybody that—certainly not the other investors, not even Robb. Everybody involved assumed that the package was complete. Losing Peter Dunmore had helped the bottom line; she'd promised him five hundred thousand and she would pay Robb half that. Unless, of course, she got all the money she needed, then she could bump him up to half a million. After all, it would be as much hers as his in the end. But getting all the money was going to be a stretch. First she needed to find the six million she'd lost in the boardroom that afternoon.

She'd been counting on raising the other five over the next six weeks, during the course of the shoot. There were still some smaller foreign markets she hadn't approached, and she had hoped to spur some interest by sending dailies with Olivia Burns looking quite fetching and heroine-like in the wilderness. She'd arranged the schedule so they would shoot the sex scenes in the first two weeks. Olivia didn't know it yet, but Sam and Robb intended on making the scenes a little more graphic than outlined in the script, catering specifically to the European networks and cable outlets. There was definitely a difference in the sensibilities of the two continents. Americans who bought movie tickets liked violence and bad rom-coms and sophomoric, scatological humor. Europeans liked period pieces and sex.

However, those financing potentials wouldn't help Sam today. She'd just lost six million dollars and was five days out from shooting.

Robb stirred beside her, turned, and opened his eyes.

"Sleepyhead," she said.

"Yeah." He stretched and rubbed his eyes like a toddler waking.

"This place smells like a Turkish armpit," she said. "What were you doing—hot knives?"

"Levi and I smoked a couple pipes when we got back from scouting."

"Where is Levi anyway?"

"He drove into Manhattan," Robb said. "Said he had to meet a guy, some business deal."

"He's a man of mystery," Sam said sarcastically. She got up from the bed and went to the minibar for a bottle of water. "You want anything?"

"What kind of beer is there?"

"Budweiser, Heineken, Stella—"

"Give me a Stella."

Sam opened the beer and poured it into a glass for him. Robb sat up in bed to drink and she arranged his pillow behind him.

"So how did it go?" she asked.

"Great," he said. "The frontier village is perfect. Plus, the guy who runs the place told us about another log cabin up in the mountains, near Haleyville. This couple owns it, and they're loaded, made a bunch of money in the market. The guy's got a hard-on for the pioneer days and he restored the place for a getaway. The wife is all excited to have it in a movie. We might get the place for nothing. What else? Oh, we found some of those great big workhorses, you know? Like they used back then. We haven't talked to the owner yet. And there's an old barn on the property too."

"That's good," Sam said. She walked to the window to pull back the drapes. There was nothing to see outside but the parking lot. Her BMW was parked along the fence at the back, a twelve-year-old sedan with over two hundred thousand miles on it.

"So?" Robb asked.

"What?"

"What happened with USN?"

Sam hesitated before turning away from the window. "We parted company," she said. "I basically told them to fuck off."

"Because of me?" Robb asked. "They didn't want me?"

"No, that wasn't it. I didn't like the way they were talking to me. They seemed to think that this was *their* movie. Well, guess what? This is *our* movie and we can't have anybody dictating shit to us. They put up a few bucks and suddenly they're in the driver's seat? I don't think so."

"But they were okay with me directing?" Robb repeated.

Sam approached and sat down on the edge of the bed. "They were fine with you. They, uh, they said they had some problems with the script all of a sudden. It's just network bullshit." She stopped. "What the fuck is that smell?" she asked. "That's not hash."

"Oh, I stepped in horse manure," Robb said. "It's still on my boots. I can't get it off."

"I'll do it, baby," Sam said. "Finish your beer. We have to meet Olivia and Levi for dinner in an hour. You want to watch some TV?"

"Okay."

She found the remote and turned the set on. "Here, find something you like," she said, handing him the clicker.

She took his Wellingtons into the bathroom and cleaned them using a face cloth and one of the little vials of shampoo. She pretty much ruined the cloth in the process but got rid of the horseshit. As she worked she heard him in the other room, clicking through the channels. He finally settled on an episode of *The Three Stooges*. It was the one where the boys find work on a movie set. Sam hoped it wasn't a case of art imitating life.

They'd arranged to meet at a bar in Union City, a place called T-Mac's situated on the ground floor of an old hotel. T-Mac's was a beer-and-wings joint, with off-track betting in a separate room in the back. The rooms upstairs had been turned into apartments; the sign out front indicated they were available weekly or monthly. No lease required.

Levi sat at the bar and drank vodka tonics while he waited for Cox to arrive. The waitress was one of those fading beauties, maybe late forties, with short blonde hair and a number of tattoos on her arms. She could still pull off the tight jeans she wore, and her V-neck sweater showed enough cleavage to keep Levi interested. She was overly friendly, maybe because he was a stranger and she'd exhausted any patter with the locals. If he hadn't been preoccupied, Levi would have considered asking her when she got off. She looked like she'd be fun for a night, and the fact that he had no reason to come back to Union City made the notion even more attractive.

Cox showed up nearly an hour late. Levi was supposed to meet the Indian farther upriver at seven, but with Cox running late, that wasn't going to happen. At quarter to he called the man to say he'd get there when he could. By that time he was into his fourth vodka and had learned in the process that the waitress, whose name was Jenny, had once been in the X-rated film business. Levi had been about to ask if she had any special skills in that area when he saw Cox's gleaming bald head in the entranceway.

Levi was relieved that Cox showed up alone this time. When they'd met two weeks earlier he'd had a Samoan with him who looked as if he could bench-press a school bus. The Samoan had stood by and not said a word but he never took his eyes off Levi for a moment.

Cox indicated a vacant table in the corner and Levi, vodka in hand, slid off the barstool and went to join him. Cox was wearing a long leather coat in the heat and shrugged out of it as he sat down. He ordered a Guinness and offered Levi a look of bemused contempt as he waited for it to arrive. After taking a long drink from the glass, he indicated Levi's clothes, the formfitting T-shirt and jeans.

"I don't see anything that suggests a large envelope on your person," Cox said. His voice was soft and held just the slightest remains of an English accent. "Surely you don't intend to offer me a check."

Levi had a drink. "You might as well know, I don't have the full amount."

"I suspected that," Cox said. He sighed as he took a cell phone from his pocket and opened it to send a text that appeared to Levi to consist of a single letter. "How very unfortunate for you," Cox said, putting the phone away.

"I brought some cash," Levi said quickly.

"*Some* cash." Cox took another drink.

The door opened and the Samoan from the previous meeting entered the bar, having presumably been summoned by the text. Wearing baggy black pants and a blood-red shirt, he filled the doorway. His small eyes squinted in the dim interior of the joint as he looked around, finally settling his gaze on the two of them at the table. With a quick nod of his head, Cox directed him to the bar, where the behemoth sat down on a stool that fairly disappeared beneath him.

"How much?" Cox asked, not looking at Levi now, as if he was no longer worthy of his attention.

"Five grand."

"Five?" Cox repeated. "You've moved the decimal point, lad. Twice, in fact."

"I'll have the rest within the week," Levi said.

"Such a familiar tune," Cox said. "And it's getting old. What am I to do with you?" Now he turned to Levi. "No, no . . . don't attempt to reply. If ever there was a rhetorical question, that was it."

Levi glanced reluctantly toward the bar where the Samoan was talking to Jenny the bartender; it looked like he was telling her he wasn't there for a drink.

"Give me the five," Cox said. "You have a week. I hope you know that you've been a great disappointment to me, lad. Therefore I don't think I can allow you to run about unsupervised any longer. You keep telling me what a mover and a shaker you are in the motion picture industry and yet at the same time you can't come up with even a fraction of the money you owe." He had another drink of the black beer and got to his feet. "If I were to suggest a title for this little film that *you and I* seem to be making—it would be *Last Chance*. Do you follow, lad?"

"Yeah," Levi said. "I follow."

The Hampton Inn had a decent restaurant called Finnegan's and that's where they met Olivia for dinner. Levi Brown called the room as they were walking out and said he would be running late. Sam and Robb smoked a small chunk of hash before going downstairs. They shared the elevator with an older couple dressed to the nines, the woman actually wearing a fox stole. Sam stood behind her and mugged, bulging her eyes like that of the dead animal around the woman's neck until Robb finally broke out laughing. The couple was not particularly amused.

The restaurant was dark, with raised oak paneling on the walls and deep-red carpet with swirls of gold leaf. A bar commanded the far wall of the place; a half-dozen men in suits sat drinking there, under a large-screen TV showing the Yankees and the Orioles.

Olivia was sitting at a table alone, a glass of Chardonnay in front of her. She wore a sleeveless dress of bone white. Her arms were toned and muscular, and Sam again felt the stab of jealousy she'd experienced in the restaurant that afternoon. She let it slide; she wasn't about to compete with Olivia Burns on that level. Maybe she'd been working out to play Martha Jones. Pioneer women who spent their days hauling water and chopping firewood and birthing babies in fields were undoubtedly in pretty good shape.

They sat down and Sam ordered wine while Robb asked for a light beer.

"Meet your new director," Sam said.

"Yes." Olivia smiled.

"This is going to be great," Robb told her. "I'm so happy you're doing this."

"*We* might not be doing it if you weren't," Sam told her. "We had exactly one actress on our wish list."

Olivia just smiled again. It appeared she was okay with things, Sam thought. But that was the problem with actors, especially good actors. How could you ever be sure what they were showing you was genuine? Sam knew a writer once, a novelist, who used to say that Meryl Streep could commit cold-blooded murder in front of a dozen witnesses, and then go on trial and persuade any jury in the world that she was innocent. She was that good an actress. Sam had suggested that if she could be that convincing, why didn't she get herself elected president? The novelist had asked why the greatest actor in the world would want a shitty job like that?

So maybe Olivia was okay with Robb directing the film, or maybe she was going along with it just because that's the way things were. At the end of the day, it really didn't matter one way or the other. She'd been hired to do a job. In that respect, she was no different than a grip or an electrician.

"Sam said you've been working with Stuart on the script," Olivia said.

"Oh yeah," Robb said. "We've been collaborating."

"We've been in touch, by e-mail mostly," Olivia said. "But I talked to him a couple days ago. The script is great."

"It's awesome," Robb said. "It's so true to the book, which is great. I mean, I insisted on that from the get-go."

"Well, there would be no point in doing it otherwise," Olivia said.

"Absolutely," Robb said. "We promised, um . . . the writer." He stalled. "Shit, the woman who wrote the book."

"Ann Furlong," Sam provided quickly.

"Yes," Robb said. "I drew a blank there. I mean, I know her very well. We promised Ann that we'd remain faithful to her vision. And we will." He hesitated. "I mean, there are a couple of areas that need to be—"

The waiter appeared with the drinks then, and he stayed to recite the specials for the evening. Sam noticed, as he talked, that his eyes never left Olivia Burns. She had that effect on people.

When he was gone, Robb took a drink of beer and looked at the menu.

"You were saying?" Olivia asked.

It was obvious to Sam that Robb, stoned out of his gourd, had lost whatever it was he was going to say.

"Something about the script," Sam prompted.

"Oh yeah," he said. "The script is great. But I wonder if we need another element in there. Something . . . really dramatic."

Olivia had a drink of wine. "What do you mean?"

"Just think about this," Robb said. "I'm just brainstorming now. But what about a scene where Martha fights off an Indian attack?"

Olivia glanced quickly at Sam, who picked up the menu

and opened it, thus excluding herself from the discussion. Olivia turned back to Robb.

"There's nothing even remotely like that in the book," Olivia said.

"I guess not," Robb said uncertainly.

"You've read the book?" Olivia asked.

"Of course I have," Robb told her. "I love the world of the book. I love it. It's just . . . I mean this is a motion picture. As a director, I need more to work with. *Visually,* you know? I think a scene where Martha and the girl—" He hesitated, trying to come up with the name.

"Sara."

"Yeah, Sara. I think a scene where they are forced to fight off this ferocious war party . . . I mean, they're alone in the wilderness. I think it could be very powerful. And visually, it would just rock. The story as it is, is kind of, I don't know . . . it's kind of inert."

Olivia glanced again at Sam, who was still hiding behind the menu.

"Think of Lara Croft," Robb said. "Now, that's an empowered woman. That's what I'm trying to say."

"Martha Jones isn't Lara Croft," Olivia said. "Is that how you see her?"

Robb shrugged and had another drink of beer. "I have to go to the little boys' room."

He got up and wandered off in search of the restroom. Sam placed her menu on the table. Olivia was once again looking at her.

"That's not how you see this film," Olivia said.

"Of course not," Sam said. "It's all part of Robb's process. He likes to throw things out there, stirring up the mix. Then he discards what doesn't work and keeps what does." Sam warmed to the image. "It's like a miner panning for gold. You sift through the gravel and sand until you find what's really precious. Um . . . Kubrick worked like that. I think it's a sign of great talent."

"Kubrick," Olivia said.

"Yes."

They ordered dinner when Robb returned and Sam made sure the conversation drifted away from the specifics of the upcoming shoot. She knew that Olivia had gone to Harvard, where she'd majored in English, so she steered things in that direction. Sam had also studied English, at Northwestern, so it was easy to fall into a discussion of the writers they'd encountered along the way. Both had been influenced by O'Connor and Henry James. Olivia was also a huge fan of Steinbeck, which explained to Sam why the actress was so enamored of *Frontier Woman*. There was an element of *The Grapes of Wrath,* or even *East of Eden,* in it.

Of course Robb, not being much of a reader, was left out of the conversation to a great extent, but he didn't seem to mind. He was still somewhat wasted, Sam knew, and he was content in that, listening to the two of them and watching the comings and goings in the restaurant. She suspected he knew that he'd said too much earlier on.

After they'd eaten, the conversation returned to the movie they were about to make and Robb, back in the loop, decided they should all have Scotch. Sam turned and signaled to the waiter. While Robb was going down the list of single malts, Levi Brown called Sam on her cell phone. She told him where they were and he said he was on his way.

"There's someone I want you to meet," he said.

"Levi," Sam said after she hung up. Robb ordered Macallan for them all.

"None for me," Olivia said suddenly. She got to her feet. "I have some phone calls to make." Sam glanced at Robb, then stood up as well. They all embraced at the table.

"We are so pumped that you're doing this," Robb told her again.

He watched her as she walked away, heading for the elevators just outside the restaurant entrance, then turned to Sam, who was frowning.

"What was that about?" she asked.

"I don't know, but there's going to be a fucking Indian attack in this movie," he said.

"I know there is," Sam told him. "But she doesn't need to know until she needs to know. Keep that in mind. She's just another employee. Would you run it by wardrobe? Would you run it by craft services?"

"Not fucking likely," he admitted. The waiter arrived with the Scotch.

"Then you don't need to run it by the cast," Sam said. "She's working for us, not the other way around."

"As long as she knows it," Robb said. He had a drink. "Does Levi know about USN?"

"Yeah. I called him from the car."

"What did he say?"

"He said fuck 'em."

When Levi arrived ten minutes later, he had with him an American Indian of about fifty. The man was short and skinny with shiny black hair combed straight back; he wore jeans and a black dress shirt with pearl snaps down the front. Levi introduced him as Marvin Nightingale.

"Marvin's the casting agent I told you about," Levi said when they were seated.

The waiter returned and Sam ordered more Scotch for everybody.

"So can you get us the extras we need or are we going to have to bring them in?" Sam asked.

"There's all kinds of talent right here," Marvin told her. "You got any idea how many little theater groups there are in upstate New York? I could get you a thousand Indians."

"We can't afford a thousand Indians," Sam joked.

"Well, I can get you what you need," Marvin said. "For speaking parts too. But I guess you got that covered."

"For now," Sam said. She looked at Robb. "The script is an ever-evolving thing, though. Who knows what might pop up. We might need a war party. You got any pissed-off Indians?"

"Shit, there's no shortage of them," Marvin said. "You ever read a history book?"

Sam had a sip of the single malt, looking over the rim of the glass to Levi. There was something he wasn't saying, maybe because he couldn't say it outright. There had been no reason to bring the guy who was providing the extras to the restaurant. Levi smiled at her, then drank before leaning forward to place his glass on the table.

"I mentioned to Marvin that occasionally an investment opportunity might become available," Levi said. "You know, that there might be a couple of spare pieces of the movie still floating around."

"I'm not sure there is in this case," Sam said, following the lead. "But on the other hand—we're always fine-tuning the budget. I've never met a producer who turned down money." She turned to the agent. "Who would be the investor? You?"

"Hell no," Marvin said. "I'm poor like a church mouse. But I know a guy. He's a big fan of the movies."

"What does he do?" Robb asked.

"You ever hear of the Running Dog Casino?" Marvin asked.

Robb shook his head. Sam was watching Marvin Nightingale with interest now. She'd been thinking there was nothing to this, and wondering why Levi had thought otherwise. But the word "casino" piqued her interest.

"I have," Levi said. "It's a big deal. They're building a golf course over there that's going to run them something like twenty million. They already have a commitment from the PGA. It will be a tour stop beginning in 2014."

"Casinos, man," Marvin said. "They're a license to print money. They got Asians coming up from New York City by the busload. Those Chinamen love to gamble. They're tight as bark to a tree in every other way, but they love to bet."

"And this casino guy—he wants to get into the movie business?" Sam asked.

"Shit, that's all he talks about," Marvin said. "Except he has no idea where to start. He's always asking me. Like I know. I told him to find a book he likes and option it. But he's not much for reading."

With that Sam glanced at Robb but it appeared that he missed the parallel. She took a drink of the Scotch and rolled it on her tongue. It really wasn't to her liking; they were approaching an hour when she preferred to get into tequila. In fact, she had a bottle in the room. For the moment, though, she was aware that both Robb and Levi were watching her expectantly.

"You know," she said, "I think it would be kind of cool to have some Native participation in this project. The script is very sympathetic to the Native point of view. The protagonist eventually develops a symbiotic relationship with a local tribe. Which is somewhat ironic, considering what happened to her husband."

"What happened to her husband?" Marvin asked.

Sam smiled. "You're going to have to wait for the movie. Or buy the book."

"I can wait."

Sam laughed at that, then turned to Levi. "Our ducks are pretty much in line when it comes to financing. But what do you think—is there a piece of the film kicking around for a Native investment?"

It was Levi's turn to play along. "I don't know. Why not have a meeting and at least talk about it?" He looked at Marvin. "Can you set that up?"

"In a heartbeat."

"What's your connection to this guy anyway?"

"I book all the talent for the casino," Marvin replied. "Singers, comics, every show that goes on there has to go through me. I've been there since they opened in 2006. Ronnie trusts me."

"What's the guy's name?" Sam asked.

"Ronnie Red Hawk."

"Ronnie Red Hawk," Sam repeated. "I like that."

# FIVE

Kari got up shortly after noon. She could hear Nicole in the other bedroom, snoring away like a drunken dockworker. She walked into the kitchen and washed down a Xanax with some orange juice while looking out over Venice Beach, two stories below. Both the beach and the boardwalk were packed with people. The tide was out and there were kids riding bikes along the packed sand by the water's edge amid young lovers strolling hand in hand. The boardwalk was filled with Rollerbladers, but then it always was, any time, night or day, the skaters recklessly dodging the tourists dressed in their baggy shorts and Tilley hats, cameras dangling from their necks. Kari hadn't been on her blades for months now. She needed to start again, to get in shape.

Today was a day for beginnings.

She made coffee and sat on the balcony watching the scene below while she waited for Nicole to get her lazy ass out of bed. They'd stayed in the night before, drinking wine and getting high with a couple guys Nicole had met somewhere on the beach that afternoon and invited over. Around three in the morning Nicole had disappeared into the bedroom with one of them, a geeky fucker with curly brown hair who looked like one of those guys who was always selling dot-com shit for millions. Apparently he wasn't one of those guys, though, because an hour later, after he'd presumably had his brains fucked out by Nicole, he borrowed twenty bucks from

Kari for cab fare. By that time the other guy, whose name was Willard, was gone. He'd made a move on Kari but she wasn't into him. He could barely put a sentence together and smelled pretty bad, as if he hadn't showered for days. Besides, he had a rat's name. Who calls their kid Willard?

Down on the beach, Kari's good buddy Freeman was doing a stellar business, sketching lightning-fast caricatures of tourists too stupid to know that he was basically mocking their appearance for seventy-five bucks a pop. Kari tried to catch his eye but he was too busy at his work—either that or he didn't want to risk looking up and seeing her, knowing she would make him laugh, busting him with his clientele. She would catch up with him later. He was always holding some killer pot and Kari was out. The two guys from the night before had shown up empty-handed. Nicole had a habit of finding freeloaders, but then she was basically one herself. Takes one to know one.

Kari drank another cup of coffee while she watched the never-ending parade on the beach. Nicole wandered out from the bedroom at half past one, slouching along in her Marilyn Monroe T-shirt and pink panties. Her blonde hair was sticking out every which way, the roots showing black. She'd obviously never removed her makeup after banging the geek, and her eyes were smudged and crusted.

"You're nice," Kari said.

"Fuck you." Nicole poured some coffee and sat down in the wicker chair next to Kari, holding the cup with both hands, her knees up.

"That fat couple from Muncie is going to see your cooch," Kari said.

"Fuck them too."

"I'm glad you got up," Kari said. "I've been starving for intellectual conversation."

Nicole regarded her darkly but kept silent.

"Your boyfriend didn't want to stay over?" Kari asked.

"I made him leave. You know I hate that whole morning-after thing. I don't mind fucking them but I don't want to feed them in the morning and I sure as fuck don't want to talk to them. What about you and Willard—did you cuddle for hours?"

"Willard and I were two ships that crossed in the night." Kari sipped her coffee. "The *Titanic* and the *Lusitania*."

"The what?" Nicole yawned. "I've never even heard of that second movie."

"They were ships, not movies."

"You know more useless stuff," Nicole said. "Where do you get it all?"

"I read books," Kari said. She looked at the Pacific, rolling on forever in the distance. "I want to go shopping. This is the first day of my probation-free life. Let's go to Rodeo."

"Shopping for what?"

"For whatever tickles my fancy."

They both showered and changed and then took Kari's Mustang to Rodeo and spent what remained of the afternoon checking out the shops. Kari bought some jeans and three sweaters and a leather jacket for Nicole, who would pout the rest of the day if she didn't get anything. They looked at jewelry at Casey's and checked out some abstract art by an obscure Chilean dude at Starrett's. The dude was actually in the gallery, hanging around his exhibition, and Nicole flirted with him for a bit before realizing he spoke not a word of English.

There were a few photographers hanging around, as always. Kari fucked with them, stopping at every turn to let them take her picture. When they saw how willing she was, they typically lost interest. There was no market for photos when everybody else had them. Besides, they wanted action shots, Kari leaving a bar drunk or—better yet—reacting to some slight, taking a swing at somebody or screaming her head off. So she smiled and posed and played nice with them, and eventually they left her alone.

They hit the liquor store on the way home and grabbed a couple burgers at In-N-Out. Cruising down Sunset in the Mustang with the top down, Nicole finished her burger and tossed the wrapper out the window.

"Jesus," Kari said.

"What?"

"Littering."

Nicole ignored the charge, and turned to reach into the backseat for her brand-new leather jacket. It was short and red, and had silver conchos on the collar and cuffs. Kari had told her it looked like it belonged to a Mexican bullfighter but Nicole had to have it. Now she held it to her face with both hands, breathing it in.

"I love the smell of leather," she murmured, closing her eyes, her expression near rapturous. "What is it about leather that smells so good? What do they do to it at the factory? I mean, you ever smell a cow? They don't smell like leather and they're fucking made of it. Cows smell like shit."

"When were you ever near a cow?"

"My grandfather had a place in the Valley," Nicole said, looking over. "His neighbor had cows. Beige cows."

"And they smelled like shit?"

"Everything out there smelled like shit. I hated it."

When they got back to the beach they parked and walked over to the boardwalk, lugging their shopping bags. Freeman was packing up for the day and Kari called to him as he was heading toward his van.

"What's up?" he said, sliding his easel into the back of the vehicle.

"What're you smoking?" Kari asked.

Freeman ran his hand over his shaved head. "I got no time to get high. Heading for a meeting at NBC right now."

"For what?"

"Some reality shit. My agent set it up."

"Since when do you have an agent?" Kari asked.

"Everybody's got an agent," Freeman said. "Nicole, you got an agent?"

"Nope," Nicole replied. "But I have a new leather jacket. See?"

"Cool," Freeman said and turned to Kari. "I got to run. What do you need?"

"Ounce of hydro?"

"All right. I'll send Bobby over with it. You can pay him, okay? But I gotta go." Freeman laughed. "I gotta go save television."

Back in the condo, Nicole walked around in her new jacket while Kari uncorked a bottle of red and cut up some cheese. It was too hot to sit outside, so they stayed in the living room with the air-conditioning cranked. They were halfway through the first bottle of wine when the buzzer sounded from the lobby.

"Bobby already?" Kari said. "That was quick."

"Bring on the boo," Nicole said. "Maybe he's got other goodies too."

Kari walked over and hit the intercom.

"It's Seth," the voice said, and Kari buzzed him in.

"You expecting him?" Nicole asked.

"No," Kari said. "Maybe the HBO offer came through. About time."

Seth arrived a minute later, looking hot and uncomfortable in a powder-blue suit and white shirt. His gray hair was plastered to his temples as if glued there. Kari gave him a hug, although she really didn't want to. He was sticky with sweat.

"You want wine?"

"Water," Seth said, and he sat down on the couch.

"Hey Sethy," Nicole said.

"Yeah," he said, looking at her unhappily.

Kari brought him a bottle of water and he drank half of it in a gulp.

"This a social call?" she asked.

"No, it isn't," he replied.

"You hear from HBO?"

"No, I didn't."

"Is there another offer, then?" Kari asked. "I'm off probation, you know."

"Funny you should mention that," Seth said, and he drank the rest of the bottle. "What were you girls up to today?"

"Little shopping, little road tripping."

"You weren't at Casey's?"

"Yeah, we stopped in," Kari said. She glanced at Nicole.

"What the fuck is wrong with you?" Seth demanded, finally losing his demeanor. "I mean, what in the name of all that is fucked up in this world is wrong with you?"

"Whoa," Nicole said. "Dude."

But Seth didn't look at her. His eyes were on Kari, who sat quietly across from him.

"Beth called me," Seth continued, dialing it back but just a bit. "You know—Beth who works at Casey's and who is my wife's close friend? And Beth tells me that a diamond necklace is missing from Casey's. And Beth tells me that one of her girls was showing jewelry to the two of you this very afternoon.

She was in fact showing you that very necklace this very afternoon. And now it is missing. So we need to figure out where that necklace went. Maybe Beth's yappy Chihuahua ate that necklace. Maybe the Santa Monica winds swept through the store and blew that necklace out over the Pacific Ocean."

"What the fuck are you suggesting?" Nicole demanded.

"You need to be quiet," Seth said. "Unless, of course, you took the necklace. Did you take the necklace?"

"I never took fuck all."

"Then be quiet." Seth turned to Kari. "Beth is rather hoping that her yappy Chihuahua pukes the thing up, or that the winds blow it back into the store. That way she will not have to call the police and mention your name and by calling the police and mentioning your name involve every news agency from here to the planet Jupiter."

Kari shook her head. "I have no idea, man."

Seth sat looking at her, his breath coming in quick little spurts. He was still sweating, in spite of the frigid temperature in the room. He was staring at her as if willing the situation to an acceptable conclusion.

"We were shopping," Kari said slowly, as if reviewing her day in her head. "I had a couple bags with me when we went to Casey's. The only thing I can think—wait a minute."

She got to her feet and went into her bedroom and stayed there for an appropriate length of time before returning with a diamond necklace in her hand.

"It was in the bag with my new sweaters," she said. "It must have dropped there after I tried it on." She glared at Seth, suddenly defiant. "I'd like to know why the fucking salesgirl never noticed. Isn't that her job?"

Seth got heavily to his feet and held his hand out. Kari placed the necklace in it.

"I will drop this off on my way home," he said and started for the door.

"Nothing from HBO?" Kari asked.

Seth stopped with his hand on the door handle. He didn't turn for a long moment, just stood there, looking at the flat white slab that was the door, as if there were something written there and he was taking time to read it. It was a full minute before he spoke.

"Nothing from HBO," he said, and he left.

Billy hated it when Ronnie made him take the limo into the drive-thru at McDonald's. The turn was so tight that he always had to back up once or twice going in, pissing off the drivers behind him, the drivers who were no doubt wondering why somebody in a stretch limo was loading up on Egg McMuffins to begin with. Billy had offered time and again to park and walk inside for Ronnie's order but the suggestion had never flown. Ronnie seemed to be of the opinion that the use of the drive-thru lane was one of his inalienable rights. Fine, but why not do it in a fucking pickup truck?

Ronnie ordered the big breakfast, as he invariably did if they arrived before noon. He asked, as always, what Billy wanted and Billy, as always, asked for black coffee only. Billy hated McDonald's food; the chicken had no taste and was the texture of gelatin, the beef was greasy and overcooked, and the eggs were just weird. Billy had an apple in his pocket and some granola bars in the glove compartment. Besides, he'd eaten breakfast three hours earlier when he got up.

Once he shoehorned his way out of the parking lot, he headed for the site of the new golf course, on the acreage to the west of the casino. Billy had the partition window up, but he could imagine Ronnie in the back, vacuuming up the huge breakfast as they drove. Later, Billy would have to clean up the aftermath—wrappers, coffee and juice cups, Styrofoam containers.

The day was going to be smoking hot again but it was icy cool in the big Cadillac. Ronnie was an air-conditioning freak. He insisted that the car be as cold as possible and his house on Mount Ransom was the same. That is, if you could call a redbrick castle with three stories, thirty rooms, eight bedrooms, and sixteen bathrooms a house. He kept the place as cold as the inside of the Caddy, in spite of the fact that he lived for the most part in the penthouse suite at the casino hotel. He might sleep at the house two or three nights a month, and to Billy's thinking, that was a lot of wasted electricity, keeping the air going. But Ronnie never thought that way, not about anything. He'd grown up with nothing, he always said, and now he was just evening things out.

The building site course was visible from a half mile away, as was the enormous sign out front that proclaimed:

THE FUTURE HOME OF RED HAWK GOLF

Billy drove in on the gravel road and parked in front of the half-constructed clubhouse. Earthmovers and bulldozers were at work everywhere and the stench of diesel exhaust hit him as he stepped out of the car. There had been no rain for days and the dust from the excavation hung in the air like a gritty mist. Billy knew he would be washing the limo later that day.

He opened the door and Ronnie stepped out, wincing as the hot, grimy air hit him full on. The difference in temperature between the inside and outside of the limo must have been forty degrees. Ronnie was wearing black nylon shorts that reached his knees and a basketball-style tank top, with a picture of a snorting bison on the front. His sunglasses were pushed up into his thick hair and now he flipped them down.

"Fuck me," he said in reference to the heat.

A short man in a white hard hat was standing alongside a worker on what would eventually be the first tee of the course, gesturing with a sweeping arm at the scalped earth that would in time become number one fairway. Ronnie started for them, glancing back.

"Billy Boy, bring me a water from the back," he said.

When Billy caught up with Ronnie, he was talking to the man in the white hat, whom Billy knew to be the foreman on the site, although he'd never learned his name. Ronnie knew it, Billy was sure, but Ronnie insisted on calling the man Squirt, even to his face. Ronnie liked to assign nicknames, particularly when the name served to diminish or embarrass the person in question. Billy considered himself lucky to have escaped with Billy Boy.

"It's going to go right there," Ronnie was telling the foreman.

"And what is it again?" the foreman asked slowly.

"A hawk."

"Made of what?"

"Granite," Ronnie told him. "I commissioned it yesterday. I found this red granite from a quarry in Kingston. Ontario, not New York." Ronnie pointed again. "Right there. It's gonna be a hawk taking flight, sixty feet high."

The foreman, thoroughly confused, took a moment. "You can't put it there."

"Why not?"

The foreman glanced at the worker he'd been talking to, then at Billy, as if Billy might help him out. That wasn't going to happen. "That's the first fairway," he said finally. "It's going

54

to be in the way. How they supposed to tee off with a sixty-foot statue in the way?"

"Let them figure it out," Ronnie said. "They can either go over it or around it. I don't give a shit what they do—it's going to be the course signature. A big red hawk. It will be incredible. The most incredible opening hole in golf."

"But you—" the foreman began, then stopped, taking time either to tailor his argument or possibly to make sense of the whole situation. "Why not put it in front of the clubhouse, or out by the entrance?"

"Because then there's no guarantee it will be on TV when the PGA Tour plays here," Ronnie said. He tapped his temple with his forefinger, emphasizing his genius. "We put it out in the fairway, and it's gotta be on TV. Matter of fact, everybody's going to be talking about it."

"They'll be talking about it all right," the foreman said.

"It's not for you to worry about, Squirt."

Billy saw the foreman flinch at the name. The man then glanced at the course, perhaps imagining the future statue blocking the future fairway.

"Did you run this by McTavish?" he asked.

"I don't need to run it by anybody," Ronnie said.

"It's his design."

"But my dime," Ronnie said. "That's the end of that story."

The foreman shrugged, as if announcing he wasn't going to argue it anymore.

"Come on," Ronnie said. "There's something else we need to talk about. The clubhouse walls are wrong."

"Wrong in what way?"

"I'll show you in what way," Ronnie said.

The foreman turned to the worker he'd been talking to earlier. The man had been standing there quietly the entire time.

"You can start the drainage for the green," the foreman said. "I'll get back to you on the other."

The worker nodded. Billy watched as the two other men headed off for the clubhouse on the hill. The worker stepped forward.

"Who was that?" he asked.

Billy turned, surprised. "Ronnie Red Hawk."

"That guy?" the man repeated. "That guy's Ronnie Red Hawk?"

"That's him."

"That guy's not an Indian."

"I wouldn't tell him that," Billy said.

Ronnie led the way up the wide brick staircase and into the clubhouse, stopping just inside the cavernous lobby. The foreman tagged along, glancing quickly at his watch as he ascended the stairs. He had a busy day and was already behind. There was a crew with chain saws on the back nine, waiting to be told which trees to cut and which to spare.

"This is what I'm talking about," Ronnie said. "These walls are smooth."

"Yeah?"

"They're supposed to be rough. You know, like the walls of a canyon. So people feel like they're out in the wilderness, like in Colorado, or New Mexico or someplace."

"It's a golf course clubhouse," the foreman said. "Not a theme park."

"It's whatever I decide it will be, Squirt," Ronnie told him. "If I decide to graze a herd of buffalo here in the lobby, I will."

"All right, give me a minute," the foreman said. He pulled his phone from a holder on his belt and moved a few steps away while he punched in a number.

Ronnie took a walk through the lobby and had a look inside the restaurant and bar area. A half-dozen workers were laying the marble floor. Ronnie stood there watching until the foreman came up behind him.

"Okay, I see what happened," the man said. "They were going to do the stone finish but then you decided that the lobby walls are going to be covered with murals."

"Oh yeah," Ronnie said excitedly. He led the way back into the lobby. "This artist from South Dakota is doing them. A Brule Sioux. Incredible talent. Incredible."

"So," the foreman said slowly, as if explaining two plus two to a toddler. "The thinking was . . . if we're not going to *see* the walls, why go to the expense of the stone finish?"

Ronnie took a moment. "You don't have to see something to know it's there," he said.

"What?"

"Canyon walls are canyon walls, whether you see them or not. Like the spirits all around us. I can't see them but I know they're there. Do you believe in the spirit world?"

The foreman exhaled. "I believe in getting this job done on time. And on budget."

Ronnie stepped to the wall nearest them and ran his hand over the smooth surface before shaking his head. "Who made the call on the finish?"

"I'm not sure."

"Find out," Ronnie said. "I want to talk to him. I'm not leaving here until this thing is resolved."

The foreman took his phone out again. As he entered in a number, Ronnie's phone rang. Ronnie answered.

"Red Hawk here."

The foreman's call was still going through and he moved away.

"Marvin," Ronnie said into the phone. "What's going on, Slick?" Ronnie listened for thirty seconds or so. "On my way," he said and hung up.

As Ronnie started for the entranceway, the foreman was closing his phone. "Wilson's coming over to talk to you about this," he said.

"About what?" Ronnie asked.

"About the walls," the foreman said, his voice disbelieving.

"Don't worry about it, Squirt. The murals will cover everything anyway."

# SIX

Sam went to the casino by herself, heading out at eleven in the morning. It was a two-hour drive from where the production company was set up in Kingston. Robb was working on the shooting schedule with Tommy Alamosa, the first assistant director. Tommy had been working in film since the sixties and didn't need Robb's assistance, but Sam was hoping some of Tommy's quiet confidence would rub off on Robb, who was a little freaked out about the directing gig. Sam didn't want him with her anyway. She suspected that the meeting she was heading for would require some finesse and Robb wasn't good in those situations.

Levi had been pushing her to pursue the casino money and he'd fully expected to come along, but Sam had told him she'd rather go it alone, sending him off on a location scout instead. Levi couldn't help flexing, in the physical and every other sense. He had a habit of turning even the most cordial of meetings into a pissing contest and she couldn't see how that might be beneficial today.

She did a MapQuest for Running Dog Casino on her iPad before leaving the hotel, but it turned out to be unnecessary. Once she was within thirty miles of the place, there were signs everywhere—loud and large, announcing the location, as well as the amenities offered. The upcoming shows were also advertised on towering roadside neon signs. Kenny Rogers was coming next week, and Jessica Simpson the week after that.

Marvin Nightingale had set up the meeting and agreed to meet Sam at the hotel beforehand. Sam had no expectations of the place but even if she had, they would have been dashed by what she found. Running Dog was a nouveau Shangri-la rising out of the Catskills like some garish mythical creature emerging from the forest. First there was the gaming house itself—a five-story chunk of limestone, steel, and glass set on the edge of a vast ravine, the slopes of which were covered with spindly birch trees amid stands of hardwood. A quarter mile away was the Red Hawk Hotel; she guessed it was twenty-five or thirty stories high, and between the two there were countless other venues—fitness centers, tennis courts, soccer fields, baseball diamonds, and a riding stable. And these were just the things Sam could identify from her vantage point in the moving car, on the sloping road leading up toward the hotel.

After pulling into the parking lot, which must have covered thirty or forty acres, she shut the engine down and got out for a better look. The place was impressive, suggesting a lot of things, not all good—depending on one's viewpoint, and their opinion of large-scale gambling in general. Sam really didn't care one way or the other about the sociological implications of the place. To her it smacked of the only thing she was interested in today, the only thing that would persuade her to make the drive in the first place.

Money.

She was wearing a long skirt she'd bought in New Mexico, and an off-the-shoulder blouse her sister had brought home from Argentina. The blouse was low-cut and she wasn't wearing a bra. She had good boobs and there were times when she wasn't above letting them do a little work for her, particularly when it came to financing. She reached into the car for the battered straw cowboy hat she'd picked up at South by Southwest a few years ago when she was shooting a video for a rockabilly band from Vermont.

Marvin was waiting for her in the hotel lobby, sitting in a plush velour armchair and reading *USA Today*. He wore a suit of some synthetic material, sky blue in color, with a red shirt beneath. No tie. Sam gave him a hug that he quite clearly was not expecting.

"You look good," Marvin told her.

"The hat's okay?" Sam asked.

"Oh yeah," Marvin said. "Indians love cowboy hats. One of the great paradoxes of our people, given the history of it all."

Sam smiled. "Where do we find Mr. Red Hawk?"

"The penthouse, of course."

They rode up in the elevator together while Marvin provided her with some background to the place. The casino was located on a tiny reservation, population less than two hundred, belonging to the Sumac tribe, an offshoot of the Mahicans, who were situated in the Albany area before moving to Massachusetts in the mid-1800s. The Sumacs stayed behind at that time and hadn't fared particularly well. Twenty years earlier, the reservation had been a pretty bleak place, according to Marvin—no jobs, no industry, myriad problems concerning alcohol and illegal pharmaceuticals. Then came the casino license and the subsequent turnaround. It had been quick and lucrative, a familiar story of success and unimaginable wealth. Some members of the tribe had handled it well and some hadn't. Marvin didn't elaborate on either; apparently he felt he didn't need to. He did say, as the elevator made a smooth stop at the top floor, that the success of Running Dog lay solely at the feet of Ronnie Red Hawk.

The doors opened into a foyer on the top floor. A receptionist sat behind a large mahogany-topped desk, typing something into a laptop. She looked up when they stepped off the elevator. Smiling widely, revealing perfect white teeth, she got to her feet.

"Hello, Marvin," she said before turning her focus to Sam. "He's expecting you."

"I'll wait here," Marvin explained. "Ronnie likes one-on-one."

Sam was surprised; she had assumed they'd be going in together. But she wasn't fazed. After all, this was her thing and as a rule she preferred to go it alone. Marvin sat down in a chair along the wall and began to flip through some magazines there. The receptionist walked over to open a large oaken door and moved aside.

Sam stepped inside and the door closed behind her, the latch clicking crisply. The office was as cold as a meat locker and roughly half the size of a tennis court, with shining maple floors and walls of some beige fabric, like muslin, covered for the most part with Native artwork. There were sculptures everywhere: some sitting on coffee tables, a few on tall glass plinths, others rising from the floor. One—of a polar bear on its hind legs—was more than eight feet tall. There was a large brown leather couch and several matching armchairs at the far end of the room, the furniture arranged in a manner that suggested a separate room or sitting area. There was a well-stocked wet bar along the wall.

A heavyset man of about forty-five, with thick red hair pulled back in a ponytail, sat behind a large desk opposite the door where Sam had entered, a phone cradled to his ear. His feet were up on the desk; he wore baggy black shorts and a tank top and red sneakers. The man half turned when Sam entered and held up a forefinger, as if to say he'd be just a minute. He was clean-shaven, his complexion not good at all, his face and shoulders covered with freckles.

Sam gave the room another quick once-over. She'd been expecting to find Ronnie Red Hawk here. The man on the phone turned away from her, spoke while looking out the large plate-glass windows to the forested hills in the distance.

"You can tell Trump to go piss up a rope," the man was saying. "I'll build it without him. I'm the one guy he doesn't boss."

Sam waited a moment longer, then turned and walked back into the foyer. Marvin looked up, frowned when he saw her.

"What's going on?"

"Where's Red Hawk?" she asked.

"He's not in there?"

"No," Sam said. "Just some white guy talking on the phone. A big dude with red hair."

Marvin laughed and the receptionist joined him. "That's Ronnie," he said.

"That's him?" Sam asked. "Ronnie Red Hawk's not Native?"

"He's Native enough," Marvin said. "Long story, but he's Native. And right this minute he's probably wondering where you went."

Sam turned and went back through the door. The red-haired, freckle-faced man who was Ronnie Red Hawk hung up the phone. As he got to his feet, he picked up a book from the desk. Sam saw it was a copy of *Frontier Woman*, the trade paperback, looking brand-new. He stepped around the desk, extending his hand. He was tall, maybe six three or four.

"You're Sam Sawchuk," he said. "I'm Ronnie."

"Very nice to meet you," Sam said.

"Let's sit over here," Ronnie said, indicating the couch.

The couch was probably forty feet away. Crossing the room, Sam removed her hat and pushed back her hair. Ronnie towered over her and as they walked Sam could feel his eyes on her breasts, swinging freely in the blouse. In the cool of the office, she could feel her nipples against the thin fabric of the top. When Ronnie indicated the couch to her, she sat and placed the hat beside her. The leather was real and soft as butter.

"Cool hat," Ronnie said. "You want something to drink? Soda or water? Hey—you want a shot of tequila? I got some great tequila."

Sam smiled. "I'm good."

Ronnie shrugged and sat down in a chair opposite the couch. He was still holding the book loosely in his left hand.

"So you've read the book," Sam said.

"Not all of it," Ronnie said. "Well, just the first page actually. I had my secretary go out and buy it an hour ago. But I read the thing on the back, you know, where they tell what it's about. I like it."

How's that for a snap review, Sam thought. The man reads the back cover and decides the book is a winner.

"Who's playing the woman?" Ronnie asked.

"Olivia Burns."

"Yeah?" Ronnie said. "Do you know Kari Karson?"

"I don't know her," Sam said. "Not personally."

"She's incredible," Ronnie said. "You should put her in your movie."

"Well," Sam said slowly, "there's not a role for her right now. She's too old to play the daughter and too young for the preacher's wife. She's pretty busy in the tabloids anyway."

"Those assholes," Ronnie said. "They should leave her alone."

"I agree," Sam said. She wanted to move off the starlet. "So Marvin tells me you're a big movie fan."

"I love movies," Ronnie said. "I got maybe two thousand DVDs. Blu-ray."

"What do you like?"

"I like everything," Ronnie said. "I don't know . . . *Scarface. Braveheart. Goodfellas. Rocky* . . . the first one anyway. I like comedies, like *Superbad* or *Pineapple Express*. Westerns. I love westerns."

"*Frontier Woman* is sort of like a western," Sam said, spotting an opening. "It's actually set in the 1840s. Call it an early western."

"I thought that, reading the thing on the back. Who's playing the Indian . . . what's his name?"

"Gregory Stone."

"He's okay," Ronnie said. "He was good as Sitting Bull in the HBO thing. You see it?"

"Yeah. He's great."

"You should make a movie with him and Kari Karson."

Kari Karson again, Sam thought. "Hey—find me a script and we'll talk about it," she joked. "Sounds like you should be in the film business, Ronnie."

"I'd be good at it," he replied. "I'm good at everything I do. I'm an incredible businessman. Incredible. You know why? Because I know what's good and what sucks."

"Intuition," Sam said. "It's huge in this business. And you can't teach it." She hesitated, cautioning herself to go slow. "You know, I've got a partner on this project, he doesn't know shit about movies. He's got money but his instincts suck. I don't have to tell you that it's tough to work with somebody like that."

"So why do it?"

"Because I need the equity. I'd dump him in a New York minute if somebody else stepped up with the cash." She paused for half a beat, like a poker player pondering whether to call or raise. She decided to go all in. "And yeah—I'm talking about somebody like you, Ronnie. There are a lot of people out there who like movies, but true instinct is tough to find."

"What's his name—this other guy?"

"His name doesn't matter. Just a guy who likes to play producer."

Ronnie leaned back in the chair and gazed at the ceiling for a long moment, as if taking time to imagine himself in a certain position in the film business. "And I would be a producer?" he asked, his eyes still cast upward.

"Absolutely."

Now he looked at her. "So, like, if the movie won an Oscar, I'd be one of the people onstage?"

"Of course."

Ronnie turned in his chair and had a long and quite deliberate look at himself in the large mirror on the opposite wall. He didn't seem embarrassed in the least that he was admiring his own reflection. "I might like to get into acting at some point too," he said after a moment. "My ex-girlfriend told me I look like Liam Neeson."

"I can see that," Sam said. If she'd been drinking something she'd have spit it up. The man sitting across from her looked as much like Liam Neeson as Sam looked like Jabba the Hutt.

He looked at her now. "How much you need?"

"I'd have to check the paperwork," Sam said, and she paused once more; she could feel her pulse rate elevating. "Ballpark, six million."

Ronnie Red Hawk never blinked. "Let's do it."

Sam, stretching like a cat, locked her hands behind her neck. "I like the way you handle yourself, Mr. Red Hawk. You know what—I think I would like a shot of tequila after all."

Ronnie openly ogled her breasts, straining against the blouse, as he heaved his bulky frame out of the chair. "You'll love this stuff. I get it sent up special from Mexico. It's incredible."

# SEVEN

Fairfield Village was a somewhat faithfully reconstructed pioneer settlement located on a two-lane blacktop a few miles off Route 17, about halfway between Woodstock and Oneonta. Virgil, driving his old pickup and hauling Mary Nelson's double horse trailer behind, found the place easily enough, arriving at a quarter to seven Monday morning. There were signs with FRONTIER WOMAN and BIG DEAL PRODUCTIONS everywhere, advertising the film shoot and advising cast and crew where to park.

Virgil pulled the Ford into a gravel lot at one end of the re-created village and turned the ignition off. The settlement was much larger than he'd expected, covering maybe fifty acres in all. The main street was composed of dirt, and featured—among other buildings—a general store, millinery, post office, courthouse, and smithy. There were fields, just beyond the town proper, planted with rye and corn and bordered with rail fences. And while the quaintness of the village felt artificial on a certain level, the fields were real, as were the crops.

A few people in period costume wandered the streets, carrying take-out coffees, the early hour and their somewhat sluggish pace suggesting they were heading for work. Whether they were involved with the film or everyday employees of the pioneer village, Virgil had no idea. In fact, he had no notion at all of what to expect now that he was there. He'd been told it was the first day of shooting and to be at the village at seven in the morning. Nothing else.

He'd brought along a thermos of coffee and some lunch, and now he poured himself a cup and leaned against the fender of the truck, waiting for whatever was going to happen next. Alongside the parking lot, off the end of the village, in what must have been a fallow field, a couple dozen large trailers were parked, all part and parcel of the film crew, he assumed. There were a lot of people hustling here and there, some carrying totes, others with clipboards or binders in hand. Some wore lightweight headsets.

After a time Virgil spotted the two men who'd approached him in his hayfield several days ago stepping out of one of the trailers. The taller one, the director with horseshit on his shoes, spotted him and pointed him out to the other, the longhaired one. Virgil couldn't recall either of their names.

Pretty soon the longhair corralled a third man and the pair of them headed over. The longhair wore cotton pants and a tight T-shirt, the better to show off his arms. The other man, carrying a clipboard, was lean and rangy, with gray hair that reached past his collar, and he wore faded jeans and a green work shirt. He was probably in his sixties, with creases around his eyes, his faced lined and weathered from too many hours in the sun. He had a relaxed way about him that the longhair didn't, the way he walked, his body language. When they were twenty feet away, Virgil remembered the longhair's name. Levi.

"You made it," Levi said as they approached, his tone suggesting that he had little confidence in Virgil showing up. "This is Tommy Alamosa, first assistant director." He jerked his chin toward Virgil. "This guy works for the guy who owns the horses."

Tommy Alamosa extended his hand. "I bet this guy has a name."

Virgil shook the hand. "Virgil."

"Glad to meet you, Virgil."

Levi never offered a handshake and Virgil was far from disappointed with that. He'd already decided the man was a poser. The older guy seemed okay, though. So far.

Tommy turned and gestured to the settlement. "We're basically taking over the village for the week," he said. "There's a paddock over there for the horses. There's feed and water and some straw for bedding, if you need it. You can leave them here or trailer them back and forth every day. Up to you."

Virgil looked at the paddock, and the barn behind. Two long-eared goats were enclosed in the paddock, and Virgil could hear the sound of chickens somewhere, possibly from the barn. There were no other horses in sight.

"You'd better check with your boss on that, cowboy," Levi said. "What's his name—Cain?"

"Yeah."

"What's his first name?"

Virgil shrugged. "I call him Mr. Cain."

"Who said there was no respect left in the world?" Tommy asked. "You want to unload the horses? We're going to put them to work this morning. I'd like to have a look at them anyway."

"In the paddock?" Virgil asked.

"That's good," Tommy said. "They'll be pulling a buckboard, a scene where the family comes to town for supplies. They can pull a buckboard?"

"They can pull a wagon." Virgil shrugged. "Not much of a stretch. Somebody trained them well."

"Not you?"

"No."

"I'll send somebody over to show you where to go," Tommy said. "You need a hand hooking the team to the buckboard?"

"Mr. Cain told me to deliver the horses," Virgil said. "He didn't say anything about hitching them to anything."

"What the fuck did you think we were going to do with them?" Levi demanded.

"I wouldn't know," Virgil said. "I'm not in the movie business."

Tommy turned to Levi. "We got a wrangler on set?"

Levi indicated Virgil. "I figured this guy—"

"You figured what—he was going to work for nothing? We need to get this straightened out." He turned to Virgil. "You interested in working for us?"

"Sure."

"He's not union," Levi said.

"Neither are the horses. Put him on a personal services contract. Sorry about this, Virgil, but we'll get it right. I have to get moving. You two can figure out the money."

He walked away. Levi waited until he'd disappeared into one of the trailers, then turned and looked unhappily at Virgil.

"What do you want?" he asked.

"Remind me—what are you paying for the horses?" Virgil asked.

"Five hundred a day."

"If it's good enough for Bob and Nelly, it's good enough for me."

Two hours later Virgil had the team harnessed to a buckboard that apparently was the property of the little settlement. FAIRFIELD VILLAGE was stenciled onto the sideboards, and someone had artfully arranged a worn canvas tarp over the lettering to conceal the name from the cameras. The cinematographer and crew had been setting and re-setting lights in front of the general store for a while, and as he waited, Virgil had driven the buckboard around the perimeter of the town several times, getting the horses used to it. It wasn't much different than pulling a hay wagon, Virgil guessed, other than the fact that there were a few dozen people around. And, of course, the lights. But the team fell into pace, and even broke into a trot a couple of times when Virgil encouraged them.

The scene, as it was described to him, would be of the frontier family—the husband, wife, and daughter—driving into town, traveling along the main street a hundred yards and then stopping in front of the store, where the man would jump down and tie the horses to the hitching post. It seemed pretty simple to Virgil but it was taking a long time to set everything up.

The director, Robb-something, Virgil finally remembered, was doing a lot of walking around, hands thrust deep in his pockets, occasionally stopping to look up and down the dirt street as if waiting for something or somebody to arrive. Inspiration maybe. Tommy Alamosa sometimes walked with him, and he seemed to be encouraging him to get on with things.

Finally, they were ready to try one, as Tommy called it. A diminutive woman wearing a long blue dress and bonnet came out of one of the trailers and approached the blacksmith shop at the end of the village, where Virgil was standing by the front wheel of the buckboard, holding the team. The woman was accompanied by another woman, this one carrying a cell phone and a couple bottles of water. It took Virgil a moment to realize that the woman in the dress was the actress Olivia Burns. She smiled and said hello to Virgil.

"I'm Olivia," she said.

"Virgil."

"Your horses are beautiful," she said.

Virgil just nodded, not wanting to get into the whole ownership thing again. Someday he might have to decide just who in the hell did own the horses.

A minute later a girl of about ten, also in a gingham dress, appeared. When she saw Bob and Nelly, she ignored everybody else and went directly to the horses, cautiously holding out her hand.

"Feel how soft their noses are," she said in wonderment.

Virgil had some carrots in his pocket and he broke one in half and gave the pieces to the girl. "You ever do this before?"

"No," she said. "I'm from Brooklyn."

"Hold your hand flat," he said, demonstrating. "Let them take it from you."

The girl did as she was told and the two horses gobbled the carrots. The little girl smiled, then looked at Virgil. "What's your name?" she asked.

"Virgil. What's yours?"

"Georgia Lee Thompson."

"And you're in the movie?"

"Yes, I'm Sara," the little girl said. She suddenly stepped back and flung her forearm across her face. "Oh mother, woe is me to be trapped in this desolate place!"

The girl stopped emoting as quickly as she'd begun and broke into laughter. Virgil smiled.

"Here he comes," he heard Tommy say, and he looked up to see a man approaching, dressed in high boots and homespun pants and a shapeless shirt of some rough material. In his hand he carried a brown slouch hat. Tommy introduced him to Virgil as Daniel Vardon.

"Daniel plays the husband," Tommy said.

The man was vaguely familiar to Virgil; no doubt he'd seen him in some movie or on TV. He was dark-haired and had deep-set dark eyes that gave him the appearance of being a thinker, whether he was or not. He was slender and short—maybe five foot six or so—and quite serious looking.

He was also terrified of the horses.

He didn't want to touch them, he didn't want to stand in front of them, he wouldn't stand behind them, and he definitely did not want to drive the buckboard with them pulling it. Apparently this aversion hadn't come up during the casting process and the director Robb was not particularly happy with the turn of events. He walked around in circles, muttering to himself, and then got on his cell phone and wandered off. Tommy Alamosa spoke to Daniel for several moments, then asked someone to get Levi Brown from wherever he was. While they waited, Tommy walked over to Virgil.

"How do you like it so far?" he asked.

Virgil shrugged. "Could be worse. Could be raining."

"Yeah, it could," Tommy said. "I have a proposition for you, Virgil."

Sam arrived on set shortly before noon. Driving up from Kingston, she'd been on the phone with Robb almost constantly. Apparently things weren't going all that smoothly and Robb, in general, didn't do well when things were going sideways. He did even worse when things were going sideways and Sam wasn't around. She kept him on the line for half an hour, reassuring him. Finally, after seeing a sign that announced Fairfield Village as being just ten miles away, she told him she'd be there momentarily and hung up.

Five minutes later, she began to see rough cardboard placards on fence posts and telephone poles with arrows in Magic Marker displaying directions to the site. There was a handful of other signs, vivid red lettering on a white background, proclaiming the name of the movie and the production company. She'd been expecting those. However, with the village finally in sight, she came upon a very large sign she had not been expecting:

FRONTIER WOMAN
RED HAWK FILMS

Sam nearly drove into the ditch.

"What the fuck?" she said out loud. It had been just three days since she'd signed the deal with Ronnie Red Hawk and already he was making signs and stamping the movie with his own name? Who did he think he was? It was the type of move Sam herself would make, and that bothered her more than a little. However, she had no choice but to set it aside in her mind for the time being. Apparently there were problems on set to sort out. She would deal with Ronnie Red Hawk down the road, after he realized he was out of his depth. For now, Sam would let him flounder for a bit before showing him the advantages of keeping to the shallow end.

First she had to get to the village and make sure they actually got something worth printing on the first day of shooting. Thank God for Tommy Alamosa, she thought. He was good at keeping things moving, and at talking people down from ledges, which is why she hired him. He had a reputation as a doper and a guy who liked women, particularly young women, but that had nothing to do with Sam, as long as he did his job. He was a pro and she needed him, with Robb's insecurities and Levi's delusions of grandeur to deal with.

When she arrived, she parked by the trailers at the end of the faux settlement and walked toward the cameras and crew gathered on the dirt street a couple hundred yards away. As she got near, she spotted Olivia Burns and the little girl Georgia, decked out in gingham frocks and sitting on the hard wooden seat of a buckboard wagon. Sam didn't, however, recognize the man sitting beside them, also wearing period costume. It sure as hell wasn't Daniel Vardon. This guy was somewhere in his forties, his face and neck and muscular forearms deeply tanned; he had light-brown hair and an expression that was an odd mixture of bemusement and sheepishness. Sam didn't know who he was, but it was quite obvious he was no actor. Nor was he Vardon's stand-in, whom she'd interviewed herself a week earlier.

Robb had been standing on the plank sidewalk looking morose, and now he beetled across the dirt street to intercept her.

"This has been a disaster," he said.

She reached out to stroke his cheek. "It'll be fine," she said. "Who's the guy in the wagon?"

"Oh fuck," Robb said. "The guy who came with the horses. Virgil-something. The asshole I told you about. He made fun of me and Levi in the field."

"Daniel didn't make it to set?"

"Oh, he's here," Robb said. His tone grew mincing. "Daniel has a thing about horses. He's scared shitless of them."

"Christ," Sam said. "What about the stand-in?"

"Guy's a fag from Boston. You think he can operate a wagon and horses?"

"Homosexuals can't drive buckboards?" Sam asked. "Does the gay and lesbian alliance know about this?" She put her arm around Robb's shoulders. "Okay, looks as if we're stuck with the hired hand. Let's make it work."

The man named Virgil was talking with Tommy Alamosa, who stood with his right foot up on the front wheel of the buckboard, shooting the shit with the guy like they were at a ball game or something. Sam made her way over to the wagon and, after saying hello to Olivia and Georgia, turned to the man.

"Hey buddy," she said. "I'm Sam Sawchuk. Listen, we really appreciate you helping us out here. Your horses are gorgeous. What are their names?"

"Bob and Nelly," Virgil said.

"Nelly likes carrots," Georgia said.

"Carrots are good for you," Sam said to the little girl before stepping closer to the horses.

"You might want to put your hand on that mare to let her know you're there," Virgil advised. "She could decide to kick you otherwise."

"Hey, I'm the producer," Sam joked. "She won't kick me."

"She doesn't read the papers, she might not know you're the producer," Virgil said. "She kicked me once and I'm the one who feeds her every day."

Sam held her smile but moved away from the mare. "So what's the plan here?" she said to Tommy Alamosa.

"Long pan of the three of them in the buckboard, approaching the general store," Tommy said, gesturing with his right hand to indicate the intended route. "Medium shot from behind of them stopping at the hitching post. That's it for Virgil. We cut to a tight shot of Daniel climbing down from the buckboard—*without* the horses—and then we go inside, the three of them entering the store."

Sam turned and looked down the street, imagining the sequence. She frowned.

"Best we got," Tommy said. "Unless you have a better idea."

"You get anything at all yet?" she asked.

"Nothing," he said. "Wardrobe had to alter a set of Daniel's clothes to fit Virgil. We've been waiting on them."

"It's fucking near noon," Sam said. "Let's shoot it."

They filmed it as Tommy described. Wearing the slouch hat, Virgil was passable as Daniel Vardon, at least from a distance. They tried a couple of medium shots of Virgil and the two actresses climbing down from the buckboard with the horses still harnessed, but they weren't usable.

"No way in hell," Tommy told Robb and Sam, looking at the footage in the video village. "Daniel's built like a dancer and this guy Virgil looks like he could toss one of those horses over a fence. Print it and let's move on."

Sam knew he was right, but still she looked pointedly at Robb. "Just a minute," she said. She needed him to establish early on that he, and not Tommy Alamosa, would be calling the shots. As usual, it took him a moment to catch on.

"Let's have another look," he said.

They ran the footage again on the monitor, with Robb watching intently, arms crossed, his thumb pressed to the cleft of his chin.

"No," he said decisively midway through. "That won't work. They're two different body types. I don't want it. Let's move inside."

Levi arrived back on site as they were setting up to film inside the store. Sam, standing in front of the mock courthouse, saw him hurrying toward her from the parking lot. She guessed what was on his mind and walked out to meet him, out of earshot of the others.

"When did you get here?" he asked at once.

"Hour ago."

"Did you happen to see anything interesting on the drive in?"

"Like a big red sign announcing our new producing partner?" Sam asked.

"I thought he was a silent partner," Levi said.

Sam sighed. "I have a feeling that 'silent' isn't in his vocabulary. What would you like me to do about it?"

"Start by taking down the sign."

"And piss him off?" Sam asked. "You know we're doing drawdowns. If I'm going to piss him off, I'll wait until after he's paid in full."

"Chrissakes."

"Look—this guy read *one* page of the book and decided to give us six million dollars," Sam said. "I have a feeling he's got the attention span of a two-year-old. So let him play movie producer for a while. Once he sees how boring it is on set, he'll find some other shiny object to chase and we'll be rid of him. Capisce?"

"Like I got a choice," Levi said. He indicated the crew converging around the general store. "Did they manage to get anything?"

"We're back on track," Sam said. "First day shit, right? Everybody needs to find their rhythm. Where have you been anyway?"

"I had to meet someone."

"You do realize we're shooting a movie here."

"It was personal," Levi said, irritated. "Plus I had to go to the bank to get money for that dumb hick who brought the horses. He has to have cash."

"I thought you were dealing with the owner."

"Just for the horses," Levi said. "This is on top of that, for the hired hand. First he held us up for an extra five hundred a day to wrangle the horses, and then five more as a stand-in."

Sam smiled. "And he's a dumb hick? Good thing we didn't hire a smart one."

"He's a prick. He pushes me too far and I'll knock him on his ass. You know where I come from, Sam."

"Right," she said. "The mean streets of Dee-troit."

"Don't fucking mock me."

"I wouldn't dream of it," Sam told him. "It's a thirty-million-dollar movie. We need horses, and we need a wrangler." She smiled. "Guy's kind of a stud too."

"Give me a fucking break," Levi said. "I need something to eat."

"I'll walk with you," Sam said. "I could use a cup of tea."

They turned and started for the craft services trailer. As they headed across the lot, a black limousine approached along the drive from the main road out front, moving slowly, as if the driver was either lost or didn't know where to park.

"That for Olivia?" Levi asked.

"Doubt it," Sam said. "Olivia's not a limo kind of girl."

"Who, then?"

Sam stopped walking and watched as the limo idled up beside them. As she waited for the back window to power down, she didn't need to speculate as to who might be inside. She knew damn well who was inside.

"Hello, Sam," the man said, the cold air from the limo's interior escaping like a blast of Arctic wind.

"Mr. Red Hawk," Sam said. "Welcome to the set."

# EIGHT

Claire took a bite of her burger and leaned back in her chair as she chewed. Swallowing, she wiped her mouth with the paper napkin, then smiled across the table.

"You know, I've never dined with a movie star before," she said.

"Well, you're not dining with one now, so you can stop it," Virgil replied.

He took a drink of beer and looked around the roadhouse called Slim's. The place was moderately busy, for a Monday night anyway; the bar was lined with young guys drinking beer and watching some show on the big screen, where contestants of questionable intelligence were attempting to jump bicycles over a pool containing a half-dozen small sharks. The guys watching were wagering on the outcome and no doubt wondering how they could land themselves on a show like that.

Roughly half the tables were occupied as well. Virgil and Claire sat by the front windows where they could see the Hudson in the distance in the fading daylight, drifting slowly past the town of Saugerties on its way to the Atlantic.

"I don't know," Claire said. "Sounds to me as if you made quite an impression, first day and all. What did you get—two promotions?"

"Yup," Virgil said. He had a bite of steak and talked around it. "From horse hauler to buckboard outfitter to a guy who pretends to be another guy. I'll be surprised if I don't win an Oscar or two."

"You're pretty funny for a movie star."

"I told you to quit that."

Claire smiled again and plucked a French fry from her plate. "Have some of these," she said, pushing them toward Virgil. "Well, it sounds as if the money's okay."

Virgil nodded. "They said they're going to need me for four or five days at least. Should take care of my taxes anyway. And I sold my young bull to a guy up by New Hartford. I'm trucking him up there tomorrow."

"Why are you selling the bull?"

"Because he's half-brother to all my heifers and I don't want him breeding them. I got a line on another bull, once I get the money for this one."

"So no movie work tomorrow?"

"They're shooting inside stuff," Virgil said. "They said I could come and watch if I was interested. I'll truck that bull instead."

"So you going to take me to the set someday?"

"Sure," Virgil said. "But you can't call me Mr. Cain there. They're under the impression that Virgil and Mr. Cain are two separate people. They think Mr. Cain owns the horses and Virgil's just the half-wit hired hand."

Claire raised her eyebrows as she wiped her hands on the napkin and took a sip of beer. "And why would they think that, Virgil?"

Virgil shrugged. "Not sure. These people like to assume things, especially when it comes to us rural folk."

"And you didn't feel any urge to set them straight?"

"It's not my job to set them straight," Virgil said. "I'm just the hired hand."

After they ate they took a walk down to the river. The air was cooler there, and there was a slight breeze from the east, rippling the surface of the water. They stopped at a pavilion by a public dock, and Claire sat atop a picnic table while Virgil walked down to the water's edge, where he stood looking out over the Hudson. A tugboat was motoring noisily upstream, its engines working hard against the current.

"Well," Claire said after a time. "Did you meet her?"

"Meet who?" Virgil asked without turning.

"You know who. Olivia Burns."

"Yeah, I met her."

"And is she beautiful?"

"Oh yeah," Virgil said. "Gorgeous. Stunning."

"All right, all right."

"Hey, you asked." Virgil turned now. "She's actually very small, and quiet. I don't think she said two words the whole time I was around her."

"Which was probably two more than you said."

Virgil nodded and picked up a rock and with a long, high arc threw it into the river. It splashed down a couple hundred feet out. "It was funny, though," he said. "When they were actually filming, she changed. It was like turning on a light switch. All of a sudden she became this other person."

"I guess that's acting," Claire said.

"I guess so." Virgil threw another rock. "I met another actress too. Now, she was beautiful. I liked her a lot."

"I don't need to hear this," Claire said from behind him.

"Okay."

She waited a few moments. "Okay, who is she?"

Virgil turned. "Her name is Georgia. Blonde hair, great smile. Smart as a whip." He paused. "She's ten years old."

"Asshole."

He smiled and walked back to her. He took her face in his hands and kissed her, then pulled away for a second and kissed her again, this time reaching behind her and wrapping the long hair at the nape of her neck in his hand. They stayed like that for a long while, then walked back up the hill to where they had parked.

"I'm heading out first thing in the morning," Claire said. They were standing by the fender of her car. "Looks as if I'll be in Rochester for the rest of the week. You can call me on my cell."

"Okay."

"Unless you move to Hollywood."

"They have phones in Hollywood. I'll still call you."

"Goodnight, Mr. Cain."

Sam sat drinking in the bar at the Hampton Inn with Levi. Several members of the crew were also there, scattered around the room, some playing darts, others just lounging and imbibing. People were still getting to know one another. Within days, they would decide who liked whom, and who didn't, and there would be hookups here and there as the shoot progressed. And maybe a few broken hearts before it was over. It was like summer camp for adults.

She and Levi had the corner of the bar to themselves, Levi nursing a gin and tonic and Sam drinking tequila shots and beer. From where she sat Sam could see the entrance to Finnegan's Bar and Grill on the far side of the hotel's lobby, the entrance where two hours earlier she'd seen Olivia Burns disappear with Ronnie Red Hawk.

"Robb coming down?" Levi asked.

"I doubt it," Sam said. "He's going over tomorrow's shot list." She knew Robb was probably sleeping, but she wouldn't tell Levi that. Sam would go over the shot list later, when she finally went up to the room, and she'd tell Robb in the morning what he needed to get that day.

"Where the hell's he staying?" Levi asked.

"Who?"

"Red Hawk."

"Here, I assume," Sam said. "The limo's in the parking lot, and I saw his driver get on the elevator earlier."

"When do we get the money?"

"We got it," Sam said.

"What?"

"He paid the first draw, twenty-five percent. It's in the bank."

Levi sat fuming, making no attempt to hide it.

"What?" Sam demanded.

"I assumed I'd be handling it. That's my job, Sam."

Sam shrugged. "He gave me a shopping bag with a million and a half in it. What was I going to do—carry it around for a day or two?"

Levi shook his head, as if in disbelief. "When's the second draw?"

"Halfway through shooting, so six weeks or so."

"Shit," Levi said.

Sam gave him a long look. "What's your problem with this? We got the money."

"I assumed I'd be handling it," he said again. "Jesus Christ. What the fuck's he talking to Olivia about?"

"He's probably asking her if George Clooney is a good kisser."

"You think this is funny?"

"I think it's funnier than you do," Sam said. She laughed and downed a shot. "But then, I don't have a crush on Olivia Burns."

"I don't have a crush on Olivia Burns."

"Sure you do," Sam said. "So does Robb. Shit, I'd probably do her myself if the opportunity presented itself." She indicated to the bartender to bring another round. "You need to get your head out of your ass, Levi. We make the movie first and let everything fall wherever it falls. Ronnie Red Hawk has a piece of the film, whether you like it or not."

Sam watched as Levi finished his drink and pushed the empty glass away. While he waited for the bartender to bring the refill, he looked at himself in the mirror behind the bar, running his fingers through his hair, pushing a strand here or there. Maybe he was still stressing over the fact that he personally hadn't been paid the money from Ronnie Red Hawk or maybe he was thinking of how far he'd traveled from the days when he was Larry Bronowski from downtown Detroit, before he had golden locks and bulging triceps and a cool name.

As she watched, though, Sam saw his expression change and she realized he was no longer looking at his own reflection but at something behind them. She turned to see a huge man at a corner table—a Samoan, it appeared. The man, who was reading a menu, had to weigh at least three hundred pounds.

"Who's the giant?" Sam asked.

"How would I know?" Levi demanded.

"I thought maybe he was crew," Sam said. "He looks like a Samoan, so he's not an actor—not one of ours anyway. We wouldn't slide a Samoan in a film about 1840s America, would we?"

Levi shook his head irritably, dismissing the matter. He continued to watch the big man in the mirror, though. He was in a bit of a mood tonight, Sam thought. She had seen him like this before and she had to wonder why he wouldn't just stay upstairs in his room when he was so prickly.

Tommy Alamosa came into the bar, and with him was one of the girls from craft services. Her name was Nikki, Sam remembered. She was tall and curvy, maybe twenty-two, which was roughly a third of Tommy's age. But right in his wheelhouse, Sam thought. Nikki had a hippie-ish quality to her; she rarely wore a bra and always had any number of items hanging from her hair—trinkets and beads and bangles. Sort of like a distaff version of Keith Richards, but about fifty years younger and hot. Tommy was catnip to women. Nikki might be the first woman on the crew he would sleep with, but Sam doubted she would be the last. Sam herself had had a fast and furious fling with Tommy the previous year while shooting *Monkey Sex*. They'd done some Ecstasy and fucked a couple of times in his hotel room. It had been fun and Sam, who turned forty that month, was flattered that Tommy had been interested in her, however briefly. Forty was way out of his age range.

"You guys want a drink?" Sam asked as the two approached.

"We're just passing through," Tommy said. "They're calling for rain Wednesday. We can shoot the schoolhouse interiors if we have to. I put it on the schedule in case. We'll need the schoolmarm and the rest of the kids."

"All right," Sam said. "How's it going, Nikki?"

"Cool."

Cool, Sam thought. Ah, she remembered those days when everything was cool. When there was nothing to do on a Monday night but to hook up with a charming guy like Tommy Alamosa and smoke some dope and fuck each other's brains out. She remembered those days and missed them. She especially missed them when the alternative was hanging out in a hotel bar listening to Levi whine.

Maybe he was reading her thoughts because he began again.

"Olivia's in the restaurant with our Indian friend," Levi announced to Tommy.

Tommy laughed. "Is she now?"

"Another guy thinks it's funny," Levi said.

"Isn't it, like, incorrect to say Indian?" Nikki asked.

"Oh, our Native American partner," Levi said. "Fucking guy's whiter than rice but we have to treat him like he's Geronimo's great-grandson."

Tommy ignored Levi's bitching and turned to Sam. "Anyway, I thought I'd give you a heads-up on the weather situation, in case we need to change the call sheet. Nikki and I are going for a walk. We'll leave you two to your dissertation on the history of the Native peoples."

"Fuck you, Tommy," Levi said.

Nikki laughed as she and Tommy walked away.

"What's she laughing at?" Levi demanded.

Sam turned to him. "The fact that she's about to take your suggestion literally?"

Virgil used Mary Nelson's horse trailer to transport the yearling bull to New Hartford. He'd brought the bull up from the summer pasture before meeting Claire for dinner and left him in the barnyard overnight so the animal would be ready for loading first thing in the morning. Virgil was on the road shortly after daybreak. With the rising sun at his back, he headed north-west on the winding two-lane stretch that was Route 145. They were calling for temperatures in the nineties again, with clouds arriving late in the day, in advance of a storm front that promised rain for much of Wednesday. But promises, Virgil knew, could be broken, especially when it came to the matter of rain this particular summer.

He was watching the weather because he was due on the

movie set Wednesday morning. The scene called for Bob and Nelly to pull a single furrow plow back and forth across a meadow that was tucked in some poplar trees a half mile from the pioneer village. The meadow was a picnic area but apparently the production company had persuaded the owners of Fairfield Village to allow them to tear it up with plowshares. Virgil assumed that meant the production company had made it worthwhile to the owners financially. He could see how that might happen; they'd basically done the same thing with Virgil.

Before leaving the set on Monday he'd mentioned to Tommy Alamosa that he didn't know how the team of Percherons would take to pulling a plow. Mary Nelson had mentioned to Virgil that she thought they'd been used in plowing competitions in the past, but he had no idea if that was true.

"Don't worry about it," Tommy had said. "A guy with a tractor has already plowed half the field. If the team doesn't work out, we'll fake it, shoot them from the far side of the field by a little rise, have them walk just outside the plowed ground. You won't be able to tell. It'll actually make a nice long shot, the farmer behind the horses with the forest in the background. Later we'll cut in some shots of the wife watching from the porch of the log cabin, which is actually twenty miles from here. We can't get too close anyway because you're going to be standing in for Daniel again. The horse thing."

The horse thing. Virgil wasn't sure why they would hire a guy to shoot scenes with horses when the guy had a pathological fear of them. But he wasn't going to dwell on it; the windfall was going to help Virgil out with his taxes and that was all he needed to know. As for shooting on Wednesday, he doubted it would happen, if the rain came as expected. The truth was that Virgil needed the rain more than the day's wages.

Outside of Cobleskill he took Route 28 heading west, passing within a few miles of Cooperstown. Virgil had always intended to stop at the baseball hall of fame but had never gotten around to it. Maybe he'd finally do it later today, on the drive home when the trailer was empty. He wondered if the hall had any artifacts from the Toledo Mud Hens, his old team. The franchise had been around, in one form or another, since the late 1800s.

The farmer who was buying the bull was named Louie Batten. He'd driven down to look at the animal a couple weeks ago, and at that time had told Virgil that the asking price—two thousand dollars—was too high. A week later he'd called and offered fifteen hundred and eventually Virgil sold the bull for eighteen, with the condition that he deliver the animal. Batten had given Virgil directions over the phone and he found the place today without any trouble.

The farm, on a gravel side road eight miles south of New Hartford, looked run-down, with an ancient wooden barn missing half its plank siding, and an Insulbrick house that was just as mean. Twenty or so rangy Hereford cows were fenced in a sun-baked front field, picking at whatever meager pasture was there.

Virgil drove over to a gate that led to the field and parked. As he shut off the ignition, the barn door opened and a scrawny kid of thirteen or fourteen emerged, dragging a bale of straw by the twine. The kid wore dirty jeans and a faded red T-shirt with a flying dirt bike stenciled across the front. He was no bigger than a sapling and it took all his strength to hoist the bale up over the top of the fence and toss it into the field. The kid turned and hustled back into the barn without giving Virgil a glance.

Wondering why the kid would be carrying bedding to a herd in the middle of summer, Virgil got out of the truck. As he did he heard the creak of a screen door and turned to see Batten standing on the sagging porch of the house, a bottle of Coke in one hand and a half-eaten sandwich in the other. He was a big man, sloppy in his appearance, with small eyes and a scar that ran diagonally from the bridge of his nose to his jawline. Coming down the steps, he stuffed what remained of the sandwich in his mouth. He wore stained twill pants and a green John Deere T-shirt, stretched tightly across his big belly. The sleeves of the shirt had been cut off, revealing large, fleshy arms with fading tattoos on each bicep.

"You made it, eh?" he asked pointlessly.

Before Virgil could reply, the kid came out of the barn again, dragging another straw bale. Batten turned a bad eye on him.

"What the fuck are you doing?" he demanded.

The kid stopped, his thin forearms quivering with the effort of holding up the bale. He dropped his eyes to the ground. When he spoke, his voice was apologetic, uncertain. "Feeding 'em, like you said."

Batten walked over and roughly jerked the bale out of the kid's hands. "Feeding 'em this?" he snapped. "This is *straw,* you moron. Cows eat hay. You don't know the difference between hay and straw?"

The kid stared at the ground. "I didn't know. I'm sorry."

"*You're* sorry?" Batten said. "I'm sorry I hired a fucking moron."

The kid glanced at Virgil, then quickly away. His face was as red as his threadbare T-shirt. He had some cringe in him, for sure, but he'd been trying.

"Get the hay," Batten told him, "before I stuff that bale of straw down your throat, you useless little shit." He watched the kid scurry back into the barn before turning to Virgil. "Fucking kids," he said.

Virgil, his eyes on the door where the kid had disappeared, made no reply. It had nothing to do with him. Approaching the trailer, Batten didn't offer his hand and Virgil didn't want it anyway. Drinking from the bottle of Coke, Batten walked around to the tailgate and had a look inside.

"This is the bull?" he asked.

"That's the bull," Virgil said. What the hell did it look like—a barn swallow?

"I thought he was bigger than that," Batten said.

"No, he's exactly that big," Virgil said. "Same size he was two weeks ago when you saw him."

"Shit," Batten said. "I don't know."

"You don't know what?"

"I just figured he was bigger than that. I like a big bull."

Virgil didn't say anything more. Batten took another drink from the bottle, finishing it before tossing the empty onto the lawn. He belched loudly and wiped his mouth with the back of his hand.

"Well, shit, what the hell to do," he said.

Virgil didn't like the way the conversation was going. They had a deal. He was about to remind Batten of that fact when the kid emerged from the barn again, this time dragging a hay bale along in the dirt. Batten looked over.

"See?" he said. "You're not too stupid to learn."

The kid never looked their way as he hauled the bale to the field. The hay was heavier than the straw, and after realizing he didn't have enough strength to lift it over the fence, the kid opened the gate and pushed the bale inside before pulling the twine from it. The herd, presumably weary of tugging at the jimsonweed in the field, approached right away and began picking at the hay. Batten turned back to Virgil.

"You drove all this way," he said. "It's not really what I want but I'll give you what I offered you first off. Fifteen hundred. I just gotta hope he turns out to be a half-decent bull."

Virgil could see the play now. He'd driven four hours, investing his time and gasoline, not to mention the wear and tear on the truck and trailer. Batten was wagering that Virgil, rather than haul the animal back home, would settle for the fifteen hundred.

"Well?" Batten persisted.

"Fuck you," Virgil said.

"What did you say?"

"I said fuck you. We agreed on a price. I'll turn that bull loose in the Catskills before I'd sell him to you for a nickel less."

"You'd better watch that lip," Batten snapped. He stepped closer. "You won't get the fifteen hundred and I'll knock your goddamn teeth out to boot."

To Virgil's way of thinking, the last comment represented a threat to his personal well-being, but he wouldn't rise to the bait. When he was younger, he might have. Now he would cut his losses, head for home.

However, as he turned to leave, he saw the skinny kid by the fence watching him. There seemed to be a question in the kid's eyes. Virgil didn't know what the question was, but he had an inkling. So he asked Batten to repeat the threat and when Batten did, Virgil hit him in the jaw as hard as he could with his right fist. Batten fell backward against the trailer and then slid to a sitting position on the ground. He groaned and then blinked several times, and he seemed close to losing the sandwich he'd just ingested. Virgil left him there and got into the truck and started for home.

With the bull in the trailer in the heat of the day, he decided not to stop off at Cooperstown. The hall of fame would have to wait. He got a bucket of water when he stopped for gas and watched as the bull drank it thirstily. Virgil decided that the animal was better off with him than with Batten anyway. Virgil would find another buyer.

It was late afternoon when he pulled in the yard at home. He drove the truck to the pasture field at the back of the farm where his beef cattle passed the summer, and unloaded the bull there beside a couple dozen young steers. His heifers were in another field, up near the barn.

Parking the truck by the house, he left the trailer hooked on for the time being. If the weatherman proved wrong, he'd be hauling Bob and Nelly to the film set at Fairfield Village in the morning. He walked to the end of the lane to pick up the mail and looked through it on the way back to the house. There was another bill from the county reminding him of his tax situation. With the deal for the bull falling through, he was even more grateful for the movie work.

In the kitchen, he grabbed a beer from the fridge and was taking a drink when the telephone rang. He reached for it and heard Claire's voice.

"You really need to get a cell phone," she said right off.

"Actually, I don't."

"You heard from the movie people?"

"No," Virgil said. He glanced at the reminder from the county and tossed it on the table. "Should I have?"

"Probably."

"Why? Where are you anyway—Rochester?"

"I'm back in Kingston," Claire told him. "Investigating a

suspicious death. Some kids found a body floating in Rond-out Creek."

Virgil paused, trying to make the connection. "And what's that got to do with the movie people?"

"Everything."

"All right," he said, already dreading the answer. "Whose body is it?"

"Olivia Burns."

# NINE

For the time being at least, virtually all the suspects were either with the production company or on the periphery of the film shoot, so that's where Claire began. The term "suspects" was not entirely accurate, as the presence of foul play had not been established. All that was known for certain was that Olivia Burns had been found early Tuesday morning floating in a shallow eddy of Rondout Creek, wearing a nylon tracksuit and sporting a lump on her left temple. Cause of death was unknown at this point.

Since most of the film crew was staying at the Hampton Inn, that's where Claire set up late Tuesday morning, taking over a small boardroom off the main lobby. When she arrived at the hotel a little before noon, Joe Brady was already there. Investigating a suspicious death was not a pleasant task; investigating a suspicious death with Joe Brady also on the case was akin to having a root canal without anesthesia.

"These people," Joe had said, approaching her.

"What people?" Claire had asked.

"Film people."

Claire wasn't inclined to listen to Joe's take on the apparent subspecies known as film people, so she'd kept walking. She got a list of everyone working for the production company from someone named Levi Brown—a thick-chested man with a mane of fashionably dirty-blond hair that looked as if it cost a lot of money in upkeep. Brown said he was one of the producers on the movie, he and a woman named Sam Sawchuk.

The personnel list consisted of two pages, so Claire simply gave one to Joe Brady and kept the other for herself. Joe set up in Finnegan's Bar and Grill, which would not open until later in the afternoon. It was as good a place as any for Joe to deal with "these people."

Claire spent the next three hours basically learning nothing.

The last person to be seen with Olivia Burns was a guy named Ronnie Red Hawk, who looked like an out-of-shape Viking but claimed to be Native American. Claire decided she would talk to him before tackling the crew list.

"She was an incredible talent," Ronnie Red Hawk told her as they sat opposite each other in the boardroom. "We will miss her."

The man had an earnest, somewhat formal way of speaking, as if he were giving a eulogy, or providing sound bites for the evening news.

"Did you know her long?" Claire asked.

"Not really. No."

"How long?"

Ronnie Red Hawk took a few seconds to consider the question, as if determined to provide a thoroughly accurate reply. "About . . . seven hours."

"Seven hours?" Claire repeated. "Seriously?"

"Yes," Ronnie said. "But I feel as though I've known her much longer. Much. I have a way of connecting with people. It's almost . . . paranormal."

"Paranormal," Claire said. She wrote the word down on her notepad, then wondered at once why the hell she did.

Ronnie Red Hawk said that he'd had dinner with the actress the previous night there in the hotel restaurant, and that afterward he'd walked her to the door of her room on the fifth floor before continuing on to his suite. He'd last seen her at around ten thirty.

"How did she seem over dinner?" Claire asked.

"Incredible."

Claire sighed. "I mean—did she seem out of sorts, frightened, depressed? Anything like that?"

"No," Ronnie said matter-of-factly, as if incredulous that anyone could be out of sorts when basking in his presence. "She was wonderful. We talked of many things. Future projects."

"Future projects?" Claire asked. "What do you do?"

"Why, I'm a movie producer," Ronnie said. He gave Claire a puzzled look, as if she'd just announced that she'd never heard of pizza, or the NFL. "I'm the president of Red Hawk Films," he added.

"I'm not familiar with the various production companies," Claire said. "I'm sure there are lots of them. Red Hawk Films—have they been around long?"

"Not long. No."

Claire started to ask if the company had been around for more than seven hours but she let it go. "I assume your company is involved with *Frontier Woman*."

"Yes," Ronnie said. "I'm one of the main producers. For instance, if we win an Oscar I'll be one of the people onstage. Accepting, that is. And, of course, I'll be making a speech."

"I think we're about done here," Claire said.

"Good," Ronnie said. "I have to head down to JFK. I have someone very special flying in."

Claire sensed that he was dying for her to ask the identity of the special person en route to JFK, so she didn't. She had a list of people to talk to and she had to keep moving. In truth, she didn't know what to think of Ronnie Red Hawk.

All she had learned in the past ten minutes was what he thought of himself.

Sam stood looking out the window to the parking lot below, where Ronnie Red Hawk's limo was parked at a forty-five-degree angle, the exhaust belching fumes out the back. Behind her, Robb was lying on the bed, holding a pillow over his face as if in the act of suffocating himself. Levi was pacing the room; she could hear his shoes on the carpet.

"If we shut it down, we're out a shitload of money," Sam said. "The insurance doesn't cover everything. Keep in mind we had to pay Furlong the first day of shooting."

"Who?" Robb asked, his voice muffled by the pillow.

"The woman who wrote the book," Sam said, turning to look at him. "Remember her?"

"Oh yeah."

"The question is—who are we going to lose investor-wise if we keep going?" Levi said. "We can recast the lead but who do we lose if we don't have Olivia Burns?"

"*If* we don't have her?" Sam asked.

"You know what I mean. Who do we lose?"

"We'll find out soon enough," Sam said. "This story is all over the news. We're going to have to prepare a statement for the press." She thought about it, how she would word such a thing. "Christ, do you think she killed herself? You think she pulled a Virginia Woolf?"

"Very possible," Levi said.

Sam suspected Levi wanted to ask who Woolf was, but he didn't. "She seemed happy, though," Sam said. "She was excited about the part."

"Was it because of me?" Robb asked. He took the pillow from his face.

"No, it wasn't because of you, baby," Sam said. "Why would you even say a thing like that?"

"Because she wanted to work with Peter Dunmore," he replied.

"Stop that," Sam said. "We don't even know that she killed herself."

"Looks like a suicide to me," Levi said.

"And as far as we're concerned, it doesn't fucking matter," Sam said sharply. "What matters is how we're going to move forward."

Sam looked out the window again, in time to see Ronnie Red Hawk lumbering across the parking lot, heading for the limo. He got in and the big Cadillac drove off in the direction of the thruway.

"There goes our man from Red Hawk Films," she said. "Heading back to the rez, I hope. I was afraid he was going to call a press conference."

"I'm surprised the cops let him leave," Levi said.

"Why?" Sam turned away from the window.

"Why?" he repeated. "He was the last one with her. Wouldn't he be the prime suspect?"

"Two minutes ago you thought it was suicide," Sam reminded him. "Besides, why would Ronnie want to harm Olivia? She's the star of the movie. *His* movie, or so he thinks."

"That's my point," Levi said. "There's something not right about that guy. He doesn't look right, he doesn't sound right. He's not right."

"He's got casino money coming out of his ears," Sam said. "So I'm willing to cut him all kinds of slack. He can call himself Ronnie B. DeMille and walk around the set with a megaphone in his hand if he wants to."

"Forget about him," Robb said. "When do we begin shooting again?"

Levi and Sam both looked at him. The question was uncharacteristically direct, coming from Robb. It was also, Sam knew, exactly what they should be asking themselves.

"As soon as we find a replacement," she began, then stopped. "No, all we need to do is announce that we're looking for somebody. You know, we could actually get some good PR out of this. And then we go ahead and shoot around the character of Martha while we decide. A lot of actresses wanted this part, and you know fucking well every one of them still does. So this is what we do—we don't even contact any of the money people. Our stance is nothing has changed. While we regret this great tragedy, we keep right on shooting, which means back at it tomorrow. Let's keep in mind that we're paying a fucking crew."

"Yeah," Robb said.

"We need to get Tommy up here and set up a new shooting schedule," Sam said. The hotel phone rang then and she walked over to it. "We can shoot the schoolhouse stuff tomorrow." She picked up the receiver, said hello, and listened for a moment. "All right," she said before hanging up. "They want us downstairs to talk to the cops," she said. "It's our turn in the barrel. I'll call Tommy's cell and we'll meet back here in an hour."

"All right," Levi said. "I need to go work out anyway. I gotta work off this stress."

"You already talk to the cops?" Sam asked.

"I'll talk to them on my schedule, not theirs."

The Hampton Inn featured a good gym, better than most Levi had experienced in a chain hotel, especially a chain hotel out in the hinterland. In general he was of the opinion that everything to be found in the rural environs of the nation was of an inferior nature. This included the food and the drinks and the general intelligence of the people themselves. Not to mention whatever passed for culture. Levi had become convinced in recent years that he lived in a country of imbeciles, with limited and select pockets of intellect based, for the most part, in New York or Chicago or possibly LA.

The gym was empty when he got there and he started at once on the Nautilus, working his legs and glutes first. He was obviously the first to use the facilities that day and the equipment was very clean and spotless. That didn't stop Levi, who detested finding tiny rivulets of sweat or, even worse, the odd pubic hair on a machine, from wiping the equipment down anyway.

After he'd been on the Nautilus maybe five minutes a woman entered, tall and blonde, with her hair pulled back in a ponytail. She wore a black leotard and running shoes and carried with her a white towel and an e-reader. She gave Levi a quick nod and went directly to one of the treadmills, where she set up the reader, pulled glasses from somewhere inside the towel, and began a slow jog.

She was a good-looking woman, maybe thirty-five, and very serious in her demeanor, focused on both her reading and her workout. By her appearance she was urban and hip and Levi doubted she was from around there. Of course she wasn't from around there, if she was staying at the hotel. After a while he left the machine and approached a lifting bench not fifteen feet from the woman. He made a show of adding weight and then lay down and did a couple dozen presses. The room had mirrors all along one wall and he could watch himself there while he worked, occasionally sneaking glances over at the blonde. His arms looked good, the triceps rolling with each lift.

Not that the woman was noticing. She was intent on her jogging and on whatever she was reading. Levi added more weight and did a few more presses, then he got up and wiped his face with a towel. Turning, he reacted as if he'd forgotten she was there.

"Not a bad facility for Hooterville," he said.

She glanced over and nodded somewhat absently, then went back to her reading.

"I work locations a lot," he said. "Most of the time you can't find decent equipment. My local gym in Tribeca is state-of-the-art, so I'm spoiled. But I can live with this. If I don't work out every day, I get antsy as hell. It's like my body rebels. You?"

"Oh, I can miss a day and survive," she said, her eyes remaining on the reader.

She wasn't overly friendly but at least she'd responded and that was enough for Levi to pursue the conversation. He saw now that she really was a babe; she had a great ass and small, firm tits. Her nose was a little perky for Levi's taste but her mouth was very nice, her lips full. One of those ice-cool blondes, probably in fashion or television even. Hard to crack but definitely worth the effort in the end.

"I'm shooting a feature film in the area," he said. "So I'm here for a couple months. Always a bit of a culture shock, coming from the city. You think you're ready for everything you have to do without, but you never are." He paused. "Where you from?"

"California."

"I can see that, you look like a California girl," Levi said. "I get out there a lot. Meetings with studio honchos, you know? Pain in the ass, but part of the gig. I'd complain but who would listen?" He paused. "What are you reading? And don't tell me it's *Frontier Woman*."

"No."

Levi laughed. "That would be too ironic. The movie I'm making is an adaptation of the book. Have you read it?"

"*Frontier Woman*? Yeah, I have."

"Did you like it?"

"I liked a lot of it," the woman said. She reached forward to increase the speed on the treadmill.

"I'm Levi Brown, by the way."

"Sandra."

No last name, Levi thought. That was fine. He could do anonymous. "So what are you reading?" he asked.

"Oh, it's a biography."

"Not the new one on Matt Damon, is it?" Levi asked. "I was at the Garden with Matt a couple weeks ago and he is pissed about that book. *Pissed*."

"It's not Matt Damon," the woman said. "It's Wendell Berry."

"Oh yeah," Levi said, wondering who in the fuck Wendell Berry was. "I haven't read it yet. Good?"

"It is."

Levi used the towel to wipe down his arms and shoulders. The woman hadn't really even taken a good look at him yet, he noticed. In fact, she hadn't glanced over at all. "So what are you doing here, Sandra? Way out in the boonies."

"Research."

"Really? What are you researching—hillbilly culture in upstate New York?" Levi laughed at his own joke. "You should come out on location. I could introduce you to some rural types that would blow your mind. Right out of *The*

*Grapes of Wrath*. There are people who actually wear straw hats to restaurants. It's insane."

The woman shut the machine down and stepped off. She removed the reading glasses and folded them with the e-reader into her towel. She really hadn't spent a lot of time on the treadmill. Levi noted that she wasn't even perspiring.

"So are you interested in coming on set?" Levi asked. "I could introduce you to the cast and you could watch them shoot a few scenes. Might be interesting for you. I mean, since you've read the book."

"No thanks."

"Right. I suppose that's old hat for you, being from LA." Levi wiped his face. "But you might like to hang out anyway." He knew he was scuffling, so he went to his standard line. "I'm a bit of a maverick in this business. I grew up in Detroit, the inner city. Ninety percent of the people I went to high school with are dead or in jail. But I made it out."

"I'm not from LA," the woman said, ignoring his mini-autobiography.

"Oh. I assumed—"

"I'm from Capay Valley," she said. "I have an organic farm there. I'm here researching some of the local vineyards."

"Oh," Levi said. "So you're a winemaker?"

"No." The woman finally smiled. "I'm a farmer. As a matter of fact, I'm pretty sure I'm one of those hillbillies you mentioned."

"I wasn't talking about you."

"Actually, you were," she said. "But I'm okay with it. Now I have to grab my straw hat and get to work."

Claire ran into Sal Delano as she was walking to the coffee shop off the hotel lobby. She was almost done there, although in terms of gathering pertinent information she'd been pretty much done before she'd started. She had worked with Sal on a couple cases of late, so she'd gotten in touch with him through dispatch and asked that he come to the hotel. He had just made investigator a couple years earlier but he was smart and had the ability to think outside the box, a term that Claire would never actually use out loud.

She bought him a coffee and they sat down in the little shop.

"You finished?" he asked.

"One to go," Claire said. "One of the producers."

Sal pulled his notebook from his pocket. "I did a little digging on the web, like you asked. Most of the stuff you probably already know. The film is *Frontier Woman,* based on a book by Ann Furlong. Budget around thirty million. I got the names of the producers, cast, all that." He looked at his notes for a moment. "Nothing racy in Olivia Burns's background. She's pretty low-key for a big-name actress. She was married once when she was just a kid, but divorced ten years ago. Seems unlikely the ex-husband would be a suspect after all that time."

"It does."

Sal had a drink of coffee. "I found one thing that might interest you. The guy who was supposed to direct this thing left the project a few days ago."

"Name?"

"Peter Dunmore."

"What happened?" Claire asked.

"According to the Internet," Sal said, "he either quit or was fired or he joined a cult."

"Good old Internet."

"Yeah," Sal said.

Claire glanced out into the lobby and saw the producer Levi Brown heading for the boardroom. He was to be her last interview. She'd wanted to talk to him earlier when he'd provided her with the crew list, but he'd declined, saying he had a meeting with another producer and the director to discuss the status of the film. He'd been somewhat dismissive of Claire at the time, but she'd let it go. Presumably he'd had a rough morning.

"Check it out," Claire said, turning back to Sal. "See if the guy has an ax to grind. And while you're at it, follow the money. How the hell does anybody get their hands on thirty million dollars? I couldn't raise thirty cents."

"I can pay you for the coffee, Claire."

She stood up. "Smart-ass. Get to work."

When she walked into the boardroom, Levi Brown was there waiting for her. He'd obviously just come from working out, presumably in the hotel gym. He was wearing track pants and a tank top and had a thick yellow towel draped around his neck. He stood looking at his cell phone, reading a text, or so it appeared. When Claire entered, he glanced at her irritably, then moved away a few steps, as if she was intruding. She heard the beeps as he replied to the message before closing the phone and turning to her.

"I don't have a lot of time," he said.

But enough time to go for a workout, Claire thought. "I'll keep that in mind," she said.

"I don't have anything to tell you anyway," he added.

"But you don't know what I'm going to ask," Claire said.

"I'm just telling you that I'm in the dark," Levi said. "So I intend to make this quick."

"Sit down," Claire said lightly. "I'll do the intending around here."

Levi Brown sat, shaking his head slightly to free his blond tresses from the damp towel around his neck. His arms were large and impressive, at least to look at, the kind of arms a man got from lifting weights, not from actual work. Arms, Claire suspected, that were solely intended to look good in a tight T-shirt, which is what the producer had been wearing earlier. Claire thought of Virgil, of his hard, muscular body, usually sporting a random cut or bruise somewhere from repairing machinery or fixing fences. She was certain he'd never visited a gym or lifted a weight in his life, and she couldn't see him shopping for T-shirts based on how they made his arms look. In fact, she was pretty sure he bought his shirts at the TSC store, probably while buying binder twine or grease fittings.

"How well did you know Olivia Burns?" she began.

"I don't know how to answer that," Levi said. "How well do we know anybody?"

"You going to get philosophical on me?" Claire asked. "I thought you were in a hurry."

"Okay," he said, as if despairing of her provincial attitude. "On one hand, I was her employer. On the other hand, we were on friendly terms."

"When did you meet?"

"About . . . two months ago. No, closer to three. Sam and I flew to Seattle to meet with her, to talk about the film."

"Who is Sam?"

"Sam Sawchuk," Levi said, frowning, as if puzzled that Claire wouldn't know this. "She's my co-producer."

"So that's where Olivia Burns is from—Seattle?"

"No," Levi said. His impatience with Claire was now palpable; he stopped just short of rolling his eyes. "She was finishing a film in Seattle—the Baumberger feature? You *must* have heard of that movie."

"We'll be better off here if you don't assume I know anything about the business you're in," Claire said.

"That's obvious."

"You might also want to drop the snotty attitude," Claire added. "Do that and we'll get along just dandy. Okay?"

The movie producer fell into a bit of a sulk then. That was fine with Claire. She'd been in his presence for only a few minutes and had already decided she didn't care for him much. Something about him suggested he'd been spoiled from a young age. She wondered if he was an only child.

"So you've known her roughly three months," she said. "Did she ever discuss her personal life with you? By that I specifically mean any problems she might have been having?"

"What kind of problems?"

"Medical problems. Depression. Boyfriend problems, drugs? Anything at all."

"No."

"Did she seem fearful of anything? Celebrities sometimes have stalkers. Did she ever ask for security?"

"No," Levi said.

"So you never got the sense that she was dealing with something out there?" Claire asked. "Something that might have been bothering her?"

"Never," Levi said. "She was a very normal person. Matter of fact, I'd say she was better-adjusted than most."

"Than most what? Actresses?"

"People."

Claire looked down at her notebook, filled basically with inconsequential statements from the crew. "When did you see her last?" she asked.

"Last night. I was in the bar across the foyer there, having a drink with Sam Sawchuk, talking about the shoot. Olivia had dinner at Finnegan's with Ronnie Red Hawk. He's . . . um . . . an investor in the film. We saw them leave the restaurant and walk across the lobby to the elevators."

"Ronnie Red Hawk is an investor?" Claire asked. "I thought he was a producer."

"All right," Levi conceded. "He's a minor producer."

"I didn't know they came in different sizes," Claire said. "Where are you on the scale?"

"At the pinnacle," he said defiantly.

Claire smiled. "So why did you fire Peter Dunmore?"

She caught him off guard with the bluff. She had no idea whether Dunmore had been fired or not. He glared at her as if she'd stuck her nose where it didn't belong and now he was being forced to humor her. "He wasn't fired. He quit."

"Why?"

"Who knows?" Levi said. "Money, artistic differences, whatever. Happens all the time. I leave that shit to the creative types."

"You're not a creative type?"

"I'm a money guy," he replied. "Without me, there is no movie."

"I can tell you're a powerful man," Claire said, not hiding her sarcasm. "Was Dunmore pissed off when he left?"

"No idea," Levi snapped. He obviously didn't care for Claire's flip assessment of him. "I just told you—that's not my bailiwick."

"Right, you're the money guy," Claire said. "What time was it when Olivia and Red Hawk left the restaurant?"

"Ten o'clock or so."

"And what time did you and Ms. Sawchuk leave the bar?"

"Maybe a half hour later?"

"And you went to your rooms then? Or someplace else?"

"To our rooms. We rode up together."

"Same floor?"

"No. I'm on the fifth, Sam and Robb Fetterman—the director—are on the seventh."

"Together?"

"They're married."

Claire hadn't known that and she made a note of it. She paused. She didn't have much else to ask the sullen producer.

"One last thing," she said. "Have you seen anybody on the periphery of this situation that you might regard as suspicious? You know, hanging around the hotel, or the filming itself. Anybody at all that doesn't fit in?"

"No," Levi said. "And Sam and I can vouch for the crew. We've worked with them before." He hesitated as something came to him. "Wait a minute. There is somebody."

"Who?"

"The horse wrangler on set. There's something off about the guy. Like a Boo Radley thing. You know who that is?"

"Yeah, I know who that is," Claire said. "You say this guy's a horse wrangler. What's his name?"

It took Levi a moment to remember. "Calls himself Virgil. But you know, he's never actually said if that's his first name or his last. And he makes us pay him in cash. Which suggests to me that the guy's off the grid, so it isn't his real name anyway."

"I'll talk to him."

"I don't know how you'd get in touch with him, but we have a number for his boss. Guy's name is Cain. I can get it for you."

"I'll find it," Claire said. "So what's off about the guy?"

"His attitude," Levi said. "Like he doesn't have any respect for anything. And he's one of those guys, got a smart mouth, trying to hide the fact that he's not very bright. You know what I mean?"

"I know what you mean," Claire said. "When you say he doesn't have any respect for anything, you mean for the movie and all that?"

"Exactly," Levi said. "He likes to act the wise guy, and you don't pull that shit where I'm from. I came close to punching his lights out yesterday. I might still."

"Punch him?"

"Yeah."

"I hope I'm there when you do," Claire said. "I'd love to watch."

When the producer was gone Claire sat at the table and went through her notebook before closing it up. Other than finding out there was something allegedly *off* about the man she'd been sleeping with the past couple of years, she hadn't really learned anything. Levi Brown had actually been right on that last count. There was something off about Virgil. Which is why Claire had been attracted to him since the moment she'd met him, even though he'd been in police custody at the time.

Walking out into the lobby, she saw Joe Brady emerge from the restaurant with a man and a woman, the man in black jeans and the woman wearing leggings and an over-size white T-shirt. They said something to Joe before moving off toward the elevators. Joe spotted Claire and walked over.

"Well?"

"Nobody saw nuttin'," she replied.

"Same here."

"Who was that?" Claire asked, indicating the departing couple.

"The producer and the director," Joe said.

"They tell you anything interesting?"

"Not really."

"They would know everyone on the crew. Did they see any strangers hanging around?"

Joe stifled a yawn. "The woman said there was some big Samoan or something in the bar last night. Nobody knew him. She thought he might have been a wrestler."

"Why a wrestler?"

"Because he was big, I guess."

Claire glanced toward the elevators. "You interviewed them together?"

"Yeah. I was trying to save some time. They're married to each other, so I killed two birds with one stone."

"Where were they last night?"

"In their room from eight o'clock on."

Claire watched as the two people in question got on the elevator. The woman turned and looked directly at her as the doors closed.

"I just talked to a guy who said he was in the bar with the Sawchuk woman until around ten thirty," Claire said, still watching the closed doors. Now she looked at Joe. "And yet they're telling you different."

"Well, they're in agreement on it," Joe said.

"Of course they are, when you interview them together."

"Must be nice, always being right, Claire."

"I'll let you know if it ever happens," she replied. She continued to look at Joe. There'd been a time when she might have expected him to admit that he screwed up, but that time was long past. Not that she cared anyway, not about that part of it. "If nothing else, we've got something to go on. At least one of those three people lied to us. So you know what we have to do now."

"Find out which one?" Joe said.

"Find out why."

# TEN

At first light Wednesday morning Virgil loaded Bob and Nelly in the trailer and headed for Fairfield Village. With the death of the lead actress, the filming had shut down for exactly one day. Tommy Alamosa had called him at eight o'clock Tuesday night to tell him he was needed the following morning.

The day was overcast but the rain that had been promised never materialized. The radio was calling now for clearing in the afternoon. Virgil arrived at the pioneer village just before eight and unloaded the horses into the corral. Tommy walked over a few minutes later carrying coffees from craft services and told him they would be shooting some schoolhouse scenes today, which led Virgil to ask where Tommy thought the two draft horses might fit in.

"I had this idea when I was flipping through the book last night," Tommy said. "I thought it would be a nice visual, the daughter riding a huge workhorse bareback along that dirt lane over there." He pointed to the far end of the village, where a mud path emerged from the heavy forest. "You know—coming to school in the morning. Would your mare be okay with that?"

"Probably not," Virgil said, thinking about Nelly's cantankerous nature. He tried the coffee, which was pretty good. "But I imagine Bob would. He's about as excitable as a rock. I put one of my neighbor's kids on his back one day last summer and Bob walked around the field like he was in the Veteran's Day parade." He took another drink. "What about the little girl, though?"

"She's all for it," Tommy said. "Girls and horses, you know? We're going to wait and shoot it later, though. We're supposed to get some sunshine this afternoon, give us a nice contrast coming out of the shade of the trees there. It won't be early morning but we can make it look like it is."

Virgil watched the horses in the corral. "I don't have a bridle for riding."

Tommy shook his head. "No, we'll want you to use the harness and stuff from before. That's what they'd do back then, take the horse from the plow and throw the kid on it."

Virgil nodded. "I didn't think you'd be filming anything today."

"After the Olivia thing?" Tommy asked. "Neither did I. I have the feeling that the theory is to keep on like nothing happened, although I don't know how you can call that nothing. But otherwise, the money might disappear, and if that happens it's a real cluster fuck. A lot of it is covered by insurance but not all of it. So it looks like we're going to shoot around the lead until they cast somebody else."

"How do they do that?"

"It won't be hard," Tommy said. "You can bet there's been a hundred agents trying to get hold of Sam since the news broke. She'll drag it out a few days, milk it for all it's worth for the press it'll get. But I'm betting they'll cast somebody by the weekend."

"And forget all about Olivia Burns?"

"Shit, they already have," Tommy said.

Virgil walked to the trailer, set his coffee on the fender, and went inside for a half bale of hay, which he tossed over the rail fence to the two draft horses. They were standing in

the shade of the fake livery stable, and they showed no interest in the feed. Virgil retrieved his coffee and walked back to
where Tommy stood, leaning against the box of Virgil's old
pickup.

"So I guess I just needed to bring Bob today."

"This way, you get paid for both," Tommy told him. "And
your wrangler fee."

"Levi whatshisname might not like that."

"Fuck him," Tommy said. He tossed the remains of his coffee in the grass. "One of the perks of my job is pissing that
phony fucker off."

After Tommy went off to set up whatever they were going to
shoot first, Virgil got a brush from the cab of the truck and
went into the corral to give the horses a cleaning they didn't
really need. But he couldn't stand around all day doing nothing. It made for a long day, but more than that, it really didn't
feel right, not when he was being paid.

As he worked, he watched the comings and goings of
all the people around the trailers and RVs at the end of the
village. As they had on Monday, the crew was laughing and
joking as they went about their business. From where Virgil
stood, there didn't seem to be any sense of mourning about
them, something that might be expected when the star of the
film had been found dead, floating in a creek, roughly twenty-
four hours earlier.

At one point, he saw Levi Brown pull up in the black Audi,
then disappear into a trailer. A few minutes later he watched
Sam Sawchuk and the director, Robb, cross the lot and enter
the same trailer.

After grooming the two horses, Virgil decided to grease
the front suspension of his truck, another job that really

didn't need doing. He was lying in the grass, most of his body beneath the Ford, working the grease gun on the tie rod ends, when he heard footsteps and looked over to see two small pink sneakers protruding from the hem of a gingham dress.

"Hello, Georgia," he said.

"Hi, Virgil."

He came out from under the truck and wiped his hands on a rag before stowing the grease gun behind the seat. Aside from the modern footwear, the little girl wore the same clothes as when they'd shot the buckboard scenes on Monday. Her bonnet was hanging off the back of her neck by the tie strings. Her fine blonde hair was mussed up from the cap. Her eyes were red.

"How're you doing?" Virgil asked.

"Okay, I guess."

Virgil watched her as she glanced around, as if not knowing where to look. What to do. She was the first person he'd seen who appeared to be upset about the death of Olivia Burns. Even Tommy Alamosa had been pretty jaded about the whole thing. Virgil wondered if anybody had talked to the kid about it. Looking at the hustle and bustle over in the town, where lights and cameras and large coils of cables were being carried into the schoolhouse, he somehow doubted it. But somebody should. She was just a goddamn kid.

"That was sad about Olivia," he said.

Georgia looked up quickly; she seemed surprised that he would mention it. "Yeah," she said after a moment. "She was nice. She was really nice."

"How well did you know her?"

"We just met," the little girl said. "But she was, like, super friendly to me. She told me that I could run lines with her anytime I wanted. And she even gave me her cell phone number. Her personal phone. She told me not to give it to anybody else. That was pretty cool."

"That means you made an impression on her," Virgil said.

"I guess." She looked at Bob and Nelly tucked away in the shade of the livery, their tails flicking at the flies now buzzing around them. "I only met her three times," she said. "I don't know why I'm so sad, but I am."

"That means she made an impression on you," Virgil said.

The little girl thought about that for a time and then smiled at Virgil. "Maybe it does," she said. "You're smart."

"You might be the only one around here who thinks that," Virgil said. "I'd appreciate it if you'd keep it to yourself."

"Okay," she said in a conspiratorial whisper.

Virgil looked over toward the trailers, wondering again why the kid seemed to be alone. "Are your parents here?"

"No," she said. "They're divorced. My dad's a musician, so he's on the road a lot. He plays the oboe. You know what that is?"

"Some kind of flute?"

"Sort of."

"Is your mother here?"

"Nope. She's in Spain. She's writing a book about the Spanish Civil War. It happened back in the 1930s."

"So you're here all by yourself?" Virgil asked.

"There's a lady who looks after me, like I'm a puppy or something. We do schoolwork too." The little girl glanced toward the horses again. "Did they tell you I'm going to be riding one of your horses?"

"Yeah."

"Which one—Nelly?"

"No. Nelly doesn't want anybody riding her."

"Why not?"

"Just the way she is," Virgil said. "You know, it's like how some people like baseball and other people don't."

"I like soccer. I can ride Bob, then?"

"Yeah. He's pretty excited about it."

"Stop it," she said. She reached into the folds of the dress. "I brought them some carrots from craft services."

"Go ahead," Virgil said. He watched as the little girl slipped between the rough cedar rails of the corral to approach the team, her hand with the carrots extended flat as he'd shown her a couple days earlier. "You want to get on him and see how you like it?"

Georgia looked toward the trailers. "Should we get permission first? I don't want to get you in trouble."

Virgil smiled. "I've been getting into trouble my whole life without any help from you."

He grabbed the harness from the back of the truck and went through the rail fence. Removing the halter from the big gelding, he fitted the horse with the Sweeney collar and bridle. It was a makeshift rigging for riding, but apparently that's what they were looking for. It seemed authentic enough to Virgil, and even if it wasn't, he doubted there was anyone around who might tell them otherwise.

He lifted Georgia onto Bob's back and started by leading the animal around the paddock a couple of times. The gelding plodded along like a milk horse on its route, so Virgil handed the reins to the little girl.

"Let them hang loose and he'll be fine," he told her.

He stood back and watched horse and rider cross the large paddock, the little girl looking like a toddler atop the massive Percheron. When Bob reached the far fence, he turned on his own and made his way back. They drew near Virgil.

"How do I stop him?" Georgia asked.

"Tell him to whoa."

"Whoa!" she shouted. The horse stopped.

"You don't have to yell," Virgil said. "He's big, not deaf."

"Sorry. How do I make him go?"

"Say giddyup to get him moving again. If you want him to turn left, say haw. Right, you say gee."

"You're making that up!"

"Give it a try."

"Giddyup," the little girl said, and the horse started walking. "Haw," she said. When the horse turned to the left, Georgia whipped around on the animal's broad back to smile at Virgil. "That is so cool!"

They did a couple more passes, with Georgia instructing the horse to stop and go and turn this way or that, and then Virgil lifted her down and pulled the harness from Bob, who plodded at once over to the shade, where Nelly had been standing the entire time, watching the proceedings, content not to be involved.

"Thank you, Virgil," Georgia said.

"You are welcome, Georgia."

He saw her look past him then and he turned to see Levi Brown approaching from the direction of the trailers, striding along the dirt road as if he were an important man on an important mission, wearing aviator-style sunglasses, his chest puffed out, his long hair trailing in the breeze.

"Here comes the cowardly lion," Georgia said. "Guess I have to go."

"What did you call him?" Virgil asked.

"He looks like the lion from *The Wizard of Oz*."

Virgil glanced at the approaching Levi and smiled. "He does, doesn't he?"

"They're ready for you in the schoolhouse," Levi said as he

neared, looking only at the little girl and pointedly ignoring Virgil.

"See you later, Virgil," she said.

Virgil winked at her as she walked away with the producer.

"What were you two talking about?" he heard Levi ask. "Was he bothering you?"

"No."

"You shouldn't be hanging around him," Levi said. "Tell me the truth—was he bothering you?"

"No," the little girl said again. "You are."

Sam sat in the trailer, her feet up on the desk beside her laptop, her BlackBerry pressed to her ear. She'd been on the phone all the previous evening until she finally turned it off around midnight, and then again all morning. There were a lot of actresses interested in playing Martha Jones on the big screen.

Robb was sitting on the couch, the script in his hand. He'd been making familiar grunts of exasperation for the past half hour. Sam had been ignoring him, and the sounds had increased in both volume and frequency in response to that ignoring. Now she hung up the cell phone and looked over at him.

"Frances Lee Scott is too old, right?"

Robb frowned. "Christ, yeah. She's like forty-something, isn't she?"

"Martha is thirty-eight in the book," Sam reminded him.

"Not hot enough," Robb said.

Sam didn't bother mentioning again that the role was of a pioneer woman eking a hardscrabble living out of the bush after her husband is killed by Indians. The overwhelming hotness of the actress playing her needn't be a factor.

"We have the Jessicas," she said. "Tait, McGee, and Alba. All very interested. Alba even offered to fly in and read for us."

"She's a total babe," Robb said.

"She looks pretty contemporary, though," Sam said. "I don't know if I see her as period."

"We could have dinner with her," Robb suggested. "Has she read the script?"

"No, but she read the book. I can send the script to her agent."

"Call her. Let's have dinner."

Tommy Alamosa knocked sharply and entered the trailer. "We're ready for a run-through in the schoolhouse," he said.

Robb exhaled heavily and got to his feet. He shook his head, looking to Sam for support. "I'm not really sure what this scene is about."

Sam glanced at Tommy before replying. "Country girl comes to school in town, is mocked by the locals. Think *Mean Girls* in long dresses and bonnets."

"Okay," Robb said uncertainly.

"I talked to our wrangler about my idea for putting Georgia on top of one of the draft horses," Tommy said. "You know—riding to school through the woods."

"I'm not so sure about that," Robb said. "Lot of fucking around for a shot."

"What's this?" Sam asked.

Tommy told her the idea.

"I like it," Sam said. "Those horses are photogenic as hell. It's a nice little insert."

"Yeah, an insert that takes half a fucking day to shoot," Robb said. "And we'll have to get someone to double for the kid. She's not going to get on that horse."

"Funny you should say that," Tommy said. "I saw her riding him around the corral about a half hour ago."

"On her own?" Sam asked.

"All by her lonesome."

"Oh Christ, then, let's shoot it."

After a while Sam got tired of talking to agents who told her how stunned and saddened they were to hear of Olivia's demise before morphing into well-rehearsed spiels of how perfect their client would be for the role. Having the same conversation over and over again got old pretty quick. Shutting her phone off, Sam decided to walk over to the schoolhouse to see how the shoot was going. There were times when Robb needed her around, as if her mere presence reinforced what little confidence he had in himself, and she sensed that this would be particularly true on this project. He really didn't have a clue what the movie was about. She knew he'd started to read the book a half-dozen times and had always given up. She thanked God one more time for Tommy Alamosa.

She wished she hadn't mentioned Jessica Alba to Robb. Now he wouldn't rest until they had dinner with her, and once they had dinner together, he would undoubtedly develop a huge crush on her, as he typically did with every beautiful actress he met, and then it would be up to Sam either to cast her or try to explain to him why she wasn't right for the role. The sad truth was if Robb wanted her bad enough, Sam would relent and give her the job. Either way, the whole thing would be time-consuming and draining, and quite possibly the wrong choice.

The Fairfield Village schoolhouse, true to the era, did not have air-conditioning, and it was steaming hot inside. They were shooting close-ups of Georgia when Sam entered, the little girl sitting at her desk in the front row, with a dozen or so more kids of different ages and sizes behind her; the boys, cowlicked or buzz-cut, dressed in buckskin or cord, the girls in bonnets, wearing homespun cotton or gingham. The scene was one where her character, Sara, tells the assembly about the death of her father. At the end of the telling, the schoolmarm approaches and embraces her.

Sam stood at the rear of the building and watched a couple of takes. Georgia was terrific as the emotional Sara, holding everything in until the last moment when she becomes overwhelmed with the memory. The kid was a natural actor. Sam had found her through a casting agent who had seen her in an off-Broadway version of *The Sound of Music* and cast her before anyone could jump in with their two cents' worth. Of course, the fact that she was too young to trigger Robb's carnal urges helped.

The blocking for the schoolmarm's approach was not working. Robb kept referring to the actress as "you" until Tommy Alamosa reminded him that her name was Lori. It was typical of Robb, Sam knew. By the end of the shoot, he wouldn't know even half the crew by name.

They finally had to move the camera to get the coverage they wanted. While the camera department and grips were making the change, every one of the kid actors pulled a cell phone from somewhere inside their period duds and began checking their messages. Every one but Georgia, Sam noticed, who remained at her desk, in character.

When they finally got the shot, Tommy announced lunch, and the cast and crew escaped the sweltering building. As Sam and Robb started for the meal tents set up beyond the parking lot, Robb noticed the draft horses dozing on their feet in the corral off the end of the livery.

"Come on," he said.

Virgil was sitting on a hard wooden bench in the shade of the building, rubbing neat's-foot oil into the leather harness traces when they approached.

"Hey pal," Robb said. "How's it going?"

Virgil glanced up, squinting into the sun. "All right."

"Listen, I had an idea," Robb continued. "I want to put the kid on one of your horses, like she's riding to school in the morning. Think you could swing that?"

"I think I could swing that," Virgil said. "Say, that's a good idea you had."

"I'm thinking it would make a nice little insert," Robb said. He hesitated; obviously there was something else on his mind. "Tell me something—you didn't already let the kid on your horse . . . ?"

"Yup."

Sam, hanging back, was watching warily.

"In the future," Robb said, "you'd better check with somebody before you do something like putting one of my actors on a horse. You understand?"

"You better make a list," Virgil said as he continued to work the oil into the leather.

"What?" Robb demanded.

"So I'll know what I need to check with you on," Virgil said. "I mean, right now I'm rubbing neat's-foot oil into this harness. Should I have checked with you on that?"

"You need to use common sense," Robb told him. "I thought you rural types were all about common sense."

"That's a stereotype." Virgil smiled. "You don't believe in stereotypes, do you, Mr.—um, what's your name again?"

"My name is Robb Fetterman," Robb said, his voice rising. "I'm the *director* of this film. Do you even understand the hierarchy on a film set? As a rule, I wouldn't even be talking to you, I'd have someone else do it." He paused but went on, as if he couldn't stop himself. "I'll try to make it simple for you. I'm the boss here, of everything. What I say goes. So you need to take that into consideration no matter what you're doing. If you're on my set, you answer to me. And if I don't like the way you're conducting yourself, I'm going to send you down the road, pal. Is that absolutely clear?"

Virgil set the newly oiled traces aside and got to his feet. "There's a problem with that. And it's got nothing to do with common sense. It has to do with leverage."

Robb had been ready to walk away but now he turned back.

"Just leave it, Robb," Sam warned.

"No," Robb said. He looked at Virgil. "I want the hired hand here to explain leverage to me."

"I can give it a try," Virgil said, and he took a moment to think about it. "Okay, I used to play baseball, and I wasn't half-bad at it. Not great, but fair to middling. Thing is—all I cared about was being a ballplayer. Now, on a ball team the manager is the boss. Same as you are here. Anything my manager wanted me to do, I would do it, no questions asked. If he told me to run five miles across broken glass in my bare feet, I'd have done it. You know why? So I could keep on being a ballplayer. Now, the difference between you and him is I don't give a shit about you, or your movie, or anything else in your world. Which means you don't have any leverage over me. So when you wander over here like you did a couple minutes ago and start telling me what an important person you are, I'm inclined to tell you to kiss my ass. You want to send me down the road, fill your boots. I've been fired by better men than you. But before I go, you're going to pay me and those horses over there a day's wages."

The director blinked a couple times, as if he'd been slapped across the face, and then turned to Sam. "He's finished," he said. "Pay him off."

But Sam was no longer paying attention. She was looking past the pair of them to the parking lot at the far end of the village, where a familiar black limousine with license plates that read RRH1 had just parked beside the production trailers. Ronnie Red Hawk was out of the limo, and he was walking around to the other side to open the door.

The actress Kari Karson got out.

"Jesus, what has he done?" Sam said.

# ELEVEN

Virgil was back home by five o'clock. He went into the house and called Claire's number and left a message on her voice mail, then went back outside, unloaded the horses, and rubbed them down before turning them out to pasture. Then he did the rest of his chores.

Afterward he walked out into the wheat field to the north of the house. In spite of the drought, the heads were getting heavy, turning yellow. In a week, they'd be ready to combine.

Virgil hoped that his movie work wouldn't conflict with the wheat harvest. If it did the movie people would have to wait; he felt no loyalty toward them, so he would have no problem telling them that. But the truth was that the extra money was coming in handy.

As it turned out, he still had a job on the film set. To say there'd been a lot of commotion surrounding the arrival of the starlet Kari Karson would be an understatement, and the fact that Virgil had just been fired by the director basically became lost in the shuffle. Virgil, of course, hadn't forgotten, but as he was loading up Bob and Nelly to head home, Tommy Alamosa walked over to ask where he was going. When Virgil told him what had happened, Tommy went off to talk to the woman, Sam. He came back a few moments later to tell Virgil it had been a misunderstanding.

"Sam said that an apology would smooth things over,"

Tommy had said. "I told her I'd be very surprised if that happened."

"Hey, if the guy wants to apologize, let him," Virgil had replied.

Tommy had laughed and that was the end of it. Later that afternoon, Virgil hooked Bob to harness and the crew shot Georgia riding the big horse out of the thicket of trees beyond the village, the little girl sitting comfortably on the broad back, the heavy leather reins in one hand and a vintage honey pail, serving as a frontier lunch box, in the other. Tommy directed the shot and they got it in two takes. Robb and Sam spent the afternoon in the production trailer with Ronnie Red Hawk and his guest to the set, Kari Karson.

"Oh, to be a fly on that wall," Tommy had said.

Now Virgil walked out of the wheat field and around the barn to see Claire, behind the wheel of her Honda SUV, pulling in the driveway. He'd told her to call him back and she'd probably been trying to do so, but Virgil hadn't been anywhere near the phone.

"Which kind of negates this whole concept of me returning your call," she said after mentioning the fact to him.

"You want a beer?" he asked.

She sighed. "You seem to think everything you've ever done wrong can be made right by offering someone a beer."

"Wandering away from a phone ain't much of a sin."

"I'll have a beer."

They sat in wooden lawn chairs under the shade of the red maple trees behind the house, a few feet from the back porch. There was no breeze at all and the heat of the day remained. Claire was wearing a skirt, no stockings, and a light-blue button-down blouse. She kicked her shoes off and asked Virgil why he'd called.

"What killed Olivia Burns?"

"She drowned," Claire said. "But she took a hard knock to the right temple beforehand. The coroner says she was probably unconscious when she went in the water."

"So what's the theory—she was out walking and slipped and hit her head on a rock or something and then went under?" Virgil asked.

"I would call that a Joe Brady theory," Claire said. "I'd say it seems pretty unlikely."

Virgil had a drink of the cold Budweiser. "So you're thinking foul play?"

"That's what I'm thinking," Claire said. "But why are you asking about it? The last time you showed this much interest in a murder case, you were the number-one suspect. Do you remember that, Virgil? Somebody killed Mickey Dupree and Joe Brady arrested you for it and then you broke out of jail and led us all on a merry goose chase all over upstate New York for a few weeks. Does any of that ring a bell?"

"Vaguely," Virgil said as he tilted his bottle back. "Did you talk to a guy named Ronnie Red Hawk?"

"Yeah. He was the last person seen with her. Why?"

"He's a producer on *Frontier Woman*."

"I know. He thinks he's going to win an Oscar. What about him?"

"Word on the movie set is he has a major crush on a woman named Kari Karson," Virgil said. "You know who that is?"

"She's an actress," Claire said. "She's always in the tabloids. Been arrested a few times. Quite a few times. What about *her*?"

"Red Hawk showed up at the pioneer village today in a limousine about as long as my barn. Kari Karson was in the limo."

Claire had a drink of beer while she considered this. "Next you're going to tell me that he wants Kari Karson to take over the role that belonged to Olivia Burns."

"You got it."

Claire tapped the mouth of the bottle against her front teeth as she looked out over the farm. "This is where I'm supposed to put two and two together," she said.

"Hey, you're the cop," Virgil said.

"It's pretty obvious," Claire said after a long moment. "And maybe a little too obvious. But it certainly bears looking into." She paused. "Jesus, do you really think Ronnie Red Hawk murdered Olivia Burns so he could put Kari Karson in the movie?"

"It doesn't matter what I think."

"It wouldn't be his call anyway, would it?" Claire asked. "I mean, there are other producers in the mix. I was told that Red Hawk is a *minor* producer, which I assume means he's not calling the shots. Are the others okay with this?"

"From what I saw today, they're not even a little bit okay with it," Virgil said. "I was there when the main producer, this woman named Sam, watched the Karson girl get out of the limo. I thought she was going to have an apoplexy, as we say back in 1840."

"Ouch!" Claire exclaimed suddenly, lifting her left foot. "Something bit me." She examined the bare foot and scratched it before shifting in her chair and placing both feet in Virgil's lap. He laid his arm across her ankles.

"They come up with a time of death?" he asked.

"Best they can say is between midnight and three in the morning," Claire said.

"And Red Hawk says he left her when?"

"About ten o'clock."

"Where did he go then?"

"To his room."

"Alone?"

"Alone," Claire said. "Not much of an alibi, is it?"

"No," Virgil said. "What do you know about the guy anyway?"

"Not nearly as much as I need to know," Claire said. "Shit, I just got stung again. Can we go inside before I get bit to death?"

Virgil gathered the empty bottles and they went into the house. Claire decided to have a shower and while she did Virgil sat down on the couch and flipped on the TV to the classics channel. *The Adventures of Robin Hood* was just starting.

Claire came down a while later, wearing a robe she kept at the house, just as Alan Hale was knocking Errol Flynn off a log and into a stream. She curled into Virgil on the couch and he put his arm around her.

"What are you watching?" she asked.

"*Robin Hood*."

"Which one? They made about a hundred, didn't they?"

"The 1938 version, with Errol Flynn. That's him in the creek. Errol Flynn was the best Robin Hood, hands down."

"He always played Errol Flynn," Claire said.

"Doesn't matter. He was the best Robin Hood."

"Oh, I don't know about that," she said.

"Who was better?" Virgil asked. "And don't say Kevin Costner."

She tucked herself in closer to him. "I suppose I have to defer to your expertise on this, now that you're in the movie business."

"I knew that Errol Flynn was the best Robin Hood before I was in the movie business, which I'm barely in anyway."

"Okay, okay. I'm too tired to argue with you anyway."

"Fall asleep and you're going to miss the sword fight between Robin and Friar Tuck."

"You can tell me about it later," Claire said sleepily. She closed her eyes but then opened them again. "Sean Connery," she said.

"What about him?"

"He was a good Robin Hood."

"He was never Robin Hood. He was James Bond. You don't know the difference between Robin Hood and James Bond?"

"Sean Connery was Robin Hood," Claire told him. "The movie was called *Robin and Marian*. Audrey Hepburn was Marian and it took place when they were older. Robin came back from the Crusades or someplace and Marian was a nun. The guy from *Jaws* was in it too."

"Richard Dreyfuss?"

"Not Richard Dreyfuss. The other guy. Shaw. He played the sheriff, I think."

"Robert Shaw," Virgil said. "And Marian was a nun?"

"Yeah." Claire pulled her robe tightly around her. "And now that I've established that I know something you don't, I'm going to sleep."

Virgil sat quietly for a moment, watching the set. Robin and his men had just discovered Friar Tuck sleeping by a stream while his fishing line bounced.

"Errol Flynn is still the best Robin Hood," Virgil said, but Claire, who had nodded off, didn't hear.

After her initial shock, Sam recovered sufficiently to treat Kari Karson as she would any other visitor to the set. With the emphasis squarely on *visitor*. Introductions had taken place in the production trailer, where Ronnie Red Hawk had presented the young woman as if she were a member of the royal family.

Kari's face was pale, suggesting she hadn't been outside for weeks, and she wore heavy black mascara and eyeliner. Dressed in black leggings and an artfully torn white T-shirt with the logo of some LA bar displayed in red slashing letters across the front, she came off as friendly and polite and just a bit nervous, shaking hands with Sam and Robb and then Levi, who came hurrying to the trailer from wherever he'd been, probably working his lover-boy routine on one of the wardrobe assistants. Ronnie Red Hawk stood to the side, beaming at what he undoubtedly considered a major casting coup.

After appraising the situation in the trailer with a heavy sense of foreboding, Sam asked Tommy, who was standing to the side with a look of bemusement on his face that quite frankly infuriated her, to show Kari around the pioneer village.

She told him to take his time.

"Please tell me you didn't offer her the role," Sam said when they'd gone. There was a pleading in her voice even she had never heard before.

"Of course I offered her the role," Ronnie replied.

"On whose authority?"

"*My* authority," Ronnie said. "I'm the producer."

"You're one of the producers," Levi reminded him.

"Do I know you?" Ronnie asked and didn't wait for an answer. "Hey, this is how I roll. I'm not one of those producers who sits around and talks about what needs to be done. There's an old saying—when all is said and done, more is said than done. Well, that's not me."

Sam wondered if it would serve any purpose to point out

to Ronnie that he'd been a film producer for roughly a week and, as such, it seemed a tad early for him to be holding forth on his philosophies of the job. She decided not to get into it; she had enough to deal with, even without this latest fucking fiasco. What she needed to do was cut him off at the knees and get Kari Karson out of there. But gently, if there was such a way.

"How old is Kari?" she asked.

"Twenty-seven," Ronnie said. "She turned twenty-seven on May fourth."

Of course Ronnie knew her birthday, Sam thought.

"The character is thirty-eight," Sam said. She realized something. "Have you read the book yet?"

"Nope."

"Have you read the script?"

"Nope."

"Christ," Levi muttered.

Sam shot Levi a look. "But you feel comfortable casting the movie?" she said to Ronnie, keeping her voice calm.

"Absolutely," Ronnie said, and he crossed the trailer to flop onto the couch there, stretching his long legs out before him. It occurred to Sam that he wasn't a man to remain on his feet for too long a time. He was wearing navy-blue satin shorts and a golf-style shirt with RED HAWK FILMS embroidered over the left breast. Sam hadn't noticed the logo before.

"It just doesn't work that way," Levi began.

"You be quiet," Ronnie snapped. His voice changed, losing its cordial tone, as he turned his attention to Sam. "You need to think back to the day you came to see me at Running Dog. Wearing your little peasant outfit, that long skirt and that low-cut blouse, giving me a peek at the twins. Carrying your cowboy hat in your hand, which was pretty appropriate because you came there hat in hand, didn't you? Remember what we talked about that day? *Instincts.* That's what we talked about. And you told me you could see that I had great instincts, and that was why you wanted me on your team. Now, you might have said that I had great instincts *and* six million dollars but you didn't. You didn't have to—we both knew the play. Well, the fact of the matter is that I do have incredible instincts and that's why I offered the part to Kari Karson."

Sam was actually happy that the gloves were off. She was sick of the pretense. "Okay," she said. "Here's the thing. She's ten years too young, she looks like she just stepped out of a zombie movie, she's spent more time in a courtroom in the past two years than she has on a movie set, and she's a fucking tabloid magnet. She couldn't be more wrong for the part."

"She'll do it for half of what Olivia was getting," Ronnie said.

Levi looked at Sam, eyebrows raised.

"How do you know what we were paying Olivia?" Sam asked.

"I talked to the accountant," Ronnie said. "I'm the producer."

Things grew quiet then, as if nobody knew what else to say, or even where to look. Ronnie sensed it and he heaved himself to his feet.

"I'm going to go find Kari," he said. "You guys need to talk this thing over. When I come back you can tell me if she has the role. If she doesn't, then me and Kari and my six million dollars are gonna climb into that big black Cadillac and drive off into the sunset." He smiled. "Just like Thelma and Louise." He paused. "Well, not exactly like Thelma and Louise. They drove off a cliff. But you get the picture."

He walked out. Sam went to the window and watched him lumber to the limo, where he would presumably get a ride to the village just three hundred yards away. She turned to see Robb now slumped on the couch where Ronnie had sat, flipping through *People* magazine. As was typical, he hadn't said a word during the meeting.

"Well?" Sam asked. "Any suggestions?"

"We're fucked," Levi said.

"I wouldn't call that a suggestion."

Levi sat down in an office chair along the wall. "Is there any chance it could work?" he asked. "What about this— we get her over to makeup and wardrobe, put a wig on her, scrape that goth shit off her face, and put her in costume. See if she can pull it off. Maybe have her read for us to boot."

"Ronnie won't go for it," Sam said. "He already told her she has the part. We tell her she has to audition and it just undermines him. She might stand for it, but he won't."

"All right," Levi said sharply. "You want to talk about him? Let's talk about him—the big redheaded elephant in the room. Come on—it's pretty fucking obvious now that he killed Olivia to make this happen. Or at least had her killed. Don't tell me I'm the only one who's figured that out."

"Nobody's even said it was foul play," Sam said. "It could have been an accident."

"You're saying you don't want to talk about it," Levi said.

"I don't even want to think about it," Sam said. "What does it accomplish? We have to make the movie."

"But what if he killed her?" Levi asked.

Sam shook her head. She was through discussing it.

"Okay, fuck it," Levi said. "What do we do about Kari Karson? Robb—are you awake over there? Do you have an opinion on this, Mr. Director?"

Robb set the magazine aside and looked over. "Did you see her?" he asked. "She's hot. I had no idea. I mean, she is totally hot."

Sam regarded him for a long moment before glancing over at Levi. She sighed.

# TWELVE

Tommy Alamosa called Virgil later that night to say that he and the Percherons wouldn't be needed on set the next day. Apparently they had decided to shoot out, as Tommy phrased it, the village interiors over the next couple of days. Tommy also told Virgil that Kari Karson would be taking over the role of Martha Jones.

If Tommy hadn't mentioned it, Virgil would have found out soon enough, as the story was the lead on the local TV news the next morning, which he watched while eating a bowl of cornflakes at his kitchen table. Congress was threatening to shut down the government over spending issues, there were ongoing problems in the Persian Gulf, Iran had reportedly tested a nuclear missile, and gasoline was pushing five bucks a gallon. But the lead story was that a much-arrested actress was in the area, filming a movie. Virgil assumed the much-arrested part was what made the story newsworthy.

After breakfast he carried his coffee outside and made his way over to the machine shed, where he needed to service the combine in readiness for the wheat harvest. After draining his cup, he pulled on overalls and went to work, adjusting the head and greasing the various fittings and changing a universal joint that was getting noisy. As he worked he kept thinking about the situation on the film set.

Even though he really couldn't care less about the movie, or most of the people associated with it, it was pretty obvious that there was something sour surrounding the whole production. In general, he would have been in favor of letting the whole bunch of them stew in their own juices, but he'd come to like the no-bullshit Tommy Alamosa, and the little girl, Georgia. Virgil suspected that Tommy could take care of himself, but the kid was—well, just a kid. And her parents were not around to look out for her. Virgil wondered if anybody was, amid the turmoil over there. Whatever the situation, it wasn't Virgil's job to worry about her. So why did he?

When he was finished with the combine, he wiped the grease and grime from his hands, went to the house to change his clothes, then got into his truck and drove to the town of Coeymans, on the west bank of the Hudson.

Buddy Townes rented a two-bedroom cabin a mile out of town, tucked in a shallow inlet along the shore of the river. The cabin wasn't much to look at; the roof dipped in the middle and the paint was peeling from the wooden siding in long, feathery strips. Some of the windows were covered with plastic to keep out the winter, although Virgil wondered why they were still sealed up in the summer's heat. Getting out of his truck out in front of the house, he heard the whine of the air conditioner and that answered his question.

Buddy's beater of a Cadillac was parked in the drive. Buddy had been a cop for nearly thirty years, and Virgil suspected he would have a decent pension. The house and car didn't suggest that, but then Virgil knew that Buddy would dedicate more of his income to liquor and female companionship than transportation and residence. He knocked on the front door of the cabin a couple of times but got no reply. It was after eleven o'clock; even Buddy should be up by now. Virgil walked around the cabin and down the sloping lawn, although lawn was a generous name for a parched patch of ground covered with spiny weeds and little grass, to Buddy's boathouse and dock. The boathouse was empty, meaning that Buddy was out on the river. No sooner had Virgil arrived at the conclusion than he heard the putt-putt of an outboard motor and turned to see Buddy heading toward him in a small aluminum boat, wearing dirty khaki shorts and no shirt, a stubby cigar clenched in his teeth, his face tanned and cracked like old shoe leather beneath a filthy white cap of indeterminate years. He smiled when he saw Virgil on the dock, and he was still smiling as he tossed him the rope to tie off while he climbed out of the boat.

"What the fuck have you got yourself into this time?" he asked.

"Why would you ask me that?" Virgil said in reply.

"The only time you come around is when you find trouble," Buddy said. "My feelings would be hurt, if I had any."

They sat on lawn chairs in the shade of the cabin, drinking cold Miller High Life from cans that Buddy retrieved from an old Pepsi cooler he'd had with him in the boat. There were a couple of walleyes, three or four pounds each, in the cooler as well, packed in the ice, and the beer cans had a slippery sheen on them from the fish.

"What makes you think I know anything about Ronnie Red Hawk?" Buddy asked after relighting the cigar that was by now barely long enough for a match.

"Because you know everything, Buddy."

"I fucking near do." Buddy gestured around himself, his arms outstretched. "And look where I am. With all my great knowledge, shouldn't I be a Fortune 500 type?"

"Is that what you want?"

"Fucking right that's what I want," Buddy said, and he took a pull off the can and belched. "Ronnie Red Hawk, eh? Well, he was born Ronald McDonald. I'm not shitting you. Or possibly Ronald Levack, depending on whether his mother ever married his father. She kept changing her story on that one, whenever she needed a new surname to start a fresh welfare claim."

"And here I thought Red Hawk was his real name."

"Like hell you did," Buddy said. "He grew up around Watertown. He was a fucked-up teenager, no father, his mother tended bar part-time and did crystal meth pretty much full-time. Little Ronald got arrested a lot, mostly small-time shit. I remember him dealing pot and Oxy to high school kids. After a while he got into jacking cars, Bimmers and Mercedes, high-end stuff, and then selling them to some sketchy fucking Algerian who shipped them to North Africa to sell to rich oil types or local gangsters or whatever. Ronald and his buddies would get maybe four or five grand for a hundred-thousand-dollar car." Buddy puffed on the cigar but it was dormant again, so he gave up on it and tossed it into the weed-infested flower bed at the back of the cabin. "He ended up doing a stretch in Attica for his troubles."

"For car theft?"

"Nah. They nailed him on conspiracy, maybe racketeering even, trying to get him to roll over on the big Algerian cheese. I never worked the case. The first I laid eyes on him was when he got out. Now, *that* was interesting. Ronnie went into stir a goofy redheaded carjacker and walked out a sure-enough Injun."

Virgil took a drink of beer. "How does that happen?"

"Opportunity," Buddy said. "Story is he fell in with some militant Native types in the joint and found out there are certain advantages to being an Indian in today's world. Now, Ronnie's always known that this Levack guy I mentioned, the guy who might be Ronnie's papa, was a quarter Native. Or at least Levack always claimed it anyway. That makes Ronnie one-eighth Indian, which apparently is Indian enough, for certain purposes. After he gets paroled, he heads back to Watertown and pretty soon he's strutting around in a buckskin jacket and wearing fucking feathers in his hair. It's a mildly amusing act, to tell you the truth. But Ronnie's more than just an act. Matter of fact, he's a pretty smart cookie. He ends up on the Sumac reservation, which at the time was a shithole of third-world dimensions, and before you know it Ronnie's managed to secure a casino license."

"With his record?" Virgil asked.

"Oh, the license isn't in his name," Buddy said. "But he was driving the bus. He did time with guys who knew this shit inside and out and he learned it well. By the time Ronnie showed up at the rez, it was like the Messiah himself had arrived. Within a year they broke ground for the casino and now the place is pumping money like a Saudi fucking oil field. They're building a golf course that's supposedly going to host a PGA Tour event."

"And what exactly is Ronnie's role there?" Virgil asked.

Buddy laughed. "Ronnie is . . . the Great Father. One hand on the throttle and the other in the cash box."

"And was this Levack guy a Sumac?"

"Probably not," Buddy said. "I have serious doubts that he was even Ronnie's father. I mean, look at the guy—does he look like an Indian to you? Can you imagine him in a John Ford movie, all that red hair and those freckles, charging over the hill on his pony, shooting arrows at the covered wagons? John Wayne would pop a fucking vein."

"They could find out easy enough," Virgil said. "DNA or whatever."

"Who's going to question it—the tribe?" Buddy asked. "Would you? One day you're living in a fucking shack, eating squirrel and hickory nuts, and the next you're collecting a big fat monthly check and driving a Lincoln Navigator. All because of Ronnie Red Hawk. You gonna be the guy who calls him out?"

With that Buddy stood up and went to the cooler for two more cans of Miller. He tossed one to Virgil and then stepped around the corner of the house to take a leak. As he unzipped he leaned backward to look at Virgil.

"So why are you so interested in Ronnie Red Hawk? Don't tell me you lost your farm at the casino."

Virgil could hear the piss hitting the baked clay ground around the corner. "I've never been to the casino."

"You have a run-in with him?" Buddy asked, returning, one hand pulling at his zipper.

"Never met the man."

Buddy sat down. "I give up."

Virgil popped open the second beer and gave Buddy a condensed version of the events of the past few days. As he listened, Buddy leaned back in the rickety chair, his eyes half-closed, the cold Miller against his bare thigh. Every now and then he would smile at something Virgil said and after he smiled he would take a drink of beer, enjoying himself immensely. When Virgil stopped talking, Buddy shifted in his chair to look at him.

"You're working on a fucking movie?" he said incredulously. "You?"

"Sort of."

"I'll be dipped in shit." Buddy had another drink. "Well, I read about them finding the actress in the creek but the rest is news to me. But then again that's why I keep on my own little patch here. So I'm not corrupted by the vile malfeasance out there in the world." He gave Virgil another pointed look. "That used to be your position too, buddy. So what's going on—you got a dog in this fight?"

Virgil gave it some thought before shaking his head.

"Claire Marchand working this?" Buddy asked.

"Yup."

"You and her still playing the old slap and tickle?"

"What are you—twelve?" Virgil asked.

Buddy laughed. "I wish." He took another drink. "So what would you like to know about Ronald McDonald Levack Red Hawk that I haven't already told you?"

"Well," Virgil said slowly, "so far all I've heard is that he's a small-time thief and ex-con with enough balls and bullshit to grab himself a big piece of a lucrative Indian casino. It's your standard rags-to-riches story. The question is—is he the type of guy who starts killing people to get his own way?"

"From what I know of him—no," Buddy said. He paused a long moment. "But he's the type of guy who would hire it out."

"Which is one and the same."

"It is."

Virgil got to his feet and stretched. His eyes fell on the ancient soda cooler in the shade and he leaned over and flipped open the lid to have a look at the fish inside. "Nice size walleye," he said. "Where'd you catch them?"

"Off Kimball's Point," Buddy said. "You know Kimball's Point, don't you?"

Virgil closed the lid and nodded. He knew the location. Two years earlier, after a day of fishing, he'd hooked a steel cylinder on the river bottom there with his anchor. The cylinder had been full of pure cocaine and Virgil had spent the next few weeks being pursued by crooked cops, vengeful drug dealers, and a mad, murderous Russian with a cowboy fixation. Virgil had been lucky to get out alive.

"So do you follow it, or does it follow you?" Buddy asked.

"What?"

"Trouble."

Virgil smiled and finished the beer. He placed the can on the arm of the lawn chair. "Thanks for the info, Buddy. And the beer."

"Why don't you come out fishing one day?"

"I'll do that."

"Bring Claire."

"Okay."

"And leave the police work to the professionals."

"I intend to," Virgil said, and he left.

Claire had never been to Fairfield Village. It was the type of place she tended to avoid, even though she had no idea what was actually there. Leaving home Thursday morning, it occurred to her that she might, if it were possible, like to visit a genuine nineteenth-century pioneer village, but to do that she would require a time machine. She was just not comfortable with the whole notion of something being *re-created*. To Claire, re-created meant fake. She refused even to wear faux fur. Of course, she didn't wear real fur either. She once dated a guy who wanted to buy her a coat made from a wolf hide. He had a fantasy of the two of them making wild love on it, and he'd assured her over and over how gorgeous she would look wearing it. Claire had finally told him that she thought wolf hides looked better on wolves than on people. The relationship, if that's what it was, didn't last much longer.

The guy, whose name was Wayne Anderson, sold ad time

to radio stations, and while he spent a lot of time telling Claire how beautiful she was, he was constantly urging her to change little things about herself. It wasn't just the wolf hide; he wanted her to wear thongs, he encouraged her to go bra-less in the summer, he bothered her to shave areas she didn't want to shave. He apparently was all right with what Claire perceived to be her character flaws—her impatience, her too-quick judgment of people, her tunnel vision when she had a task at hand. It seemed that these traits would lose their significance once she got naked and donned a fur coat.

Virgil Cain, on the other hand, never asked anything of her. And while he rarely told her she was beautiful, he showed her that to him she was, with his eyes and his touch. She loved his calloused hands, his fingers like fine sandpaper on her skin. It was true that most of the time she didn't get a hell of a lot out of him verbally, but that just made what she did get that much more tangible.

Claire's sister, Eileen, had visited from North Carolina in the spring. She and Claire and Virgil had gone to Bearsville for Easter Sunday lunch and afterward Virgil had begged off, as he had a neighbor coming to the farm that afternoon to help him castrate some bull calves. Apparently it was a two-man job; given the nature of the task, Claire imagined it would be at least that. After Virgil had left, Eileen had started in on Claire about their relationship. Eileen liked Virgil, she insisted—and that Claire believed because her sister had flirted with him throughout the meal—but she couldn't see things between the two of them going anywhere. Virgil was stuck and unlikely to get himself unstuck anytime soon. Claire had nowhere to go with him.

Claire replied that she was okay with having nowhere to go, as she liked where she was. Then she ordered dessert.

Stopping at the station to pick up a cruiser, she noticed Sal Delano's Camaro in the lot and went inside to talk to him. He was in the corner of the main office, drinking coffee with Marina from dispatch. Claire was pretty sure Sal had a crush on Marina from dispatch but for a smart guy he was on the clueless side when it came to women. Marina was interested and Claire had told her more than once that she would have to make the first move. For the time being it was still a stalemate.

The two fell silent as Claire walked over and sat on the edge of Marina's desk. She suspected she'd caught them in the midst of some adolescent-type flirting.

"Anything on the departed director?" she asked.

"I finally got him on the phone," Sal said. "He's in France with his wife and kids. He doesn't have anything good to say about the producers of *Frontier Woman,* but I definitely didn't get the impression that he was, you know—homicidal. Plus, he says he was already in Europe at the time of death. Which would be easy enough to check out."

"Let's do that," Claire said. "And we can cross him off the list. Not that we have much of a list anyway. Anything interesting moneywise? I assume there's insurance involved when something like this happens."

"The film is insured," Sal said. "In this case, the insurance would cover whatever they'd already shot with Olivia Burns. Which wasn't much. So it doesn't seem like a big deal."

"The actors themselves aren't insured?"

"Apparently not."

"But I'm always reading how these movies can't get insurance because so-and-so has a drug problem."

"They insure the film, not the actor," Sal said. "That's what I'm hearing. And I talked to someone from the insurance company that holds the policy on this."

"Keep looking," Claire said after a moment. She slid off the desk. "I'm heading off to the nineteenth century. You kids carry on . . . or whatever."

Sal blushed and Marina smiled. Claire left.

Fairfield Village was pretty much as she would have imagined it, if she'd spent any time doing so. Log buildings, plank sidewalks, dirt streets, people walking around wearing long dresses and wool trousers in the ninety-degree heat. It looked as if the film production company had pretty much taken over the entire town. It was easy to spot the movie people; they were the ones wearing shorts and tank tops, with any number of clamps and clips and cables hanging from them. Claire had been on a film set just once before. Her cousin had a job as a still photographer on a movie about a mysterious virus that was threatening to wipe out all life from planet Earth. The movie was filmed in Connecticut and starred Meg Ryan. Claire didn't think it was ever released. The experience of being on set had been interesting for the first couple of hours but turned boring after that. Claire had ended up going to a bar in town with her cousin's girlfriend, where they drank beer and shot pool until he got off work.

Most of the film people were gathered around the fake courthouse in the center of the village, so Claire assumed they were shooting inside. She approached a woman wearing a short skirt and clogs who was struggling to push a rack of clothes along the dusty main street.

"Where can I find Ronnie Red Hawk?" Claire asked.

"Never heard of him," the woman said without breaking stride.

The woman was either lying or inordinately stupid, Claire decided. Anybody working on the set would surely know by now of Red Hawk's involvement, given the events of the past couple days. Claire let it go; maybe Red Hawk wasn't as interesting to the crew members as he was to the law. She turned away from the courthouse and started for the row of trailers at the far end of the street.

As she drew near, the door to one of the trailers opened and Levi Brown stepped out. He saw her at once, and it seemed to Claire as if he resisted an urge to turn and go back inside. Instead he forced a smile and came down the steps to meet her. Before he spoke, he gave his head a quick little shake, tossing his long hair back so that it settled on his shoulders. It was a reflex with him, Claire thought, something petty and vain.

"Detective," he said. "Something I can help you with?"

"I'm looking for Ronnie Red Hawk," Claire said.

"Yes, I guess you would be," Levi said. "Well, he's not here."

"Would you know where he is?"

"He went back to his casino, or so I heard. Rumor has it he's preparing a suite for Ms. Karson for the weekend. No doubt he's filling bathtubs with champagne and butchering some exotic roadkill for her to nosh on."

As Levi smirked at his own cleverness, Claire was reminded of his arrogance when she'd interviewed him the day before. Twenty-four hours hadn't changed him, but then why would it? People rarely changed much over the course of a lifetime, much less with the passing of a single day.

"Why did you say you guess I would be?" she asked.

"What?"

"When I told you I was looking for Red Hawk, you said you guess I would be."

Levi flipped his hand in the air, as if shooing a fly. "Just a hunch."

"Based on what?"

Levi shrugged. "Based on the fact that you're investigating Olivia Burns's death, and that he was the last person seen with her."

"That's all?"

"All I can think of."

"What about the fact that Red Hawk showed up here the very next day with the actress he wanted to replace Olivia Burns? What about that?"

The producer nodded slowly, as if considering the connection for the first time. "That is a little suspicious, now that you bring it up."

"You're an interesting guy," Claire said. "You're not as dumb as you pretend to be but not nearly as smart as you think you are."

She saw that she'd actually wounded him. His lips tightened, and he ran the fingers of his right hand through his mane, looking past her toward the village. He held the thousand-yard stare, his nostrils flaring, as if he was punishing her with his silence.

"Don't take it too hard," Claire said, unable to stop. "There probably aren't too many people out there as smart as you think you are."

Now he looked at her. "Why don't you go fuck yourself, Detective? I don't have to listen to this. I told you where he went." He turned toward the steps of the trailer, as if to go back inside.

"You'd better curb that tongue," Claire advised. "And there's one more thing. Did you tell me that you sat in the bar at the Hampton Inn with Sam Sawchuk until around ten thirty the night Olivia Burns died?"

He stopped. "That's right."

"She and her hubby claim they were in their room from

eight o'clock on. What do you make of that?" Claire paused. "Better yet, what should I make of that?"

Levi shook his head and kept shaking it while he formed a reply. "I don't know, I guess they were mistaken. People don't usually write down exactly when they're doing what." He was suddenly inspired. "What time is it right now?"

"Pardon?"

"Don't look at your watch," he said. "Tell me what time it is."

Claire smiled but she didn't play along.

"You see?" he asked. "If somebody asked you two days from now what time we talked today, you wouldn't know for sure, would you?"

"I might."

"I doubt it," he said. Smiling, he raised his left hand and with his forefinger tapped his temple twice. "See? Maybe I'm not quite as dumb as you think." While his hand was in the air, Claire had a clear look at the Rolex on his wrist.

"You just keep thinking that," Claire said. She glanced up at the sun. "By the way, I'd say it was a few minutes past two right now. You know—if some curious person were to ask me a couple days from now what time we talked."

She saw that he didn't want to look at his watch, but he couldn't help himself. His face fell when he saw the time.

"I'd also tell that curious person that you haven't explained the discrepancies in the timelines you and your friends gave to the police," Claire continued. "You want to give it another shot?"

"No," the producer said, sullen again. "I told you the truth. You'll have to talk to them. They could have been confused by the question." But then another notion came to him. The man was an assembly line of half-baked inspirations. "You know—everybody was in shock after hearing the news about Olivia. You might want to take that into consideration. We're human beings."

"I'll keep that in mind," Claire said, "when I talk to your confused friends."

"Are we finished here?"

"God, I hope so."

The Running Dog Casino was as familiar to Claire as the pioneer village was not. She'd been there socially a couple times, before deciding that casino gambling really wasn't her thing; she preferred live-action, particularly the thoroughbreds when they ran at Saratoga every summer. But she'd been to Running Dog in a professional capacity a number of times. A thriving casino was like a boomtown and as such it attracted all kinds of grifters, dopers, scam artists, prostitutes, and lowlifes in general. Every month there were innumerable calls for the state police, the charges ranging from car theft to soliciting to the odd stabbing or shooting in a parking lot or underground garage. And while many Native reservations had their own police force, the Sumac reservation did not. In the past, the place had been too poor to support one, and now everybody was too rich to bother. The casino had its own security, which was pretty corrupt in and of itself, but with more serious matters it allowed the state police to take care of things. On the state's dime, of course.

She'd called ahead to say she needed to talk to Ronnie Red Hawk, not wanting to drive for an hour and a half to find that he wasn't around. A receptionist had put her on hold for nearly ten minutes, then returned to the line to tell Claire to come on over. She'd hung up before Claire could ask if Ronnie was actually going to be made available to her.

Upon arriving, she was informed that he wasn't. The information came from a skinny Native who introduced himself as Marvin Nightingale. He claimed to be the talent coordinator for the casino before adding that he would be representing Ronnie today. He met Claire in the main foyer of the Red Hawk Hotel and led her into a restaurant a few feet away. When he offered to buy her a coffee, Claire declined.

"Where is he?" she asked.

"Couldn't say," Marvin replied. "Guy like the Red Hawk, he could be anywhere. He's building a golf course, he's running a casino, he has many charities here on the reservation. And sometimes he just disappears, like Crazy Horse would, off into the hills to seek counsel from the spirits."

"And what do you do here?" Claire asked. "Other than talk a lot of shit?"

Marvin's face fell. "That was uncalled for," he said before apparently deciding to rise above the comment. "I book the acts for the casino. I've been with the place since it opened. You want tickets to Faith Hill next month? I can get you front row, free of charge."

"No thanks."

"Have you ever been to the amphitheater? It's a world-class facility. Neil Diamond said the acoustics there are better than Carnegie Hall."

Claire nodded. "I've been there. I busted some shithead for dealing coke to some college kids over there one night. I think Carrot Top was performing."

"You must be mistaken," Marvin said. "We have a strict no-drug policy here. And our security system is top-of-the-line. We have Gulf War veterans, ex–Navy SEALs, working here. This place is as clean as a hound's tooth. You're thinking about someplace else."

"I'm thinking about going out to my car and running your name through my computer, Mr. Nightingale," Claire said. "Let's quit screwing around here. I called ahead to say I needed to have a little talk with Ronnie Red Hawk, and some woman on the phone told me to come along. Now you're telling me he's not here. All this is doing is pissing me off. So either you turn up your boss or I'm heading back down that mountain to find a judge willing to sign a warrant for his arrest. And that means he and I will be having our little talk after all. We just won't be having it *here*. You got that?"

Fifteen minutes later Claire was on the top floor of the hotel, sitting across an outsize desk from Ronnie Red Hawk himself.

Ronnie was wearing baggy brown pants and a hooded sweatshirt with a print of an eagle across the chest, his lank red hair hanging loosely to his shoulders. He'd told her when he had shown up in the foyer that he was extremely busy, so Claire did him a favor and got right to it.

"Did you kill Olivia Burns?"

"I can't answer that question," Ronnie said at once.

Which gave Claire pause, at least for the moment. The receptionist in the outer office had given her a cup of very good coffee and she took a sip of it. "Why not?" she asked after swallowing.

"It's simple," Ronnie said. "If I killed the woman, I would answer no. If I didn't, I would obviously also answer no. So what good would it do either of us if I answer?"

Claire had to admit there was a certain distorted logic to that. After all, what had she expected from the man—a confession? She rotated the coffee cup on the arm of the chair. "Might be good just to get it on record," she suggested.

Ronnie showed his palms. "All right. No."

"How long have you known Kari Karson?"

"Personally? Three days."

"Isn't personally the only way you can know someone?" Claire asked.

"Oh no," Ronnie said. "Spiritually I've known some people for centuries."

"Have you put any of them in a movie?" Claire asked.

"Don't mock my beliefs," Ronnie snapped. "I'm doing you a courtesy here. You don't have a warrant, which means I'm not under any obligation to talk to you. Correct?"

"Correct," Claire said. "Did you cast Kari Karson in this movie?"

"I'm one of the producers, so yeah, I was definitely involved in the process. Filmmaking is a collaborative undertaking, Detective."

"So she wasn't your idea?"

"What if she was?" Ronnie replied. "Casting Kari is a brilliant idea. I'm known for brilliant ideas. Do you expect me to deflect the credit from myself?"

"I get the feeling you're not much of a deflector when it comes to taking credit," Claire said, taking another drink of coffee.

"A less secure person might take offense at that," Ronnie told her. "Not me. Take a long look around you. Everything you see is because of *me*. All these Indians are rich because of *me*. Because I had a vision. I'm not about to hide my light under a bushel, act like this all happened by accident. I see things other people don't. That sounds like I'm boasting but I'm not. To tell you the truth, my abilities are so inherent that it's almost as if I have nothing to do with them. Like your beautiful brown eyes, for instance. You can't take credit for them. They're just there."

Claire smiled, not so much at the compliment but at the smooth manner in which he'd managed to slide it into a monologue about himself. "We're getting off topic here," she said. "Remind me—just how long have you been involved in the movie business?"

"Not long."

"Not long," Claire repeated. "Can you be more specific?"

"Couple of weeks."

"And how did you come to be involved with this particular movie?"

"The producers came to me looking for money," Ronnie said.

"Why you?"

"I suspect because they know I *have* money," Ronnie replied. "Where would you go for money—to a pauper? Of course, I also suspect that they thought they could hit me up for a few million, give me a little tour around the set, and then tuck me in a corner somewhere and invite me to the premiere next year. Well, that's not how I roll."

"You're a hands-on guy?"

"I am that."

"Were your fellow producers happy to discover that you'd be involved in the day-to-day filming?"

"Probably not. Their happiness level is of no concern to me."

"What about yours?" Claire asked. "Were you happy with Olivia Burns in the lead role?"

"She was a good actress."

Claire remained silent, watching him expectantly. From what she'd seen of him the two times they'd met, she knew he couldn't keep quiet very long. So she waited; she wanted to see where his brain took him when he wasn't responding to her prompts.

"Not just a great talent, but an interesting woman as well," Ronnie continued. "Very smart. We had dinner together the night she died. Well, you knew that. She asked a lot of questions about the reservation here, about my people."

"And about you?"

"Of course."

"I suspect you told her how you made all this happen," Claire suggested.

"You bet I did."

Claire leaned forward to place the empty cup on the edge of the desk. "Did you tell her about your carjacking career and how it landed you in prison at Attica?"

She fully expected him to flash anger at the question. In fact, a part of her wanted him to react. She needed to see what was behind the monstrous ego, the matter-of-fact persona he put forth seemingly without effort. Instead she got nothing. Although that wasn't quite true either. He sat looking at her with something akin to sadness in his eyes, as if she'd disappointed him somehow.

"My past is an open book," he said. "Anybody with a computer can read about it. The *New York Times* did a four-part piece about me a few years ago. They sent this blonde babe here, a condescending Jewish chick, thinking she would find some sordid story of greed and opportunism. Instead she ended up writing a tale of redemption. And make no mistake—Americans love tales of redemption. It gives them hope in their own little lives." Ronnie paused. "Well, maybe not all Americans. Thinking about it, I've never met a cop who cared about redemption. With you people, it's all crime and punishment. Isn't that true?"

"Oh, I believe in redemption," Claire said. "I wouldn't be able to get out of bed otherwise. But I can't allow myself to get sidetracked by it. So, while I'm sure your little journey from car thief to casino magnate makes for an inspirational tale, I really don't give a shit. I'm being paid by the state of New York to find out who killed Olivia Burns. You got any thoughts on that?"

"You've got a smart mouth," Ronnie told her. "You're quite obviously trying to piss me off. Well, you're not going to do it. What you're going to do is get up and leave my building. On your way off my reservation, take a good look around. I have *janitors* that make more money than you. And you come up here thinking you're smarter than me? You're in way over your head."

Claire got to her feet. "You do like to ramble on, Mr. Red Hawk. You don't say a hell of a lot but it takes you quite a while to say it. Before I leave, would you like to take another shot at my question—who do you think killed Olivia Burns?"

Ronnie reached into a drawer and brought out a Snickers bar, which he proceeded to unwrap. "I haven't the slightest idea," he said, taking a bite. "Now get the hell off my reservation."

Claire walked to the door before turning back to him. "Someday," she said, "when I'm finished ruminating about redemption and crime and punishment and after I've figured out who it was that killed Olivia Burns, then I might come back and ask just when it was you decided that this is *your* reservation."

She smiled at Ronnie Red Hawk and left.

# THIRTEEN

Virgil got a call from Tommy Alamosa on Thursday night, asking him to bring the Percherons to a rural address a few miles west of Haleyville the next day.

"There's a log cabin there up in the hills," Tommy said. "It's going to play the main homestead in the film. We start shooting there Monday but we thought we'd come up Friday afternoon and get some second-unit stuff. Exteriors, the cabin at dusk, the horses grazing in the field while the sun goes down, stuff like that."

He asked Virgil if he could be there by noon and Virgil agreed. The cabin was in a broad meadow about five miles off the main road running into the little town, the meadow itself another mile or so behind an impressive fieldstone home of recent construction. The house was a massive A-frame, with a few acres of manicured lawn stretching out before it, and a detached garage large enough for a dozen vehicles. To the rear of the building was a large steel barn, red with a green roof, and a paddock where a half-dozen quarter horses grazed.

Using a map he'd drawn from the directions Tommy had given him, Virgil drove the truck and trailer past the mansion and onto a dirt road that led up into the hills to the cabin. He didn't need the map; somebody, presumably from the production company, had planted signs reading FRONTIER WOMAN starting at the main road, showing the way.

The property looked authentic enough, with split-rail fences and a woodshed and a small barn and smokehouse. The meadow was open on three sides with what appeared to be deep hardwood forest to the north, which Virgil assumed served as a windbreak. The cabin itself was small, built of rough-hewn logs and chinked with what appeared to be real mud and grass. It was maybe thirty feet square, and featured a stone chimney off one end and a low porch across the front.

There was nobody there when Virgil arrived, so he parked in the meadow and unloaded Bob and Nelly into a small pasture field contained by the rail fencing. As the horses began to pick at the plush grass there, Virgil set out a couple buckets of water for them and sat down in the shade of the trailer to wait.

Tommy Alamosa showed up a little after two o'clock in a cube van with a cameraman and a couple of grips. Also with them was a woman Virgil recognized from the food trailer on the set back at Fairfield Village. She was a kid, tall and loose-limbed, with breasts like a centerfold's and long, shapely legs. Her dark hair was pulled back in a French braid, revealing a number of piercings in each ear from the lobes to the tops. Her name was Nikki, Virgil knew; he'd talked to her a few times at the pioneer village. As he watched, she walked around to the back of the van, where the grips were unloading equipment, and pulled out a couple of stainless steel coolers, which she toted over to the shade of the little barn.

Tommy, drinking a can of Red Bull, walked over to Virgil and shook his hand.

"Find it okay?" he asked.

Virgil nodded, then indicated the little cabin. "What is this place anyway?"

"You see that big fieldstone on the drive in?" Tommy asked. "The guy that owns it is some rich dude, story is he made a lot of money in the market back in the nineties and got out before things went to shit. He's got a jones for the old west. Apparently he owns a ranch outside of Tucson that's all done up like the 1880s. The mansion over the hill yonder is his summer home, and he built this little homestead as a get-away. Apparently he and his wife ride their horses here and spend the night sometimes. Just like the pioneers, Virgil—well, except for the billion dollars in the bank. Come on, I'll show you the place."

He and Virgil walked over to the cabin. There was a coded lock on the door—the only modern convenience Virgil had seen—and Tommy punched in a number and pushed it open. The interior was sparse and very clean. Rough plank floor, a wood table surrounded by four bent-back chairs, a Navajo rug in front of a large open fireplace, oil lanterns atop the mantel. There was a single bedroom off the rear of the main room with a queen-size bed and scarred pine bureau.

Virgil had a look around and then turned to see Tommy sitting at the table lighting a cigarette, then dropping the spent match in the empty Red Bull can.

"The guy doesn't mind you taking over his retreat?" Virgil asked.

"According to that dickweed Levi Brown, he was dead against it," Tommy said. "But then Levi charmed the wife. Again, the gospel according to Levi. Apparently she's a lot younger than the old guy, and Levi thinks he's God's gift to the ladies. So he got her all excited about her place being in a big Hollywood movie and she just had to have it."

"Is this a big Hollywood movie?" Virgil asked.

"It's a fucking rat's nest, is what it is."

Virgil crossed the floor to look out the window by the front door. The grips were still unloading the truck, while

Nikki had set up a folding table by the barn and was laying out sandwiches and fruits and vegetables.

"So what are we doing today?" he asked, turning to Tommy.

"Basically we're going to do a three-sixty around the place, shooting it from all angles and different lengths. Inserts that they can use when they edit the thing. We're running behind, though. The crew has to dress it first and they were supposed to be here this morning. Tractor trailer broke down on the thruway."

"So we wait," Virgil said.

"Like being in the army," Tommy said.

Virgil sat down across from him. "Were you in the army, Tommy?"

"Reluctantly," Tommy said, squinting as he pulled on the smoke. "Drafted. I ended up working on some film stuff, what you might call propaganda, and because of that I never shipped out to Vietnam. Didn't exactly break my heart."

"I wouldn't think so," Virgil said. "So you've always worked in film?"

"Since I was sixteen. Began toting cable for a lunatic German director who would smack me with a crop if I didn't move my ass."

"Speaking of directors," Virgil said, "where's ours?"

"Oh, I sent him back to the hotel to rest his muddled head. I'll direct this, it's just second-unit stuff." Tommy leaned back and looked at the ceiling, then exhaled heavily, as if releasing the tension from within. "Man, I am way too old for this shit. The director's a fucking idiot, the lead actress doesn't know what movie she's in, and the producers spend their days whistling past the graveyard, pretending everything's hunky-dory."

"How'd you get hooked up with them?" Virgil asked.

Tommy laughed. "Shit, I could ask you the same question."

"I was on my farm bringing in a load of hay," Virgil said. "Turned around and there they were. The director and the other one."

"Like Lana Turner in Schwab's drugstore," Tommy said. "I met Sam a couple years ago on a thing we were shooting in Atlantic City. We got along pretty good, got high a couple times, talked about film. She's a savvy chick, on a lot of levels, but blind as a bat when it comes to the nitwit she married. They had a good director hired for this, guy named Peter Dunmore, but they did an end run on him. I think Sam had it planned all along, to get the hubby a big-time directing gig. For some reason she thinks the sun shines out of his ass, and nobody can figure out why. The fucking guy—it's his first rodeo and he's practically catatonic. But you know, in a weird way, it's not his fault. He's not very bright and he has no clue what the movie is about, so why would you expect him to be any good?"

"What about the new actress?"

"Man, they threw her into the deep end of the pool and then went for lunch," Tommy said. "Did you read the book? The role is this rawboned, hardscrabble farm wife, and she's playing it all petulant, like it's a reality show and she's being imposed upon, stuck out in the wilderness without her iPad. Problem is, she's getting nothing from her director, so she's fumbling around in the dark. I don't know, maybe she'll figure it out on her own. She's not a bad actress, you know. Batshit crazy, but that doesn't mean she's not talented."

"Why did they cast her?"

"Because an Indian with red hair made them. That's a first, even for me." Tommy shook his head, as if still in disbelief.

"Sam told me that he gave them an ultimatum. Sam's the smartest one of the bunch, when she's not babysitting her husband at least. She saw the writing on the wall with this, though, and they caved. It was either that or go looking for more financing on a film that's getting a lot of bad press." Tommy smiled. "Aren't you glad you signed up?"

"I didn't sign anything," Virgil said. "I'm just the dimwitted hired hand."

"Yeah, right," Tommy said. "You can sell that somewhere else."

"By the way," Virgil said, "I thought Abner Doubleday was supposed to show up somewhere."

"They cut his part," Tommy said. "They've been cutting stuff all along because Robb wants to film some action stuff. Stuff they're going to need a lot of shooting days for. So Abner got the boot. Just as well, they probably would have cast an actor who couldn't throw a baseball and you'd have to fill in again."

"He never invented the game," Virgil said.

"I know," Tommy said. "But bullshit becomes legend and legends die hard. Speaking of bullshit, watch your back around Levi Brown. He doesn't like you."

"Gee, and I think the world of him," Virgil said, smiling. "What's his story anyway?"

"He's a champion poser in a business that's lousy with posers. Nothing about him is real. Sam says he grew up on skid row in Detroit and he's been inventing himself ever since he got out. With the hair and the muscles and the attitude. Even changed his name apparently. But he can't wash the punk off himself, or the fact he's a two-faced prick. He's been bad-mouthing the director to me and I'm sure he's bad-mouthing me to him. And probably to Sam too. Truth is, I wouldn't trust any of them as far as I could throw one of your horses."

"So they're not thrilled to have Ronnie Red Hawk on board?"

"Shit. That's another thing. Not only are they major-league pissed that he brought in Kari Karson without consulting them, they're also pretty fucking sure that Red Hawk killed Olivia Burns. Or knows who did. Which means they're scared shitless of him. Fucking hall of mirrors, man."

"You figure he killed her?"

Tommy looked at Virgil for a moment. "It makes sense, doesn't it?" he said. "But it almost makes too much sense. I've been doing this for forty-odd years and I've never heard of a producer whacking an actress to cast somebody else. But then, times have changed, man. The whole fucking world is sideways these days."

They heard the rumble of a diesel engine then, and both looked out the window to see the tractor trailer rolling into the drive out front. Tommy plopped his cigarette butt in the can and got to his feet.

"Let's get this place dressed and shoot some film," he said. "We might get some nice coverage once the sun begins to dip beneath the mountains. Magic hour."

Virgil spent the next couple of hours watching the crew refurbish the little homestead. The buckboard from the pioneer village was rolled off the trailer and parked alongside the barn, clothes were hung on a hastily strung line, wooden buckets and a half cord of firewood were placed on the porch. Several red chickens arrived from somewhere, along with a Jersey cow and a couple of jumpy calico cats, both of which ran directly into the barn and disappeared for the rest of the day.

While the crew hustled, Tommy Alamosa walked the perimeter of the place with the cameraman, deciding what to shoot and how to shoot it. Several times he had Virgil move Bob and Nelly from one place to another, sometimes in the foreground of the proposed shot, others off to the side or behind. Finally, Tommy and the cameraman wandered off into the hills to consider their options for some longer shots. Virgil let the two horses loose in the little corral beside the barn and stood there watching them. After a moment he heard footsteps and turned to see Nikki approaching, carrying some quartered apple pieces in her hand.

"Hey Virgil," she said.

Virgil nodded to her and she stepped to the rail fence. "Okay to give them some apples?"

"Sure."

Bob and Nelly had already spied the food and were on the move. The woman reached over the fence and fed them, one out of each hand, the horses gobbling the chunks of apple greedily.

"We had horses when I was growing up," she said.

"Where was that?"

"Bedford County," she said.

"Pennsylvania?"

"Yeah." As soon as the apples were gone, Nelly turned away but Bob stuck around, basking in the attention of the stranger. Nikki rubbed his forehead with the heel of her hand. "Not like these guys, though," she said. "These two are, like, awesome."

"I think Bob likes the limelight," Virgil said. "This your first movie?"

"Oh, no," she said. "It's like my sixth or seventh. I've been doing this since I was eighteen."

174

"You're an old-timer."

She looked over at him and then laughed, as if she wasn't sure at first he'd been making a joke. Her one front tooth was crooked, pushing just slightly in front of the other. She was a very pretty girl, and seemed unaware of it, which naturally made her even more attractive.

"What about you?" she asked. "How long you been doing this?"

"I'm a rookie," Virgil said.

Nikki gave Bob a final rub, then turned to look at the little cabin across the yard. "It is so cool here," she said. "Can you imagine living in a place like this?"

"I do live in a place like this," Virgil said.

"Really?"

"Pretty much. Except I have electricity. And cattle. And a mortgage."

"You see?" Nikki said, laughing. "Fucking civilization, man. It ruins everything."

She indicated the table of food she'd set up. "Come and grab something to eat if you want," she said.

"Thanks."

"You like avocados? I got avocados coming out of my ears," she said. "We bought them for Olivia because Levi said she loved them. Although now that I think about it, he probably read it in some tabloid."

She gave Virgil a little smile after that, as if she was aware of her tone and didn't care.

"Not a fan of Levi's?"

She shrugged. "He's okay. He thought I might be interested in hooking up with him, and when I wasn't, he got pretty offended by it. Like he was doing me a solid—big-time producer fucking the craft services girl." She shook her head at the memory. "What is it with guys like that anyway?" She stopped and turned toward Virgil. "Jesus, you're not a friend of his, are you?"

"Not even close."

"Good. You two don't seem very much alike."

"Did you get to know Olivia Burns?"

"Not really," Nikki said. "I mean, I met her, and she was real nice, but it wasn't like we had a long conversation or anything. I asked her the first day of filming if there was anything special she wanted and she said no." She laughed. "She never mentioned the avocados. And that was really the only time we talked. Oh, I did see her the night she was killed."

Virgil had been half listening. He'd been looking past her to where Tommy Alamosa and the cameraman were returning, walking down the grassy slope toward the little homestead. Now he turned to Nikki.

"You saw her that night?"

"Yeah. Outside the hotel. She was out walking and she was on her cell, so I didn't bother her."

"What were you doing?"

"Tommy and I were having a little picnic down by the river." She giggled. "Or something like that. We ran out of wine, so I boogied back to my room for another bottle. That's when I saw Olivia."

"Did you tell the police?"

"No. Tommy said not to. I didn't actually lie. The cop who talked to me was kind of dopey and he never asked me much. I didn't see anything suspicious and Tommy said it would just muddy the waters. Whatever she was doing was her own business."

"But she was killed the same night."

"Yeah. Bummer."

Virgil watched the young woman for a moment. It didn't appear that she was being flip. "What time did you see her?"

"Maybe midnight?"

"And she was alone?"

"Oh yeah. Shit, I'm not sure of the time. We were kinda wasted, you know? We smoked a joint and you know—one thing led to another."

"How long have you known Tommy?"

"We just met on this," she replied. "He's fucking awesome. You know he worked with Warren Beatty back in the seventies? And Jack Nicholson and, um, what's her name . . . Keaton?"

"Diane or Buster?"

"*Diane,*" Nikki said, smiling. "Wise guy. Anyway, he's worked with everybody. He's got the best stories. They're lucky to have him on this, especially with Robb the make-believe director."

"Not a fan of his either?"

"That fucking guy," she said. "Comes into the trailer, stares at my tits, and calls me 'you.' Like, you want to ogle me but you can't learn my name? What a twit."

Tommy was drawing near now. Nikki smiled at Virgil. "I gotta go make some sandwiches. Don't tell Tommy I told you about seeing Olivia, okay? He told me not to say anything. He says one of the things he learned over the years is to know when to keep your mouth shut."

She headed back to the table of food. Over by the house, the crew had just about finished their work. There was now a flower bed out front, complete with newly planted petunias and marigolds. More firewood had arrived, large sections of unsplit hardwood, piled by the tree line to the south.

"We're going to set up on that ridge over there," Tommy

said as he reached Virgil. "Can you let the horses loose in the pasture behind the house?"

"Sure."

"Just let them wander wherever they want. We'll shoot down from the ridge, with the horses grazing in the foreground, then swing around by the road there and shoot up, when the sun's disappearing. Those clouds stay away, we should get some awesome stuff."

"Okay," Virgil said.

Tommy stood looking up into the hills, as if imagining the shot. "How do you like Nikki?" he asked casually.

"Nice girl."

"Tell you something, Virgil," Tommy said, still looking off in the distance. "I've been reading *Playboy* magazine since I was old enough to work a box of Kleenex. None of those girls in that magazine is a patch on Nikki. Not one." He turned, smiling. "Okay, let's go to work."

# FOURTEEN

Ronnie positioned his office chair so he could see the road leading into Running Dog, thirty stories below. He'd sent Billy with the limo to the film set that morning, in case they wrapped early for the day, or if they finished with Kari before schedule. He didn't want Sam Sawchuk or the other one—Levi—to whisk her back to Kingston, where the rest of the crew was staying. Ronnie wanted her to himself for the weekend.

He could have remained on location for the day if he wanted to, but he didn't like being around Kari there, where her attention was constantly diverted, whether it be by the hair or makeup people, or the director or the producers. Also, Ronnie didn't like the way the director looked at Kari, like some mouth-breather. In fact, Ronnie didn't like the director at all, but that was another matter. There was something phony behind his eyes. There was no question he was frightened of Ronnie and Ronnie was okay with that.

After he'd given them the ultimatum, the two producers had been sullen for the rest of the day, but then they seemed to come around, which made sense, as there was no reason to pout about something they couldn't change. Besides, they would see soon enough that he'd been right. Ronnie had watched them shoot a scene in the general store at the pioneer village, a scene where Kari's character orders gunpowder and shot after the Indian raid that killed her husband.

The dialogue in the script was very stiff and formal and Kari had trouble with it, inserting contractions that weren't supposed to be there and adding little things like "you know" to the end of a sentence. Ronnie had noticed some of the crew rolling their eyes behind Kari's back. He decided he would put a stop to that or it would be their heads, not their eyes, that would roll. Also, he made a mental note to have the script worked on so it better suited Kari's style.

When he saw the limo coming up the winding road, he hurried to the elevator and made his way down to the ground floor. He was wearing a black Armani suit with a T-shirt underneath, not wanting to appear too formal but not, at the same time, giving Kari the impression that he was a slob.

He was standing on the ceramic sidewalk outside the hotel when the limo rolled to a stop. He was so excited he was actually vibrating at his core. Kari Karson was finally at his hotel. Ronnie knew a little about dreams coming true but this one had seemed unattainable. It was a lesson for him, he decided. There was nothing on this earth beyond his reach.

However, when the limo door opened, to his surprise a young blonde woman got out. She was maybe twenty-five, with bangs that hung down over her eyes and numerous gold bangles on her wrists. She blinked in the sunlight, her eyes resting on Ronnie for a split second before sweeping across the hotel and the surrounding buildings quickly, as if appraising the place.

Kari stepped out of the car then, wearing oversize sunglasses and torn blue jeans and a loose-fitting cotton shirt. Her hair was tucked beneath a Dodgers cap. She seemed to pause when she saw Ronnie waiting there.

"Hey," she said.

"Welcome to Running Dog," Ronnie said. It was a lame

greeting and he immediately regretted it. Why hadn't he come up with a cool line earlier, while he was waiting?

"Yeah." She came forward and gave him a quick hug, turning her cheek at the last second to discourage any notion he might have of kissing her.

When she stepped back, Ronnie hesitated for a moment, thinking he might get an introduction to the blonde with the bangs. He wasn't at all happy to see her there, but he would at least like to know who the fuck she was.

Billy, who had opened the limo door, now was moving to the rear to open the trunk. As he began hauling bags out of the Caddy and stacking them on the tarmac like a stevedore on a dock, Ronnie turned and motioned for one of the bell-hops to help.

"Better bring a cart," Ronnie said to the bellhop, then watched as more bags emerged. "Or two." He then took a step toward the blonde and stuck out his hand. "Ronnie Red Hawk."

"Oh," Kari said. "This is Nicole."

The blonde named Nicole shook his hand. "Hey."

Ronnie couldn't see her eyes behind the bangs. "What do you do, Nicole?" he asked.

"Nothing, if I can get away with it." The woman laughed and turned toward the back of the car, where Billy was helping the bellhop stack the bags on the carts. "I'll take the red one with me," she told him.

Ronnie looked at Kari, putting the blonde out of his mind for the moment. She couldn't change the fact that Kari Karson was at his casino, which was all that mattered for now. "I want to show you around. I have your suite ready. We can get Nicole a room . . . um, if she's staying."

"She can crash with me," Kari said.

That wasn't what Ronnie wanted to hear, but apparently he'd have to be okay with it. For the time being anyway. "Is she your assistant?" he asked.

"Nah, she's my homey," Kari said. "She's just here to hang."

Again, that didn't quite mesh with Ronnie's plans. He had thought that he and he alone would be hanging with Kari for the weekend. But he wouldn't let this latest development discourage him. Actors had entourages, he knew, and if Kari's consisted of just one skanky blonde, he should be grateful. If she got in the way, he'd deal with it at the time.

"Let's get you checked in and then I'll give you the tour," he said. "Maybe Nicole will want to rest up."

He could only hope that Kari got the not-so-subtle message. Ronnie accompanied them to the suite on the twenty-ninth floor, and while they waited for their luggage to come up on another elevator, he went from room to room, pointing out the amenities therein. He'd had the large refrigerator stocked with seafood and fruit and various snacks, as well as champagne and wine and beer and liquor. There was a case of Grand Marnier because he'd read once that it was Kari's drink of choice.

After the luggage arrived, Ronnie told the two women that he'd meet them downstairs in twenty minutes for a tour of the casino and the grounds. He was sitting in front of the hotel in a four-man golf cart, the black finish polished to a gleaming shine, when Kari came down by herself a half hour later. She was still wearing the torn jeans but she'd changed into the red T-shirt Ronnie had left in the master bedroom, with RED HAWK FILMS on the front, now splashed across her perfect breasts. The girl was no fool.

Starting out in the cart, Ronnie gave her a quick look at the exterior of the gaming palace itself, but they didn't go inside. She would be recognized at once if they went in, and that meant sharing her with all the gamblers there, the sweaty little Chinamen and the blue-haired old ladies and the deadbeats from the surrounding towns blowing their welfare checks on the slots. Ronnie hadn't brought her to Running Dog for that.

They drove past the casino to the art gallery in the square, where they went inside and looked at the Native pieces. When Kari expressed admiration for a painting of an Indian and his pony—a blatant and somewhat mediocre Charles Russell rip-off—Ronnie bought it for her. Realizing he had no money on him, he told the man behind the counter to send the painting to Kari's suite and the bill to his office. The man, of course, knew better than to send the bill, but it played well in front of Kari Karson.

From the art gallery they took the gravel road up into the hills to the site of the partially constructed golf course. Ronnie parked on a rise overlooking the eighteenth hole, where it ran down to the clubhouse.

"You play?" he asked.

"Mini golf once," Kari said. "We were blasted, so I don't remember much about it. You had to shoot the ball over little bridges and through windmills, shit like that."

"This will be a world-class course," Ronnie told her. "It's going to be a PGA Tour stop, which means the best golfers in the world will play here. It will be incredible."

Kari looked at the expanse before her, the dirt pushed into mounds, drainage pipes spread here and there, earthmovers climbing over the landscape like noisy beetles. She exhaled and turned to glance back toward the casino complex. It looked even bigger from that vantage point.

"Like, what does this place make in a year?"

"You wouldn't believe it," Ronnie said. "Hundreds of millions. You know the *Forbes* list?"

"Yeah. You're on it?"

"Not yet, but I will be." Ronnie offered his palms forward and skyward, like a preacher giving a benediction. "When I came here, this place was a wasteland. Physically, spiritually. And look at it now."

"It doesn't seem all that spiritual."

"Oh, but it is," Ronnie said quickly. "It's not something you can see. How could you? But a spiritual reawakening has occurred here. And I'm the one who brought it into being. But I'm not saying that to be boastful."

"It sounded a little boastful," Kari said, laughing.

Ronnie turned to look at her but it seemed she was just teasing him. So he laughed along with her, just a little, to show he was a sport. She indicated the gaping hole in the ground to the right of the clubhouse.

"What's that?"

"The lake," Ronnie said. "They're installing a poly lining and a heater. The water will be crystal clear year-round. Incredible."

"I wouldn't put it there," Kari said, looking down at the site. "I'd put it over there, on the other side of that building. What is that building?"

"The clubhouse."

"I'd put it on the other side."

"Why?"

She shrugged. "I don't know. That way you could see the trees in the background. Maybe you could see them reflected in the water."

Ronnie considered the notion for a time before changing the subject. "I thought we'd have dinner in my suite," he said.

"Just the two of us. I have fresh lobster. Or buffalo steaks, if you wish. I know you're not a vegetarian."

"How do you know that?"

"I know everything about you."

"Hang on to your hat, but sometimes magazines lie," she said.

"So you are a vegetarian?"

"No fucking way," she said. "I have to have meat. I meant, just in general. Don't believe everything you read."

Back at the hotel, Ronnie walked her to the elevator, then said he had to go back to work for an hour or so. He told her he'd see her at his suite around eight.

"It will be fun," he said.

"Can't wait," she told him and stepped into the elevator.

Ronnie watched her as the doors closed and then he went back outside and climbed into the cart and headed for the golf course. He hoped the foreman was still on the site. Ronnie needed to tell him to move the lake to the other side of the clubhouse.

"Fuck," she said when she walked into the suite.

"He's in love with you," Nicole said. She was lying on a white leather couch in the living room, a glass of Dom in her hand. She had changed into shorts and a wifebeater. The TV was on, some black-and-white film from Turner Classic Movies. Barbara Stanwyck and Gary Cooper.

"What makes you say that?"

"Duh," Nicole said. "Look at this fucking place. There's like thirty pounds of prawns on ice in there. If that ain't love, what is?"

Kari kicked off her sandals and sprawled in a chair beside the couch. After a moment she reached for the champagne on the glass coffee table. It was nearly empty and she drank from the bottle, spilling a little down her chin. "I don't want to fuck him," she said, wiping her mouth with her hand.

"Then don't. Lincoln freed the slaves."

Kari had another drink, killing the bottle. "Why don't you fuck him?"

"What's in it for me?"

"Free champagne, bitch. Go get us another bottle."

Nicole got lazily to her feet and crossed to the stainless refrigerator in the open kitchen area across the room. "You want something to eat?" she asked.

"Bring the prawns."

Kari peeled the red T-shirt off while she waited. She smelled the fabric and looked at the manufacturer's tag before tossing it aside. Made in China, of course. So much for the Native way.

"You're right about one thing," Nicole said, returning. "He doesn't look like any Indian I've ever seen." She set a plate of cold prawns on the table and poured Dom for them both. "He got you the gig, though, didn't he?"

Kari had a drink and made no reply. Instead she reached for a couple of the fat prawns. She ate one and washed it down with the champagne. "I can't believe you came up here empty-handed. No X, no coke."

"I told you I couldn't score any X," Nicole said. "What about the big chief? There's got to be drugs around here. Fucking place like this, oozing money, don't tell me there's no dealers around."

"I'm not asking him for X," Kari said.

"Why not? You're already beholden to him."

"Beholden? Who says that?"

Nicole gestured to the oak dining table across the room. "I

was reading your script. Somebody in there was beholden to somebody else. Shit, you even read the fucking thing?"

"Yeah, I read it," Kari said. "I fast-forward the scenes I'm not in." She had another drink and then got to her feet. "I'm going to have a bath. You can sit there sucking back free Dom and thinking of an excuse I can use not to have dinner with that fat fuck tonight."

"I'm on it."

"While you're at it, you can think about why you came up here with no drugs. You do realize that you're beholden to *me*."

"I didn't say I had *no* drugs," Nicole told her.

Kari was in the doorway that led to the master bedroom. She stopped and looked back.

"You little bitch," she said. "What'd you bring me?"

After her fractious interview with Ronnie Red Hawk at the casino, Claire drove back to Kingston and spent an hour or so at her desk, making phone calls and returning e-mails. She called Virgil a couple of times and got no answer. She'd tried him the night before as well, with the same result. She didn't leave a message because there was no way to do so. She'd threatened to buy him an answering machine, if in fact anybody still made such a thing, but she knew he would never use it anyway. Giving up, she went home, scrambled a couple of eggs for dinner, and slept in her own bed on Pearl Street for a change. The next morning she got up early and headed for Watertown.

She took 87 to 90 and followed the thruway west to Route 12, heading north. It was oppressively hot, once again, but she drove with the windows down, the air-conditioning off. She sifted through her CDs and, passing the countryside, she listened, in succession, to Bonnie Raitt and Lucinda Williams and Norah Jones. By the time she reached Watertown nearly four hours later, she had moved on to John Prine, whose stuff Virgil had introduced her to. As she pulled into the parking lot of the Watertown Police Department, Prine was singing about a great compromise. The song was ostensibly about a woman who'd spurned the singer, but Claire was convinced that it was about something bigger than that. She just hadn't figured out what yet. She could ask Virgil, who undoubtedly had a theory about it, but she'd rather solve it herself. And then tell him.

The building was constructed of red cinder block, and it resembled a community college more than a cop shop. It was located in a leafy area in the southwest corner of the city, a considerable distance from the downtown core, where Claire always thought that a police station should be.

Inside she was directed to the chief of the department, Bernice Heisman. She was tall and fit, maybe fifty-five or so, African American. She was dressed casually in khaki pants and a short-sleeved shirt with the department's logo on the pocket.

"Heisman like the trophy?" Claire asked, shaking hands.

"No relation," the woman said.

They sat down in a sun-filled office that looked west, toward the thruway. Chief Heisman had pictures of family on her desk, and another shot of herself dressed in an evening gown while attending some official function, it appeared.

She opened the laptop on her desk. "I sent you an e-mail about an hour ago," she told Claire, "in response to your query from yesterday." She glanced over the computer at Claire. "I guess I could have waited for you to show up."

"I felt like a drive," Claire said by way of explanation.

"The impatience of youth."

"I'll take that as a compliment," Claire said. "The youth part anyway."

Heisman hit a couple more keys on the laptop. "What I sent was basically what you probably already have. Ronnie McDonald slash Levack was a pothead and petty thief who got nailed on a racketeering charge with the stolen car ring. He took the fall mainly because we didn't get the big boss, some Algerian national who was running the thing out of Montreal. The Algerian never left Canada while the operation was ongoing, and then he skipped before the feds could extradite. But I'm sure you got all that information from the database."

"I did," Claire said.

"So you really were just out for a Sunday drive?" Heisman said. "I don't think so. What are you looking for from us?"

"I was hoping to talk to someone who had some face time with Ronnie," Claire said. "The guy thinks he hung the moon, but he's a bit of an enigma. Just the fact that he looks the way he does and calls himself a Native American is enough to make you want to scratch the surface a little."

Chief Heisman closed the laptop. "Bill Sully," she said.

"Pardon?"

"That's who you need to talk to. He was on the city force here for thirty years. He retired a couple years ago but I know he arrested Ronnie multiple times. If anybody could tell you anything, it would be him."

"Where can I find him?"

Heisman swiveled in her chair to look out the window. "Sun's shining. He'll be at the Watertown Golf and Country Club." She glanced at her watch. "Probably finished eighteen. You hurry, you just might catch him having lunch in the clubhouse."

The golf course was on the south side of town, up a winding street that passed the city zoo. In spite of the day's heat, there were a number of people out walking along the shoulder of the narrow road; they seemed to be of the opinion that the road was theirs and Claire was forced to slow down a couple of times to allow oncoming traffic to pass.

The course was an older design, to Claire's eyes, the fairways lined with ancient oaks and maples, the bunkers filled with white sand that glistened under the hot midday sun. The clubhouse was a modest frame building that might have been a private residence at one time. A number of people were eating lunch on an outside deck when she pulled into the parking lot. One of them was Bill Sully.

He was tall and young-looking for a retiree, with thick dark hair trimmed short, military style. He was dressed in green shorts and a beige polo shirt with an Adams Golf logo on the pocket. He was nonplussed by Claire's sudden appearance but then—after his lunch partners made a few cracks about Claire being his girlfriend, there to drag him off the links—he suggested they talk inside.

It was cooler there in the air-conditioning and they took a booth at the back of the dining room. The interior was nearly empty; apparently the membership preferred the fresh air, in spite of the humidity. Sitting down across from her, Sully motioned with his forefinger to his left ear.

"My hearing isn't great," he said. "Especially with my buddies yapping away. Collateral noise, you know."

A waitress approached and asked Claire if she would be eating. She realized she was hungry and ordered a grilled cheese and an iced tea. Sully asked for a light beer. After the waitress left, Claire told him why she was there and then waited as Sully thought for a while about what to say. He had a deliberate manner about him that was common to cops who'd spent a lot of time testifying under oath.

"I knew him from about sixteen on," he finally began, then corrected himself. "Actually, before that, because I was at his mother's house on a few domestics, and I remember Ronnie being there then, always hiding in the corner. His mother lived off and on with this asshole Levack. He used to slap her around when he was drinking. He'd get drunk on her paycheck, then smack her when the money was gone."

"He didn't work?"

"He was a trucker, when someone would hire him. I think he was on the dole most of the time."

"McDonald was the mother's maiden name?"

"Yeah," Sully said. "Sometimes Levack was there and sometimes he wasn't. There were other boyfriends. That's why nobody ever really knew for sure who Ronnie's papa was. Got to be hard on a kid, not knowing that."

Claire's iced tea arrived and she took a sip. It was extremely sweet, almost like syrup. "This Levack was Native?" she asked.

"Good question. He claimed to be when it served him. Looking at him, it would be hard to say, but he could have had Native blood in him." Sully laughed. "The real Indians around here never wanted to believe it, they didn't want anything to do with him. The guy was a whiner, one of those types that figured the world was picking on him."

"He still around?"

"No," Sully said. "I don't know what happened to him. He disappeared when he was out on his own recognizance on battery charges against Ronnie's mother. He skipped and nobody saw him again. I'm sure there are still warrants out for him, from twenty years back."

"What about Ronnie's mom?"

"She died. Had to be, I don't know, eight years ago, maybe ten. Before Ronnie hit the big time."

"Ronnie must have hated Levack, the way he treated her."

"It was a strange situation," Sully said. "You would think that but then Levack would do stuff like take Ronnie fishing. I'd see them down by the rapids, like a real father and son. So I got no idea what Ronnie thought. No wonder he was screwed up, living in that house. I know Levack tried to make Ronnie into a tough guy but that wasn't Ronnie. He never even played sports, that I remember. He was a sneaky little bastard, always up to something, at least before he went to jail."

"And afterwards?"

"He changed inside," Sully said. "Most guys don't but Ronnie came out different. He quit acting like a punk and started acting like he was *somebody*. Like he was entitled. But too entitled, you know?"

"This was when he decided he was Native?"

"Yeah. And it made him strut."

Claire had another drink of the tea and then set it aside. She would ask for water when her sandwich arrived. "He get into trouble with you guys after he came out?"

"Never. Matter of fact, he wasn't around very long. I sort of remember him dressing like an Indian and acting the part, and then he was gone. It was a couple years later we heard about Running Dog. Even then, we were thinking—*Ronnie?* They must be talking about a different guy."

"Does he come back here?"

"To town? No. But he bought a huge tract of land east of

here a few years back, couple thousand acres of bush. I've heard he goes there, it's like a retreat or something. I think he built a house there, or cabin or something."

"Was he violent at all?" Claire asked. "Did you ever know him to hurt anybody?"

"Violent, no," Sully said. His beer had been sitting on the table untouched. Now he took a drink and carefully wiped his mouth. "But I'll tell you a story."

# FIFTEEN

Virgil stood in the entranceway to the barn and watched the scene across the yard. It was late Monday morning and the film crew was set up around the pile of firewood behind the log cabin. The actress Kari Karson, wearing a long cotton dress and buttoned-up boots, with a bonnet hanging off the back of her neck, was trying unsuccessfully to split a length of firewood from the pile.

Virgil suspected that the woman had never held an ax before, unless it had been on the set of a slasher movie, and he also suspected that the wood she was trying to split was extremely hard, and green cut to boot. The director was taking none of this into consideration, if in fact he had any notion of it, which seemed pretty unlikely. Instead he'd been not-so-subtly ridiculing the actress for the past ten minutes, as if that might remedy the situation.

The workhorses, Bob and Nelly, were grazing in the field beyond the action, where Tommy Alamosa had wanted them as backdrop to the shot. Now, as Virgil watched from the barn, Bob decided to wander over to get in on the action, social creature that he was. The director noticed.

"Get that fucking horse out of here," he barked. "Where's the guy?"

Virgil, being the guy, walked over.

"We want the horse in the *background,* not sticking his

head over the fence and ruining the shot," the director said. "Did anybody explain that to you?"

"They did," Virgil said. "I don't believe anybody explained it to Bob."

A couple of crew members got a kick out of that, and the director's face reddened. "That's funny," he said. "I got a comedian for a wrangler and a fucking actress who can't cut a piece of wood in half."

Kari Karson was now looking at the director darkly, as if considering other uses for the heavy maul in her hands.

"Why don't you show her how?" Virgil said.

"What?"

"If it's so easy, why not just show her?"

The director took a moment, aware that the whole crew was watching. And so was Kari, who had shifted her attention now to Virgil, staring at him openly, curious.

"Because it's not my job to split wood," the director said. "I went to film school so I don't have to split wood, or paint props, or haul cable. You understand? I'm the fucking director, and right now I'm directing you to move your fucking horse out of the fucking shot."

Tommy Alamosa had been standing quietly by, probably hoping that things would subside, but now he stepped forward, looking to defuse the situation. Virgil shook his head at him before turning back to the director. "Did they teach you anything in that film school of yours about being civil to your actors?"

"Guess what?" the director said. "You're not an actor."

"I'm talking about Bob," Virgil said. "He doesn't appreciate that kind of language."

"Fuck you," the director said before turning to Tommy. "Call lunch. And get this straightened out."

Tommy called lunch. When the crew had wandered off, he approached Virgil. "Having fun?"

Virgil smiled, but before he could speak, Kari Karson walked up behind him and put her hand on his shoulder.

"Thanks," she said and walked away.

Tommy shook his head in amusement. "Well, Walter Raleigh, how you going to keep that ham of a horse on the other side of the field?"

"I'll spread some grain out along that fencerow," Virgil said. "That'll keep him there long enough for them to get the shot."

"If she manages to split the goddamn wood," Tommy said. "We might have to use the stand-in again and shoot it from the hill. She doesn't get her shit together, this movie's going to have more long shots than the Kentucky Derby. Let's get some lunch, Virgil."

"Go ahead," Virgil said. "I'll get some oats from the trailer for Bob. Push comes to shove, I can tie him off with a light lead. It won't show from that distance."

Virgil got a bucket of oats and set it by the gate before walking back to the little cabin to have a look at the woodpile. There was a selection of hardwood there—white oak, elm, ash, maple. Who knows where the production company had come up with it? The log that the actress had been whacking futilely away at was white oak, freshly cut, it appeared. She couldn't have split it with a hundred-pound maul. The elm was just as hard and gnarly as well. Virgil sifted through the pile and found a half-dozen logs of white ash, clear with no knots. He set them on the block and with the maul split each of them lengthwise, stacking the pieces off to the side of the pile. The ash had a straight grain and Virgil knew it would split easily, whether green or cured.

When he was finished he wandered toward the food tent to find Kari Karson. Walking past the trailers, he spotted her sitting outside one of them, drinking a can of soda and smoking a cigarette. It was warm there in the sun and she'd removed her character wig and unbuttoned the dress and pulled it down around her waist, revealing a period chemise that bared her arms and shoulders. She also had the hem of the dress pulled up to her thighs. Her legs were spread forward in the dirt and when she saw Virgil she remained like that, watching him openly as he approached.

"What can I do for you?" she asked.

"Nothing," he said. "I'm going to grab a sandwich. Why don't you come over to the cabin in a bit? I have something to show you."

He half expected her to question him, but she didn't; she just nodded and pulled on the cigarette before flicking it into the dust between her feet. There was something tough about her, or maybe she was just good at acting that way under the right circumstances. But there was a look in her eyes that Virgil had seen when the director was dressing her down that should have given the man pause, although Virgil suspected the man was too oblivious to notice.

Virgil got a ham sandwich and a cup of coffee from the meal tent and walked over to the little log cabin to eat by himself. He was sitting in one of the ladder-back chairs there, his boots up on the railing, watching the clouds drift across the noon sky, when she approached.

"Who are you—Henry Fonda?"

It took Virgil a moment and then he smiled. "*My Darling Clementine*."

"You're good," Kari said. "Wyatt Earp, sitting in front of

the saloon. That thing he did with his boots on the railing, like a little dance."

"Now, how would you know that movie?" he asked.

"So you can know it and I can't?" she asked. "That's a little condescending."

"You're right," he admitted.

She stepped up onto the porch and leaned her backside against the railing, facing him. The cotton dress was still around her waist, tied there with the sleeves. Virgil couldn't blame her; it was hot as hell in the little meadow, with not a hint of a breeze.

"When I got the part, my acting coach told me to rent *Drums Along the Mohawk*," she said by way of explanation. "Same era as this thing here. Henry Fonda and John Ford, right? So I'm checking them out on IMDb and there's *Clementine*. And *Fort Apache* too, but I didn't care for that much. Fonda was a dick in that one."

"You checked out what?"

"IMDb," she said. "The Internet site."

"Oh, that."

She laughed. "Oh yeah, you're hip. You probably got it bookmarked on your iPad."

"I use a Bob Feller baseball card for a bookmark," Virgil said. "And I don't have an iPad."

"I know you don't," she said. "It's working for you, cowboy. What did you want to show me? You're not a pervert, are you?"

"Not that I know of." Virgil got to his feet. "Come on."

He led the way to the pile of firewood, with the actress following. Virgil handed her the heavy maul, then selected one of the half pieces of ash he'd cut earlier and placed it on the block.

"I can't do this," she said.

"Sure you can. Lift it above your head and let it drop on the log. You don't have to swing it."

She did what he said and the log split easily, with a sharp snap. The two pieces fell away from the block and landed in the dirt.

"Well, shit," she said. "Why couldn't I do that before?"

"Because you were trying to split a piece of white oak that Paul Bunyan couldn't cut." Virgil pointed. "There's a dozen or so pieces there. Should be enough for the scene."

"Let me do another," she said.

Virgil placed another of the halves on the block. She dropped the maul on it with the same result. She smiled over at Virgil, and then flexed, showing him her biceps.

When the crew came back after lunch, the director announced that he'd come up with a plan, which, Virgil suspected, likely meant that someone else had come up with a plan and the director was taking credit for it. The idea was for one of the carpenters to cut the logs three-quarters of the way through with a saw, allowing Kari, theoretically anyway, to split them.

"No, I can do it," she told the director.

"Except you can't," he reminded her. "We watched you try. After we watched you try to deliver a line without saying *like* every other word."

She walked past him, grabbed one of the ash half logs, plopped it on the block, and split it with ease, stooping down to toss the two pieces onto the pile. Casually resting the heavy maul on her shoulder, she turned back to the director.

"Like, how's that?" she asked.

The director glared at her, his expression suggesting he'd been tricked somehow. He glanced around suspiciously at the crew, his eyes finally falling on Virgil, leaning against the cabin wall.

"What did you feed that girl for lunch?" Virgil asked.

Late in the day, when filming was done, Virgil was loading the two workhorses in the trailer when Tommy Alamosa approached, carrying a sheaf of papers.

"Tomorrow's call sheet," he said.

"What's up?" Virgil asked.

"Same as today. We need the horses here as background. No acting required."

"Try and tell Bob that." Virgil looked at the sky. "If this weather holds, I'll be combining tomorrow. My wheat doesn't care about your movie."

Tommy laughed. "And neither do you. When will you know for sure?"

"Long as it doesn't rain, I already know," Virgil said. He thought a moment. "I can't get at the wheat until the dew burns off. Tell you what—it's only an hour's drive from my house. I can have them here first thing in the morning and pick them up at night. If all they need to do is stand in the field, that is. If they need to be moved, then somebody would have to do it. I'd prefer that someone is you, Tommy. I don't want that peckerhead director or the other one with the hair anywhere near my horses."

"I thought they weren't yours."

Virgil smiled. "They're not. But it still holds."

"We can make it work," Tommy said. "By the way, the peckerhead thinks you pulled some kind of hillbilly voodoo with that firewood earlier."

"Let him think it," Virgil said. He gestured toward his truck and trailer. "I've got some hay and a bag of grain in my truck. I'll leave it in the barn there. You'll have it for tomorrow, if you need it."

Tommy agreed and then went off toward the trailers with

the call sheets in his hand. Virgil carried a half-dozen bales inside the barn and stacked them off to the side. There was a considerable amount of movie-related equipment stored there—dollies and ladders and white screens of some sort mounted on wooden frames. Virgil went back out and returned with the bag of feed, which he tossed on top of the hay. He felt her presence before he heard her.

"Hey."

She had changed from the long dress into a tank top and shorts and her dark hair was pulled back behind her neck. She smelled of musky perfume and pot.

"I never thanked you," she said.

"No need."

And then she was on him, her arms around his neck, her full lips on his, her tongue flicking wildly inside his mouth. It took Virgil a moment to react, then he stepped back and held her by the wrists.

"Whoa," he said.

"What's wrong?" she asked, attempting to lean into him again.

"It was just a lesson in wood splitting."

"Where do you live?" she asked. "Around here?"

"Sort of."

"On a farm?"

"Yeah."

"Can I go home with you tonight?"

"I don't think that's such a good idea," Virgil said. "I'm not set up for visitors."

"What the fuck does that mean?" she asked. His hands were still on her wrists and she lifted the right one to her mouth and kissed his knuckles. "I don't want to go back to the casino," she said softly. "I don't like it there."

"Why not stay in Kingston with the rest of them?"

"Why not stay with you?" she asked. "You can teach me farm stuff. Don't you like me?"

"I like you all right."

"You want a blow job? I'll do it right here."

Virgil decided it was a good time to change the subject. "What's wrong with the casino?"

"What's wrong?" she repeated. "That red-haired Indian wants to do me, that's what. He thinks I owe him because he got me the part. He's trying to win me over with champagne and jewelry and food. He's big on food."

"Just tell him no."

"I've been telling him but I got a feeling he isn't used to hearing it. I've never seen an ego like his and I live in fucking Hollywood. He actually thinks he's a movie producer and the thing is, he doesn't know shit. I bet you he's never heard of *My Darling Clementine*. He's a fucking stalker, is what he is. And he's scary."

"In what way?"

Kari twisted her wrists to escape his grip and stepped back. "I think he always gets his way. It's like he thinks he's above the rules. I don't like being around him."

"Then go to Kingston."

"Shit. I left my girlfriend there."

"At Running Dog?"

"Yeah. She was supposed to come with me to set but she got too fucked up last night and wouldn't get out of bed this morning. So I'll go back there tonight but that's it." She smiled seductively, dropped her voice. "Unless you want to change your mind and take me with you."

"What about your girlfriend?"

"She can handle herself. Maybe she'll fuck the Red Hawk. She likes money."

"You can't stay with me."

"Why not? We'll have fun. I guarantee you."

Virgil shook his head. Kari walked over to the entrance to the barn and glanced toward the trailers before turning back to Virgil. "You got a wife, is that it?"

"No."

"Girlfriend?"

"Yeah."

"So you're scared of her?"

He shrugged. "She carries a gun."

"That's kinda cool," Kari said. She walked toward him. "Can we kiss again? There's nothing wrong with a little kissing, is there?"

"It can lead to harder drugs."

She smiled. "You're funny."

"And I'm leaving," he said. "I got chores to do."

"Chores," she said. "I like that. It's romantic."

"I've always said that."

"Don't make fun of me," she said, but she smiled. "Okay . . . for now." She turned and walked out.

Levi stood by the driver's side door of the craft services truck, his eyes on the little barn in the meadow across the way. Ten minutes earlier he'd watched Kari Karson follow the horse wrangler inside. A few minutes before that he'd approached the actress, asking her to have dinner with him in Kingston that night. She'd turned him down without breaking stride, heading for the barn, dressed in shorts and a tank top that showed off her cleavage. She'd looked at Levi like she didn't recognize him.

Now he stood by the truck wondering what she was doing inside the barn with the fucking hired hand. Was she fucking the hired hand? Christ, that didn't seem possible. The man was a rube and she was an internationally known actress, albeit one with a dodgy reputation. Besides, Levi couldn't know for sure that it was just the two of them inside. Maybe Tommy Alamosa was there too, maybe with a couple others, and they were getting high or drinking beer. Nikki wasn't around the craft services truck; maybe she was there. Levi still couldn't figure why she was banging Tommy. Why would a hot young thing like Nikki be interested in a guy old enough to be her grandfather?

While he waited, he looked at himself in the truck's side mirror. He'd stayed in Kingston that morning and got his hair trimmed and highlighted. He looked good, he knew. He turned his head to look at his profile. The slightest hint of a double chin was just forming. Working out didn't seem to help. He thought about growing a goatee, keeping it trimmed close, just enough to cover the minor defect in his appearance.

He glanced toward the barn again. Who the fuck was she to say no to him? He was a producer on a film she really had no business even being in. She should be kissing his ass all over the set. She'd spent the weekend at the hotel up at the casino with Ronnie Red Hawk, who basically looked like a fucking ogre beside Levi. Was she sleeping with him? Levi had to assume so; after all, Red Hawk had hand-delivered her the role. Maybe she was a freak, maybe she liked fucking marginal people, which was why she was in the barn right now with the hick who tended the horses.

At that moment she emerged from the building and started across the property for the trailers, where the limo was waiting. As she walked she ran her fingers softly across her lips. What was that? When she got to the stretch Cadillac, she got inside. It looked as if she'd be going back to Running Dog after all. But what had gone down between her and the hired hand? Levi wondered if the man had come on to her, if she'd had to tell him to fuck off. He wanted to approach the car and ask her, but he couldn't stand the notion of being rejected by her twice in a matter of fifteen minutes.

When the limo pulled away, he walked over to the main trailer and went inside. Sam was sitting at the end of the couch and Robb was lying there with his boots up on the armrest and his head in her lap. She had a damp cloth in her hand and was gently wiping his forehead.

"He all right?" Levi asked.

"Yeah," Sam said softly. "He's just had a long day."

Levi went to the minifridge and brought out a Corona. "Any limes?" he asked.

"Don't think so."

"Of course there's no limes," he said, sitting down. "Why would anything go right? So what's going on? Are we getting anything worth keeping out of that little bitch?"

"Ooh . . . that's kind of harsh," Sam said. "You and Ms. Karson have a tiff?"

"Shit. I don't give her the time of day."

"The dailies actually look all right," Sam said. "I suspect there's going to be a lot of ADR, but I have to admit that the camera likes her. And it is what it is, right? We have to make it work at this point."

"I'm pulling a performance out of her," Robb mumbled. "But it isn't easy. I had to teach her how to cut fucking firewood today."

"I saw the footage, though," Sam said. "She looked great. And it's a nice moment, her at the woodpile, swinging that ax. It speaks of the character."

"You can thank me for that," Robb said. "To make it worse, I think she's stoned out of her mind half the time." He sighed at his burden. "Speaking of which—did you bring the hash, babe?"

"It's back at the hotel," Sam told him.

"Shit. Is there any ice cream?"

He lifted his head from her lap and Sam rose at once and went to the cupboard for a bowl. Levi watched as she doled out several scoops of strawberry ice cream from a container in the freezer and carried it over to Robb, who sat up three-quarters of the way, like a little kid in bed, to eat.

"She likes to slum," Levi said.

"What?" Sam asked.

"She was just in the barn with the hired hand," he said. "I don't know what was going on but use your imagination."

"That fucking guy," Robb said, slurping the ice cream.

"Who cares what she does?" Sam asked. "As long as she shows up on time and knows her lines, I don't care if she screws the horses."

"Wouldn't put it past her," Levi said. "I think she's a little slut."

"This isn't high school," Sam said.

"You know damn well she's doing Big Chief Red Hawk," Levi said. "And now the horse wrangler?"

"I hate that fucking guy," Robb said. "The sooner we shoot those horses out, the better. I'll find an excuse to fire him in front of the crew. He thinks he's so fucking smart. I have boots smarter than him."

"There was something going on between him and Kari in that barn," Levi insisted.

"You've really got it in for her tonight," Sam said. "You sure something didn't happen between the two of you?"

"Shit," Levi said, draining the beer. "I don't even talk to her. I got enough to do, trying to keep the money flowing on this thing. Besides, my standards are a little higher than that. I don't waste my time on starlets."

Sam went to the cupboard and retrieved a bottle of tequila she'd opened earlier. The day after they'd agreed to cast Kari Karson as Martha, Ronnie Red Hawk had sent over a case of his private stock, just up from Mexico, or so he claimed. Sam poured herself a shot and then turned to look at the two men, her back against the cupboard. She did the shot, making a face as the liquor went down. She reminded herself to tell craft services to bring in some limes.

"Where are we at?" she asked.

"We start the cabin interiors tomorrow," Levi said.

"Just Kari and Georgia then?"

"For tomorrow. Daniel's back the next day. The yard scene, where he buys it."

"When do we shoot the attack?" Robb said, his interest piqued. He finished his ice cream and sat up on the couch. Sam moved over to gather his empty bowl and the spoon.

"There's no attack," Levi reminded him. "He's out in the yard drawing a bucket of water and takes an arrow through the chest."

Robb looked pointedly at Sam.

"We were thinking that scene might need jazzing up a little," Sam said, looking at Levi. "We don't want to miss an opportunity here. Something along the lines of Daniel takes the arrow and staggers back to the cabin, then he and the mother and daughter fight off the raiding party. In the end, of course, Daniel succumbs to his wounds. Cue the violins."

"In the book, the women aren't even there," Levi said. "They're at the church thing."

"This isn't the book," Robb said. "Think about it—it's more powerful if he dies in their arms, with arrows flying. The husband, the father. And then they're forced to fight off the savage hordes."

"How would two women manage to do that?" Levi asked. "Fight off the hordes, I mean."

Robb wasn't listening, though. He was looking at Sam. "What if they rape her? Maybe they catch Kari in the barn and they rape her." He became inspired now. "Yes! And the husband buys it coming to her rescue. That's it. We could make it really graphic. Man, I'd love to shoot that."

Even Sam was hedging now. "Maybe," she said doubtfully.

"Call Stuart. Tell him to write it."

"Okay," she said slowly, refusing to look Levi's way. "He can rough it out, see what we think."

"Now we're talking," Robb said. "I'm ready to shoot some action. Chopping firewood doesn't do it for me."

"You ever shot anything like that before?" Levi asked. "A rape scene?"

"Sure he has," Sam interjected. She reached for the bottle of tequila. "He's shot everything. Okay?"

Levi turned to her for a moment and shrugged; he knew by now she would invent whatever history she needed to for her husband.

"Okay," he said, and he left.

# SIXTEEN

Virgil was back at the cabin in the hills by first light with the horses in tow. Driving up the winding road in the half darkness, he'd been thinking there'd be nobody there when he arrived. He would unload the horses and head for home and his waiting wheat crop. He had a long day ahead of him.

But Tommy Alamosa was sitting on the front porch of the cabin when Virgil wheeled the truck and horse trailer into the yard. Tommy had a cup of coffee on his knee and was pulling on a joint as Virgil got out of the truck.

"Good morning," Tommy said as he exhaled.

Crossing the yard, Virgil smelled wood smoke and looked up to see a thin fume curling from the cabin's chimney. There was a mist hanging over the meadow, the air damp with the dew, and the smoke was barely visible against it. Virgil indicated the cabin.

"You spend the night?"

"I did," Tommy said. He offered the joint in Virgil's direction and when Virgil declined he carefully extinguished it on the sole of his shoe before tucking it into his shirt pocket. "Sometimes I need a break from certain people."

"Not naming names."

"No, sir," Tommy said. "I got coffee on inside. I fired up the old stove."

"I had a cup," Virgil said. "I'll unload the horses and head back." He looked at the sky again. "The weatherman says it's

211

going to be a good day for combining. Of course, he's wrong about half the time."

"Then why listen to him?"

"He's right the other half."

Virgil opened the wooden gate to the pasture and turned the horses out into the field, where they began at once to graze, keeping close to the fence. Tommy walked over and leaned on the top rail as Virgil came back through the gate and closed it behind him.

"You need to move them," Virgil said, "just throw a little grain in a pail. They'll follow you."

"We're shooting all interiors anyway," Tommy said. "The only time they'll be in the shot will be out the window. We'll just let them wander and if they need to be moved, I'll take care of it. You coming back tonight for them?"

Virgil, watching Bob and Nelly tugging at the grass, nodded.

"So you'll be combining wheat all day?" Tommy asked.

Virgil nodded again.

Tommy sighed, as if envious. "Trade you jobs for the day?"

"Not a chance," Virgil said.

He left the horse trailer in the field where the production trailers were parked and headed for home. The sun was just rising and he drove into it, descending toward the broad valley of the Hudson. The road was winding and steep in places and he had to keep his speed to forty miles an hour for the most part.

The eastern sky, as he drove, was hazy behind the rising sun, but there was no real cloud cover. He estimated he would need two days of dry weather to get his wheat off. It hadn't rained in a month, but of course all that meant was that it was overdue. It occurred to Virgil that he'd chosen two professions in his life—baseball player and farmer—that required him to depend a lot on the weather. Which meant he'd devoted a good portion of his time to worrying about something he had no control over. And here he was worrying about it again, even while concluding that it made no sense.

He'd been surprised to find Tommy Alamosa sitting on the porch at dawn. Staying at the cabin, without power or amenities, wasn't something he'd expect from Tommy. But then Virgil barely knew the man. It certainly wasn't an alien concept to Virgil, getting away from people. And when he considered the ones Tommy had in all likelihood been referring to, it made even more sense. But Virgil was still a little uncertain about Tommy, especially in light of what Nikki had told him about the night Olivia Burns had been killed. There was more to Tommy Alamosa than met the eye, but then that was true about everyone.

Arriving back at the farm, he put all thoughts of the movie business out of his mind. When running a combine, any number of things could go wrong during the course of the day, and thinking about something other than the job at hand was tempting fate. As fate would have it, though, Virgil's day passed without a hitch. The combine, in mothballs since the previous year, ran perfectly. The wheat ran nearly forty bushels to the acre; the heads were large and ripe in spite of the drought. The heavy dews each morning contributed to that. By day's end he'd managed to harvest more than half of the thirty-acre field.

So he was feeling pretty good as he headed back west to pick up the horses. And it made him feel even better when he remembered that he'd made another five hundred dollars that day, just by grazing Bob and Nelly in some rich guy's meadow in the hills. He'd soon have enough to pay off his taxes, and maybe start looking for some new equipment. His seed drill, for instance, was held together with duct tape, wire, and reckless hope.

It was nearly seven o'clock when he arrived back at the movie set. He was hoping they were finished with the horses for the day; he wanted to get them loaded and back home. He was also hoping they wouldn't be needed the following day, but if they were, he would deliver them. It would mean another five hundred in Virgil's pocket.

As he pulled up to the set some members of the crew were milling about by the trailers, but there was no camera in view, so he assumed they were finished shooting. He'd been hoping he could load up and get out of there without having to talk to anybody.

But then, getting out of the truck, he saw Kari Karson in the entranceway to the barn, just a few feet from where she'd practically tackled him twenty-four hours earlier. She was wearing torn jeans and a loose-fitting man's shirt, her black hair brushed back and tied at the nape of her neck. She was standing, her head down and her hands thrust deep in the pockets of the jeans, and she was talking to someone.

That someone was Claire.

Virgil stopped short when he saw her. She was standing sideways to him and now she turned toward him. She gave him a long look.

"Hello," she said.

"This is Virgil," Kari said. Her voice was unsteady.

"I know who it is," Claire said.

Virgil looked from Claire to Kari. Realizing he'd interrupted something, he nodded to them and started for the team.

"I'm just here for the horses," he said, indicating Bob and

Nelly, grazing in the meadow not more than a hundred feet from where he'd left them twelve hours earlier.

The two women continued to talk, out of earshot, as Virgil went about his business. By the time the loading was done, Kari was walking slowly away, heading for the trailers, where a couple of passenger vans were waiting. A few crew members were still there as well, piling things in the vehicles. Virgil walked over to Claire, who was standing in the doorway to the barn, watching him.

"What was that about?" he asked.

Claire looked at her notebook before flipping it closed. "I just got back from the Running Dog Casino. They found a dead girl in one of the suites. A woman named Nicole Huntsman."

"Foul play?"

"Not sure at this point."

"So why were you talking to Kari?"

"It was her suite," Claire said. "The two women were BFFs, as the kids say."

Virgil raised his eyebrows.

"Best friends," Claire explained.

"What happened?"

"It's a little mysterious but it looks like an overdose, for the time being anyway. A quantity of heroin in the room, and a hypodermic needle on the floor beside the tub."

"What makes an overdose mysterious?"

"I'm not sure that it is," Claire said. "But Kari Karson just told me she'd known this girl for five years and had never seen her touch a needle. And Kari claims she never saw any needles in the suite."

"What about the heroin?"

"She's kind of vague about that. The suite's in her name

and technically she could be looking at a possession charge. With her track record, and in the middle of making a movie to boot. She says, though, that Nicole might have had drugs in her possession. She herself is clean, she says, but I have a feeling she'd be real nervous if someone asked her to pee in a cup."

She started to say something else but they were interrupted by an electrician from the crew, who entered the barn lugging a coil of cable over his shoulder. Claire stepped out of his way, watching silently across the broad meadow, her brow furrowed in thought, as she waited for him to deposit the wire in the corner and leave.

"You're not buying the overdose theory," Virgil said.

"Why do you say that?" she asked, still looking away.

"You're squinting with your left eye, like you do when you get stuck on a crossword."

Smiling, she turned to him now, as another crew member approached, this one carrying a plastic tote. "You say you're heading for home?"

"I am."

"If I follow you, will you buy me a beer?"

"You got a deal."


They sat in Virgil's kitchen at the scarred harvest table. When she had come in, Claire had removed her badge and her Glock from her belt and put them on the kitchen counter. She was wearing a skirt and now she sat stretched out in the wooden pressed-back chair with her legs crossed, her feet on the chair beside her. Virgil never got tired of looking at her legs.

"So what makes you think it's something else?" he asked as he put down two bottles of Bud and sat across from her.

"I probably wouldn't think that," she said, "if Ronnie Red

Hawk wasn't looming large on the scene. There's obviously a theory out there that Ronnie might have been involved in Olivia Burns's death. And if he was, it was for one reason—to get her out of the way. Right?"

"That would be the theory."

"Okay," Claire said, taking a long drink of the cold beer. "What if Ronnie had reason to want Nicole Huntsman out of the way as well?"

Virgil thought about it a moment. "Because she was cramping his style with Kari Karson."

"Yeah."

Virgil paused. "Seems a little thin."

"I might agree with you," Claire said. "Except I drove up to Watertown yesterday, trying to find out a little about Ronnie Red Hawk before he became Ronnie Red Hawk. And I ended up talking to a retired cop named Sully who knew Ronnie pretty well back in the day. He had a bunch of interesting stories about Ronnie, more about his attitude than his criminal career, which was pretty run-of-the-mill. Dealing hash, jacking cars. But there was something he told me that really resonated today."

"What was that?"

Claire had another drink and placed the bottle on the table. "Ronnie did his stretch in Attica for the stolen car ring. The boss man was some guy with rich oil contacts in North Africa."

"An Algerian," Virgil said.

Claire hesitated. "How'd you know that?"

"Buddy Townes."

Claire shook her head. "I keep forgetting about your curious nature, Mr. Cain. Maybe you and Buddy should start a detective agency. Get yourselves a cool car and a theme song."

"My liver couldn't handle it."

"Anyway," Claire said, then she paused. "You got anything to snack on?"

"Pretzels."

"Sure."

Virgil went into a cupboard above the fridge and found the pretzels, dumped them in a bowl, and set them on the table before sitting again. Claire grabbed a couple and then continued.

"So Ronnie and the boys were stealing high-end rides and selling them to the Algerian, and he was transporting them on cargo ships out of Montreal to Africa. We're talking Mercedes, Porsches, Bimmers—no Chevy Malibus or Dodge Neons. It was a small operation but a going concern. But here's the thing—the guy who first brought Ronnie in on this was a meth head named Syracuse Sid."

"Syracuse Sid?"

Claire was munching on a pretzel and she swallowed before she replied. "His first name was Sidney and he hailed from Syracuse. I'm guessing he didn't invest much time in picking a nickname. But he was the big frog in this little pond. Summer of 2002, they stole a lot of cars from rich cottagers in the Adirondacks. They'd watch a place until they saw everybody heading out in the family boat for the day, then they'd hit the cottage first, find the car keys inside, and jack the vehicle without having to rip the dash apart or smash the ignition all to shit. Which saved the Algerian kingpin a lot of money in repairs."

"How would they get the cars to Montreal?"

"The assumption was that the family would be out on the lake for a couple of hours minimum, and usually more like three or four. So they kept within a range of an hour or so of the border crossing at Wolfe Island. Cross on the ferry before the theft was reported and take the thruway into Quebec, and down to Montreal. All in all, it was a pretty lucrative deal except for one thing: Ronnie was the second-string quarterback, which meant he wasn't making near the money Sid was. And when the maybe-father Levack wasn't smacking Ronnie's mother around, he was hammering into Ronnie that he should never settle for being the understudy in anything."

"So Syracuse Sid was in the way," Virgil said.

"Not for long," Claire said. "They found him in the trailer park where he lived. Lying in bed in his trailer, been dead a couple days. This is where the story gets a little too familiar. It looked like an OD at first. There was a large quantity of meth on hand. But the toxicology report came back suspicious. So they tested the meth itself."

"And?"

"Shit was laced with Warfarin."

"Rat poison," Virgil said. "Which, I assume, isn't a standard ingredient in meth."

"No, but it's a good way to kill somebody without being in the room with them. In fact, it turned out that Ronnie was conveniently in Albany for the weekend. And he had hotel bills and restaurant receipts to prove it. Which is suspicious in itself—not many car thieves are that scrupulous about their deductibles. In the end, nobody was ever charged with anything and I have the feeling the local cops didn't pursue it all that strenuously. The general consensus was that Syracuse Sid was not an individual destined for a long life anyway."

Virgil broke a pretzel in half and put one piece in his mouth. "So if Ronnie wasn't your number-one suspect before, he's moving up the list."

Claire shrugged. "Maybe the woman died of an overdose. I told you Kari Karson admitted that she dabbled in drugs."

Virgil finished his beer and went for another. Claire, who'd been doing most of the talking, had barely made a dent in hers. He twisted the cap off and tossed it on the kitchen counter before sitting again.

"Kari mentioned that Ronnie was pressuring her," he said.

"She told you that?"

"Yeah."

Claire picked up a pretzel and examined it as if it were a piece of evidence. "That's interesting. She didn't mention it to me, and I'm a police officer investigating a death." She looked up at Virgil. "I didn't know you and Kari were so tight."

Virgil had a drink and said nothing.

"Pressuring her to do what?" Claire asked.

"What do you think?"

"Did she tell you that the girlfriend was along as a buffer?"

"Not in so many words," Virgil said. "But I got that impression."

"You and Kari," Claire said, not letting it go. "How long have you two been sharing secrets?"

"I never did any sharing," Virgil said.

"You never do." Claire lifted the beer bottle to her mouth, but instead of drinking, she clicked it against her teeth as she thought. "So—what else can you tell me about Kari?"

"She's a good kisser."

"You kissed her?" Claire demanded.

"No, I didn't."

"Then what?"

"She kissed me."

"Where?"

"In the barn."

"I mean *where*."

"On the lips."

Now Claire took a gulp of the beer and set the bottle loudly on the table. "And then what happened?" she asked sweetly.

"I told her I had a girlfriend who packed heat for a living."

"You think this is pretty funny," Claire said.

"You're making it that way," Virgil replied. "I thought we were discussing murder suspects. You have two dead bodies on your hands."

"It'll be three if you kiss her again."

"I never kissed her the first time."

"Okay, we need to stop this," Claire said. She rubbed her eyes with her fingertips a moment, then looked over. "But we *will* get back to it."

"Okay."

"So she told you that Ronnie Red Hawk was putting pressure on her. What else?"

"She said she didn't want anything to do with him."

"Did he threaten her?"

"Don't think so," Virgil said. "I kind of got the impression it was the other way around. He was smothering her with kindness. She doesn't strike me as the type who would respond to that."

"Kari expert that you are," Claire said.

"Thought you were going to stop that."

"I am," she said. "Eventually." She took a drink of beer. "So he wasn't overtly threatening her. Ronnie seems like the passive-aggressive type anyway, so that really doesn't surprise me. But I could see him being intimidating on a subliminal level. Although killing someone with a deliberate overdose really isn't all that subliminal, is it?"

"Neither is drowning somebody in Rondout Creek," Virgil

said. "By the way, did Olivia Burns have a cell phone with her the night she died?"

"If she did, the killer took it. Or it's still at the bottom of the creek. Why?"

"Because one of the crew members saw her talking on a cell phone and walking toward the creek."

"Which crew member?"

"Nikki. She works on the truck that does the food. She was with Tommy Alamosa that night—he's assistant director or first assistant, something like that. He basically runs the show."

"I talked to him the next day," Claire said. "He never said a word."

"Maybe he didn't know at the time," Virgil said. "They were having a little party down by the creek and she went back to the hotel for a bottle of wine. That's when she saw Olivia. But she did tell Tommy at some point and he told her it was best not to get involved when it had nothing to do with them."

"She say what time it was?"

"Midnight or so."

"And what were they doing down there?"

Virgil smiled. "I suspect what Buddy Townes calls the old slap and tickle."

Claire sighed at the adolescent term, typical of Buddy. She glanced at her beer to see it was nearly empty, and finished it. "Olivia Burns did not have a cell phone registered in her name. Which is extremely odd in this day and age." She looked pointedly at Virgil. "Well, maybe not for a stubborn farmer living in the past, but for a film actress on a movie location? Very odd."

Virgil didn't rise to the bait.

"So that means she had someone else's phone that night,"

Claire continued. "If we could find out who that someone is, then we could figure out who called her. Or who she called."

"They can do that, even without the phone?" Virgil asked.

"They can. We need the number and the server." She hesitated. "So Tommy Alamosa was out there on his own while this girl Nikki went back to the hotel. Why didn't you tell me this before?"

"I haven't seen you," Virgil said. "Besides, I was told it in confidence."

"You're allowed to break a confidence when there are killers at large," Claire said. "I'm going to have to talk to them both about this. And I'm going to have another look at this Tommy guy. We ran his name before, like everybody in the crew. He's got a couple of cocaine possession convictions from thirty years ago, out in California."

"That's got nothing to do with this."

"No, it doesn't," she admitted. "But I'm going to talk to him. You like him, don't you?"

"I do."

"I won't mention your name."

"You can tell him I told you. Because I did."

She nodded and stretched before lifting her legs from the chair beside her and straightening up. She rotated her shoulders in an effort to loosen them up.

"I could use a back rub, Mr. Cain."

"I could do that."

"Give you something to do while you're apologizing for kissing the movie star."

"I'm not apologizing for something I didn't do," Virgil said. He paused. "I'd like to know what's going on. For the most part, I couldn't care less about those people. But there's a little girl in the middle of it all. And she's kind of all alone."

"So you've been watching out for her?" Claire asked.

"Maybe a little," he said. "Somebody should."

She watched him for a long moment. "I think you have a knight in shining armor complex, Mr. Cain."

"So do you, Claire," he said, getting to his feet. "You want a back rub or not?"

"I do," Claire said.

"You going to stop talking about the actress?"

She smiled. "Depends how good the back rub is."

# SEVENTEEN

When Virgil arrived at the log cabin in the hills two days later, the actor Daniel Vardon was there, dressed in buckskin breeches and a slouch hat, preparing to get cut down in the yard by the marauding Indians, although the actors playing the marauders were not on location yet.

Bob and Nelly were required again as background, which meant another slow day for Virgil. He'd finished his combining the day before, so he was actually caught up at the farm for the time being. He would soon have plowing to do and it wouldn't be long before the second cut of hay was ready to come off, but for now he would take advantage of the money offered by the film business.

Upon arriving, he released the two Percherons into the pasture field behind the cabin and sat on the tailgate of his pickup to watch as the crew rigged Daniel's clothing with a heavy cork pad for the arrow that would strike him down. Tommy Alamosa was standing by, talking to the head prop guy, and after a while he walked over to where Virgil sat, lighting a cigarette as he approached.

"Hey Virgil."

"How do they do this?" Virgil asked. "They really going to shoot an arrow into him?"

"That's what they're going to do," Tommy said. "The prop guy will shoot it from a few feet away. Special bamboo arrow that sticks in that pad beneath the shirt, with the blood pack.

They'll speed it up in post. And then shoot it from behind, and from the side, with the arrow sticking through him. Back in the day, they'd shoot the guy standing there with no arrow, then shoot him with the arrow already in him, and then edit it with a quick cut and some sound effects so you'd swear you saw the arrow hit him. Remember *F Troop*?"

Virgil smiled. "Larry Storch. The arrow through the hat?"

"That's how they did it."

"Don't tell me you worked on *F Troop*."

"No, but I was on the lot at the time. I was a gofer on a Howard Hawks western. Highlight of the shoot for me was when John Wayne sent me into town for a couple bottles of bourbon one day. He and Bob Mitchum got drunk as lords that night and were pretty green around the gills the next day. Hawks blamed me because he couldn't blame the two of them. Mitchum would have knocked him on his ass."

"You and the Duke, eh?"

"Me and the Duke," Tommy said, pulling on the cigarette. "He was a good guy, remembered everybody's name, always on time. You just didn't want to talk politics with him. And you sure as hell couldn't spark a doobie in his presence. He'd have called the cops."

"Speaking of cops," Virgil said. "You hear from Detective Claire Marchand?"

"I talked to her the day after they found Olivia. Not since."

"You're going to," Virgil said. "She knows you and Nikki were down by the creek that night. And she knows that Nikki saw Olivia."

Tommy fell silent. He looked at the cigarette in his hand, flicked the ash into the dirt at his feet. "How does she know that?"

"I told her."

"I see. And who told you?"

"If it wasn't you, it must have been Nikki. Right?"

"I guess so." Tommy shook his head unhappily. "I gotta say, you don't seem the type to go running to the cops, Virgil."

"I didn't run anywhere. But I figured Claire should know that Olivia was talking on a cell phone before she was killed."

"So you have some connection to this cop?"

Virgil nodded. "We shower together from time to time."

Tommy had a last pull on his smoke and then dropped it to the ground and put his heel on it. He watched the prop guys across the yard. "There was nothing to it. I mean, Nikki didn't see anything suspicious or she would have come forward. Thing is, I have some history with the police from my rebellious younger days. I'd rather not draw attention to myself, if you know what I mean."

Virgil nodded but didn't say anything. If Tommy was looking for Virgil's blessing, he wasn't going to get it.

"What I'm saying is that I've been arrested a few times," Tommy elaborated.

"Me too."

"Does your detective girlfriend know that?"

"Hell yeah. She arrested me."

Tommy shrugged. "Then you know what I mean. I didn't want my record brought to the attention of my employers. I need this job. I've been broke pretty much every day of my life and I need the paycheck. You think I'd be working for these fuckwads otherwise?"

"Probably not," Virgil said. "I'm working for them for basically the same reason. Anyway, I just thought I'd give you a heads-up. The cell phone is what she's interested in. Whoever Olivia was talking to that night could be the key."

Tommy nodded, letting it go. Virgil couldn't be sure if he

was pissed off or not but he didn't really care. He wouldn't have done anything differently.

A van pulled up then, parked maybe thirty feet away in front of the barn, and a man in a cowboy hat got out and walked around to open the rear doors.

"Our weapons guy," Tommy said.

The man reached into the vehicle and brought out four long leather cases, which he leaned against the open door of the van. He then produced an open tote filled with powder horns and brass flasks and shot.

Tommy watched, then turned to Virgil. "The genius director has decided that our frontier mother and daughter are going to fight off fifty or sixty Indians all by themselves. How's that for reality TV?" He shook his head at the notion. "Which means that Will there has to teach Kari and little Georgia how to handle some antique weapons." He glanced toward the scene in front of the cabin. "I have to go. Looks as if we're about ready to shoot some arrows into poor Daniel."

Virgil watched as the weapons guy carried his goods into the barn, where he removed the muskets from their cases and leaned them in a row against the open door. The man was probably seventy or older, tall and sinewy, with gray hair that reached past his collar and a loping ease to his stride. He looked like he came from the same period as did his guns. Daniel Vardon, now lying in the dirt a hundred yards away, with fake blood dribbling from his chest, looked much less authentic. The director, who hadn't been anywhere in sight while they were setting up the shot, had now appeared and was waving his arms about; apparently he was unhappy about something.

Virgil heard footsteps behind him and turned to see Georgia approaching. It was the first time he'd seen her in anything other than her period costume. She wore red flip-flops and pink jeans and a T-shirt with some pop singer's face on the front.

"Hey Virgil," she said.

"Hello."

"Guess what I'm doing today?"

"Learning how to shoot?"

"Yes." She watched as the weapons guy went about getting things ready and then exhaled heavily. "I've never shot a gun before. This wasn't in the original script. It wasn't in the book either, but I don't think Robb ever read the book."

"You don't think he read the book?" Virgil asked.

Georgia leaned into him and dropped her voice to a whisper. "I don't think he's read any book."

Virgil smiled. "You nervous?"

"Little bit." She looked at the muskets lined up and ready a moment longer, then turned to Virgil. "I haven't seen you. I guess our schedules haven't meshed."

Virgil smiled at the phrase. "I guess not."

"I was saving apples and carrots for Bob and Nelly. I ended up eating the apples myself."

Virgil gestured to the horses grazing in the pasture beyond the cabin. "I bet they're still in the market for carrots."

"I'll take them some later," Georgia said, looking toward the trailers. Levi Brown was approaching. "Here comes Bert Lahr. I have to go."

"Good luck," Virgil said.

She gave him a little smile, but it was thin and disappeared quickly, defeated by her anxiety about the guns. He wondered again why she didn't have someone with her, a kid that age.

"Hey," he said. "Would you mind if I tagged along?"

This time the smile was genuine. "Would you?"

The weapons guy, whose name was Will, led them to a little clearing in the trees beyond the trailers, away from the filming in the yard. He set up a folding table and laid out the four muskets with the powder flasks and other equipment before walking a target on a tripod a hundred yards or so farther back into the brush.

After a time Kari Karson showed up dressed in street clothes as well, her dark hair hanging damply to her neck, as if she'd just gotten out of the shower. She was quiet, uncharacteristically withdrawn, as would be expected of someone who'd just lost a friend to an overdose, Virgil thought. Levi hung around too, acting as if he were in charge. He had a walkie-talkie and was connected to someone on the set who would tell them when it was all right to fire the guns, so as not to disrupt the filming. He wore a nylon jacket, in spite of the heat, and seemed determined for a while to demonstrate his knowledge of firearms to the man named Will. The man named Will did not appear to be overly impressed with Levi, who, slighted, suddenly noticed Virgil standing off to the side.

"You can go," he said. "This has nothing to do with you."

Georgia piped up before Virgil could reply. "He needs to hear how loud the guns are," she said. "'Cause they might scare Bob and Nelly."

Virgil smiled at the quick response. She was a smart kid. Levi glared at her, then back to Virgil, as if suspecting a conspiracy of some kind, but said nothing further.

"Well," Will said in a quiet drawl, glancing at the two actresses, "I'll show you how they did this in the nineteenth century."

He very slowly and methodically went through the process of loading the muskets—using the powder flasks, the wadding, the shot, and the ramrod—and then demonstrated how to fit the firing cap to the nipple beneath the hammer. Then he had both Kari and Georgia fire two of the muskets with just the caps, no powder or shot, which is how they would shoot them during filming.

Kari had handled firearms before, albeit modern weapons, in various films, and she had no trouble catching on. Georgia was a quick study too, but it was soon obvious that the musket was too heavy for her to hold out from her little body for more than a second or two. Not only that but the gun was so long she couldn't reach the end of the barrel to load it.

"You got something smaller?" Levi asked.

"They don't make a junior musket," Will said with a touch of sarcasm.

Levi flinched; he liked to present himself as an important cog in the machine and it was obvious he wasn't thrilled about being treated like an idiot. Virgil couldn't care less about him, but he could see that Georgia was upset that she couldn't handle the gun. She was an earnest kid and she wanted to do well. Virgil watched her for a moment before turning to Kari.

"Where's the scene being shot—inside the cabin?" he asked.

"You stick to your horses," Levi said.

Virgil ignored him.

"Yeah, in the cabin," Kari said.

"So Georgia props the musket on a windowsill," Virgil said. He had another thought. "To load it, she could stand on a chair."

"Yes!" Georgia exclaimed.

Kari nodded. "It would make a nice shot." Virgil could

see her slowly emerging from her funk. For all of the negative publicity following her around, she was serious about
the work. "Standing on the chair, pouring the whatchama-
callit . . . gunpowder down the barrel." She glanced at Virgil.
"You should be directing this thing."

"We don't want it to look phony," Levi said. "I hate those
scenes in a movie."

"Like a woman and a little girl fighting off a hundred Indians?" Kari asked.

"What you guys come up with here doesn't matter anyway," Levi said in response. "It's the director's call."

Kari smiled. "We'll just have to convince him it was his idea."

"How're you going to do that?" Levi demanded.

"Same way everybody else does, I guess," she replied.

Levi fell into a pout, shrugging his thick shoulders as if to
show that he didn't care what they did at this point. Will suggested that it could work, and he offered to help Georgia in
the cabin later, going over the loading.

Kari indicated the target in the trees. "Well—we going to
do some shooting or is this all just make-believe?"

"We can fire the weapons if you want," Will said in his
deliberate manner. "They've got some kick. I won't allow the
little one here to try it."

"No, I'm good," Georgia said.

"Give us a demonstration," Kari said. She was flirting with
Will now. Virgil suspected she flirted with everyone. Everyone but Levi, whom she'd barely acknowledged.

Will loaded one of the guns and walked a few steps away
from the others. Pulling on some lightweight hearing protec-
tion, he glanced back at Levi, who hesitated and then took
the cue. He said something into the walkie-talkie and after a
moment he nodded to Will.

"Plug your ears," Will said.

Standing sideways to the target in the distance, legs spread, he lifted the gun, squeezed the trigger lightly, and put a ball close to the center of the paper. He looked critically at the shot for a moment, then silently reloaded the musket and turned to Kari.

"Give it a try?"

She balked before turning to Virgil. "You go, cowboy."

Virgil gave her a look before stepping forward to take the gun from Will. It was even heavier than he'd anticipated but he pulled it up, took aim, and hit the edge of the target a couple inches from Will's shot.

"Good shot, Virgil!" Georgia shouted.

"Dude," Kari said.

Will looked at Virgil. "You've fired one of these before?"

"No," Virgil said. "But I grew up in rural Quebec. If you couldn't shoot a hockey puck and a rifle by the time you were five, people looked at you funny."

Virgil heard Levi, standing a few steps to the rear now, snort through his nose. It was evident he was feeling left out.

Will reloaded the musket and handed it to Kari, who gamely hoisted it to her shoulder and, with the end of the barrel wavering, pulled the trigger. The recoil set her back on her heels. The target was not threatened. She passed the gun over to Will and rubbed her shoulder.

"Holy shit," she said.

An instant later the clearing was filled with a roar of gunfire, coming from behind them. Virgil turned quickly. Levi had pulled a .45-caliber semiautomatic handgun from inside his coat and was in the process of emptying the clip in the direction of the target, hitting it several times. Georgia clamped her hands over her ears while Will looked on unhappily.

When he was finished, Levi smiled as he slipped the gun back into the holster inside his jacket. "And that's the way we do it in the twenty-first century."

"You're a goddamn idiot, boy," Will told him. "Any century."

# EIGHTEEN

After Levi shot up the forest, Will gathered his muskets and ammunition and headed back to the barn. Kari and Georgia announced they were going to their trailers to read over the revisions to the script. It seemed that everyone was intent upon putting distance between themselves and Levi, and in this Virgil was no different. He wandered over to where they were still filming the death of the father in front of the cabin. It took them until midafternoon to shoot it from the various angles and with different lenses. Virgil estimated that Daniel Vardon hit the ground at least thirty times before he was finally considered truly dead, at least dead enough for Robb, who kept asking for more takes. By the time they called print for the final time, Vardon was visibly pissed.

After lunch Georgia walked over from her trailer and fed Bob and Nelly the carrots she'd been hoarding. Virgil was sitting in a folding chair in the doorway to the barn alongside the muskets and the rest of the shooting paraphernalia left there by Will, who'd gone for something to eat. Georgia joined him there, pulling up another chair.

"Are you bored?" she asked.

"Yeah."

"Me too."

"I thought you and Kari were reading the script."

"We were," the little girl said. "We got new sides this morning." She sighed. "I have to shoot an Indian tomorrow."

"It's just a movie."

She nodded, looking over at him. Virgil had the chair tilted back against the barn door, with his right leg hooked over his left. Georgia made an effort to imitate him.

"What are sides anyway?" Virgil asked.

"Pages of the script."

"Why don't they call them pages?"

"They just don't."

Virgil laced his fingers behind his neck and looked up at the sky. "We could sure use some rain."

Georgia again copied his move. "We sure could."

They sat there like that for a while, side by side, the little girl glancing over from time to time to see if Virgil had changed position.

"How come we could use some rain?" she asked.

"My hay needs it for one thing. And my corn too."

"You have a farm?"

"Yeah."

"You never told me that," Georgia said.

"Did you think I kept Bob and Nelly in an apartment in the city?"

"No!" She shook her head. "I think they would hate that."

"Me too," Virgil said.

"Can you imagine them on the elevator?"

Virgil laughed. One of the production vans pulled onto the property then and parked near the trailers. Tommy Alamosa got out and when he spotted them by the barn, he started over.

"I would like to see your farm someday," Georgia said.

"Okay."

"Maybe once filming is done?"

"Sure."

"Good," the little girl said. She watched Tommy as he approached. "What did you think of Levi shooting his gun off?"

"Not much," Virgil admitted.

"What's his problem?"

"I think maybe his nose was out of joint because nobody was taking him seriously," Virgil said. Tommy was twenty feet away now. "That's my theory."

"I think he's an imbecile," Georgia said. "That's my theory."

"You might have something there," Virgil said. "Hello, Tommy."

"You guys watching the day go by?" Tommy said.

"Yup," Virgil replied.

"Yup," Georgia echoed.

"We're done for the day," Tommy said. "The Indian raid is next and the Indians won't be here until morning." He looked at the little girl. "Will's going to take you and Kari in the cabin and go over the weapons stuff again real quick and then the van's heading back to the hotel."

"Okay," Georgia said. She got to her feet and stuck her hand out to Virgil. "See you later, Virgil. I hope we get some rain. We sure could use it."

Tommy watched her march away toward the cabin, then he turned to Virgil. "That kid might be the smartest one on the whole damn production."

Virgil smiled and nodded his head.

"Tell me something, Virgil—can those horses of yours run?"

"Most animals can run. Why?"

"Oh, these new scenes. It's been decided that after the womenfolk fight off the savages they make a mad dash in the buckboard for the fort."

"What fort?"

"There's always a fort, Virgil," Tommy said. "You know that."

"I guess there is. Where's this one?"

Tommy waved vaguely off to the west. "About thirty miles back in the hills. Called Fort Howard. It was a tourist attraction for a while but I guess it went tits-up a few years ago and it's been sitting there empty ever since. Sam and Levi made a deal with the owners for us to shoot there. Apparently it's set back in the trees, though, and I don't know if there's a dirt road or open field or whatever to run the horses and buckboard across. If not, we'd have to film the fort and then shoot the horses running somewhere else and edit it together."

"I expect I can get them to run," Virgil said, glancing at the two workhorses grazing in the meadow. "They run around my pasture field when they feel like it."

"I'm heading over there now for a look," Tommy said. "Want to come along?"

"Sure."

They took one of the production company's rental trucks. Tommy entered the rural route address for Fort Howard into the GPS unit and they started out. Before long they were on a two-lane blacktop that wound up into evergreen forest so thick it blocked out most of the sunlight. It was like driving at dusk.

"According to the owners, it was a real fort at one time," Tommy said. "Built during the War of 1812. The Iroquois burned it but it was rebuilt later on."

They drove for a half hour or so and came upon a faded sign announcing that the fort was five miles away. Tommy steered the truck down a narrow gravel road and a few minutes later they arrived at the remains of Fort Howard, tucked away in an overgrown clearing with forest on three sides.

The fort itself was smaller than Virgil had expected, maybe a hundred yards long and half that wide. The place resembled the frontier garrisons Virgil had seen in the movies, with pointed log walls and two huge gates in the front. Whether that was the original design or a later concept based on what a tourist attraction should look like was impossible to say.

They parked in front of the gates and both men got out. The grass around the base of the fort had grown long and matted, choked with dandelions and stinkweed. Some of the logs forming the walls were rotted partway through, sagging in place. In front of the fort was a large expanse of open field, with sparse patches of gravel in evidence here and there.

"Must have been the parking lot for the tourist trade," Tommy said. He pointed off across the lot. "There's a lane leading into the brush."

Virgil glanced over. The lane was little more than a path, with overhanging limbs and tall grass growing in its center. But it could be cleared without much effort.

Tommy regarded the grounds critically. "We could run the buckboard and team out of the woods and across the lot here," he said. "And right through the front gates. The Indians in hot pursuit, pouring out of the woods, with the gates closing just in time. Cut and print. Bob's your uncle."

"What about the gravel?"

"We'll paint it brown and it'll look like dirt," Tommy said. "Nothing that can't be done, Virgil." He started for the building. "Let's have a look inside, see if there's room enough to stop the team once they come through the gates. This place is pretty small."

The big gates in front were secured from inside but there was a door around back that had presumably been an employees' entrance back when the place was a commercial venture. The door was unlocked.

The place was laid out inside like a small village, with a smithy and stable, general store, and barracks for the troops. Ramparts on all four walls served as the roofs for the various buildings. There were hitching posts and water troughs for the horses, as well as a plank sidewalk that was in decent repair.

"What are you shooting here?" Virgil asked.

"Fucked if I know," Tommy said. "They're still writing it. None of this was in the original script, or the book. I can tell you one thing—we're going to need some soldiers. You can't have a fort without soldiers. Be like shooting a beach movie without Gidget." He looked up at the shaky ramparts above them. "The carpenters are going to be busy, making all this safe. I'm pretty sure Robb is planning a big fucking battle scene, the soldiers against the Indians. Well, he's about to find out you can't shoot *Braveheart* on a buck and a quarter."

Virgil wandered into the stables. There were a dozen stalls there, along two rows, with a mow above that actually had a quantity of musty hay stowed in it. The floor was mud, caked hard and cracked. A wooden grain bin ran along the front wall. Virgil lifted the lid and scared off a skinny rat, which disappeared into a hole in the floor.

When he went back outside Tommy was sitting on the wooden steps in front of the general store, rolling a joint. He lit it and took a pull, squinting up at Virgil as he approached.

"Where's Sam going to get the money for soldiers and all the work we're going to have to do around here?" he asked after he'd exhaled.

Virgil leaned his elbows on a hitching rail and looked at the heavy wooden gates across the yard. "Ronnie Red Hawk?"

"Maybe," Tommy said. "I think that's a pretty deep well. And I know he's paying in cash, which means he's laundering. But they're tiptoeing around the guy. If you think they weren't scared of him before, they're fucking terrified now, with the dead chick turning up at his hotel."

"Is that why Levi's carrying a gun?"

"He is?"

"He pulled it and shot holes in the forest, trying to impress the black-powder guy."

Tommy had another toke and then pinched the joint off. "I heard the racket. Maybe he's worried about Red Hawk. And maybe he should be. The theory is that Red Hawk got involved in this so he could get close to Kari Karson. And now Kari's gone back to the Hampton to stay. Can't blame her, after what happened to her friend. But Red Hawk has got to be pissed off about that turn of events. And if he was killing people before, when he presumably was a happy camper, who knows what he might do now that he's pissed?" Tommy laughed. "Robb might have a real-life Indian attack on his hands. Be careful what you wish for. Right?"

"All I wish for is rain."

"I envy you that," Tommy said. He leaned back, his elbows propped on the top step. "Man, I hate getting old, Virgil. Especially when I get stuck on a production like this. This thing had potential, you know. The script was really good before they started fucking with it. We got an idiot director and a gun-toting producer and stupid fucking—" He seemed to run out of things to list, and he provided the rest with a flip of his hand in the air.

"You're saying it won't be any good?"

"It might *look* good," Tommy said. "Adam is a good cinematographer and he's getting some great stuff. But I don't see any emotion in any of it." He paused. "We might have to shoot the dog."

Virgil turned toward him. "I haven't seen any dog."

Tommy smiled. "It's an expression. Supposedly Peckinpah said it, shooting some TV thing back in the fifties. They had a bad guy menacing a family, *Cape Fear*–style, but the guy wasn't coming off as all that bad. And if your audience doesn't hate your bad guy, what have you got? So Peckinpah said, have him shoot the family dog. That did it."

"Everybody likes a dog," Virgil said.

Levi stood in the trailer, watching out the window across the lot, where Nikki, the girl from craft services, was talking to the cop with the attitude, Claire Marchand. Sam was at the table behind him, sending e-mails on her laptop and downing shots of Ronnie Red Hawk's tequila.

Marchand had arrived a half hour earlier. Sam said that at first she'd asked to speak to Tommy Alamosa but he was off looking at the fort they'd acquired for the shoot. Then she said she wanted to talk to Nikki, who had driven to a local farmers market to pick up something or other for craft services. Marchand had then waited in her car for Nikki to return.

"What the fuck is going on?" Levi asked.

"Where?"

"That bitch has been quizzing Nikki for ten minutes. Nikki's a fucking bimbo, she doesn't know anything. So what are they talking about?"

"Maybe they're swapping recipes," Sam said. "You think twenty soldiers is enough?" She paused. "No way—we're going to need more than twenty. Twice that, you think? How many Indians do we have?"

"I don't know."

Sam poured a shot of tequila, knocked it back, and reached for a wedge of lime in a bowl on the table. "Am I bothering you with these questions about the movie we're making?" she asked.

"I don't like cops hanging around," Levi said.

"That's what happens when dead bodies keep showing up," Sam said. "So how many soldiers do we need?"

"Ask Robb," Levi said, finally turning to her. "This is *his* wet dream, isn't it? Where we going to get the money to shoot a fucking battle? It'll take a week, at the very least."

"We're going to have to cut something."

"Like what?"

"I don't know."

Levi, looking out the window again, thought about it. "What about the big harvest scene, where they have the dance at night, with the fiddlers and all that? There's got to be a few days scheduled for that, right?"

"But I love that scene."

"If you love something, let it go."

"You really aren't adding a whole lot to the conversation here," Sam told him. "Am I all alone in this?"

Marchand was moving away from Nikki now, heading toward her car.

"You are for now," Levi said, and he went out the door.

He caught up with Claire as she was opening the car door. "Hold on," he said.

She turned and watched him approach. "What can I do for you?"

"Do we have a problem?" Levi asked.

"Who do you mean when you say 'we'?"

"Why are you asking my crew questions?"

"Because I'm investigating two mysterious deaths," Claire said. "And that's how it works. I ask questions in an effort to gain information. Have you ever watched a cop show on TV?"

"There's a line between asking questions and harassing people," Levi said. "We're running a multimillion-dollar production here. Nikki doesn't know anything about anything. So stop bothering her."

"First of all, I couldn't care less about your million-dollar production," Claire said. "And secondly, I don't think I was bothering her. But it sounds as if I'm bothering *you*."

"You're harassing my crew."

"I'm doing my job. You want to talk shit about harassment, I'll give you my captain's name and number and you can give him a call. Otherwise, stay out of my way. Go brush your hair or something."

"I'm watching you," Levi said lamely.

"Let me know if I do anything interesting," Claire said and got into the car.

Virgil spotted Claire in an unmarked cruiser when he and Tommy Alamosa returned to the set from Fort Howard. She was sitting behind the wheel writing something in her notebook as they pulled into the lot and parked by Virgil's truck and horse trailer. Virgil gave her a wave and then went about loading Bob and Nelly for the drive home. When he left the location, Claire was out of the car, talking to Tommy by the trailers.

She couldn't have talked to Tommy for very long. By the time Virgil arrived back at the farm, unloaded the two horses into the pasture, filled the water trough, threw some grain to his calves, and headed back for the house, Claire was sitting on the side porch. She'd even stopped and picked up a large pizza on her way.

"You realize I raise beef cattle," Virgil said when he saw the box.

"I do."

"I have steaks here."

"I felt like pizza," Claire said. "You want to cook a steak, go ahead."

They ate the pizza on the picnic table as the dusk came on. Virgil opened a bottle of white wine he'd had in the fridge for a while. He couldn't remember where it came from, but in all likelihood, Claire had brought it. She rarely showed up empty-handed.

"So you talked to Nikki and Tommy?"

She nodded, chewing. "And Levi Brown."

"Why him?"

"It wasn't my idea. He accused me of harassing people and hindering his production. He doesn't like me very much. I'm beginning to think that I won't be invited to the premiere."

"You can take my place."

"Keep in mind he doesn't like you very much either." Claire poured more wine for them both. "Nikki is one hundred percent certain she saw Olivia Burns walking down by the creek that night. And just as certain that she was talking on a cell phone. I need to find that phone. I had the boys drag the creek again but they didn't come up with anything other than some fishing lures and old car parts."

"If the killer was smart, he would have taken the phone," Virgil said.

"I've considered that."

"Then again, it might have been nothing," Virgil said. "She might have been talking to her mother."

"Maybe she was," Claire said. "But it's going to nag at me until I know for sure. And I realize I might never know for sure."

"So let's say she was talking to Red Hawk," Virgil said. "That doesn't prove he killed her."

"No, but it would prove that he lied to me. He said he never talked to her again after leaving her outside her room at around ten thirty. If he called her a couple hours later, why wouldn't he tell me that?"

"I don't know."

"Neither do I," Claire said. "The thing is—I need one more piece of the puzzle to really go after him. And this could be the piece."

"If it was him."

"If it was him. If it wasn't, the fact still remains that I need to know who she was talking to that night. If it turns out to be unrelated, then so be it. I can cross it off my list. But I don't believe for one second it was unrelated." She shrugged, as if dismissing the subject for the time being, and took a bite of pizza. "You taking the Clydesdale twins back to the location tomorrow?"

"Percherons. And no, the women are fighting Indians tomorrow."

"Really? That's not in the book."

"It's going to be in the movie. You see—we're not filming the book, we're filming an interpretation of the book."

"You're beginning to scare me."

After finishing most of the pizza and all of the wine, they talked a little more, then sat together in comfortable silence. The next thing Virgil knew, Claire was waking him up. It was a little after ten o'clock when they went inside and got in bed.

Virgil woke at dawn. He got up and dressed quietly, careful not to wake Claire. Downstairs he made a pot of coffee and carried a cup with him out to the barn. The morning air was cool and sharp, although it wouldn't last, he knew, once the humidity hit again. He ran the water for the horses in the front field and then walked back to look at his young calves at pasture behind the barn. The pond there was getting low; if it didn't rain soon, he'd have to haul a trough back there, run some plastic pipe, and pump water from the well.

He took a stroll back to the other pasture in front of the bush lot at the back of the farm, where he grazed his yearling steers. The pond there was spring fed, and Virgil had never known it to run dry. He did a head count on the cattle, out of habit more than anything; he'd never lost an animal or heard of anyone who had.

By the time he started back up the lane, the sun was climbing in the sky. The temperature had probably risen ten degrees since he'd walked out of the house forty-five minutes earlier. He had hoped to plow his wheat field today, but now he wondered if the ground would be baked too hard for that. The clay in Ulster County turned rocklike during a drought, and there were times when even iron plowshares couldn't cut it. Approaching the barn, Virgil began to think about returning to the house, slipping upstairs, and getting back into bed with Claire for an hour or so. As he thought about it, his pace quickened unintentionally, and so he was hugely disappointed when he rounded the corner of the machine shed and saw her striding with purpose toward her car, her coat under her arm and her cell phone tucked to her ear as she fumbled with her keys.

By the time he reached her, she'd shut the phone down and slid it in her jacket pocket and opened the car door to toss the coat inside. She was wearing the same clothes as the night before, her shirt untucked. Her hair wasn't wet; she hadn't even taken time to shower.

"I was coming back upstairs," he said.

"Have fun."

"It would be more fun if you were still there."

"Aren't you sweet?"

"First time I've been accused of that," Virgil said. He nodded toward the pocket where the phone had disappeared. "What's going on?"

"I had them expedite the toxicology report on Nicole Huntsman," Claire said. "Turns out it wasn't an overdose." She paused. "It was bad heroin."

Virgil took a moment. "That's interesting."

"Isn't it?"

"So where you off to?"

"My place first," Claire said. "For a shower and change of clothes. Then I'm heading for the Running Dog Casino to see what Ronnie Red Hawk has to say about this."

"Alone?"

"I'll take someone with me," she said. "See who's hanging around the station. Anybody but Joe Brady."

"You don't have enough to arrest him," Virgil said.

"Thanks for your input, Inspector."

"Well, do you?"

"Probably not," Claire admitted. "But enough to accuse him. And with a guy like Ronnie, you never know what might happen. He thinks he's above the law. Shit, he thinks he's above everything. He might get all caught up in his ego and confess and then tell me to prove it."

"You be careful," Virgil said.

"I always am."

"I mean it."

She stepped in and kissed him on the mouth, her hand on the back of his neck. She held her lips on his for a long moment.

"I know you do," she said and got in the car and drove away.

# NINETEEN

From the farm Claire drove into Kingston, to her house on Pearl Street. She went upstairs and had a shower, made herself a cup of tea, grabbed an overripe banana from a bowl on the counter, and headed for the station. When she got there, the first person she ran into was Joe Brady, the one person she didn't want to see. She had no intention of taking Joe with her to talk to Ronnie Red Hawk. Even if Joe had some strong points—and Claire couldn't name one offhand—interviewing a suspect wasn't one of them. He would be a distraction and a disruption and a pain in the ass in general. Not only that, but Joe had personal hygiene issues and Claire wasn't about to spend half a day in a car with him.

"Sal around?" she asked.

"He's off," Joe told her. "What's up?"

"Nothing."

"You need a wing man?"

"No."

"Why you looking for Sal?" Joe asked. "What're you working on?"

Claire looked around the station. A couple of young cops she didn't know, in uniform, were leaning over a computer on the far side of the room. They could have been working, or they could have been downloading YouTube videos. Claire didn't want to take a uniform with her anyway. She needed Ronnie Red Hawk to be relaxed and cocky, convinced of his superiority. Given his past record with the cops, the sight of a uniform might throw him off his game. And Claire wanted him *on* his game.

"I'm working on keeping cool in this heat," she told Joe and walked out the door.

She signed out an unmarked cruiser and, as she was walking across the parking lot toward the car, she saw Joe come out of the station. Seeing her, he started over. There was something in his pace that convinced Claire that he was determined to tag along for the day. She hurried to the cruiser, got in, and drove off without looking back.

She took the thruway to the Saugerties exit before heading northwest. There was construction on Route 32 and it was slow going for ten miles or so. Claire settled in behind a truck loaded with logs and idled along, her mind drifting. She thought about Virgil's offer of going back to bed. Maybe she should have accepted. What was an hour going to mean one way or another? Thinking about it, she decided to call him. She'd tell him she wanted a rain check, although she knew he would remind her that it hadn't rained in months. Looking over at the passenger seat, however, she realized that her phone was in her jacket. And her jacket was in her own car back at the station. She'd left her tea there too, in the cup holder, all in her haste to get away from Joe Brady.

"Shit," she said.

She considered turning back but decided against it. The traffic going the other way looked just as bad, or worse. Not only that, but she might not be able to dodge Joe again. She was connected to dispatch through the car radio and could get along without her cell for half a day. Your average teenager couldn't, but Claire could.

The drive was slow and it was eleven o'clock on the nose when she pulled into the parking lot at Running Dog. At roughly three minutes past, Ronnie Red Hawk's receptionist informed her that he was gone.

"And what does 'gone' mean?" Claire asked.

"Just gone," the woman said. It was a different receptionist than the one Claire had met the last time she was there. This one was older, with gray-streaked hair that reached halfway down her back, and a jangle of turquoise-and-silver jewelry on her arms and around her neck.

"Does that mean you don't know where he is, or you won't tell me where he is?" Claire asked.

The woman replied by ignoring the question. She began to type something into the Mac computer in front of her. Maybe she was doing a Google search for Ronnie Red Hawk, thinking that might turn him up.

"What about Nightingale?" she asked. "He around?"

"Who?"

"You're really going to play this game?" Claire said. "Whats-hisname Nightingale, skinny guy with slicked-back hair. Thinks he can win people over by offering them Faith Hill tickets. *That* Nightingale."

"Marvin," the woman said and reached for the phone.

Marvin Nightingale must have been close by; he stepped off the elevator five minutes after the receptionist made the call, wearing black jeans and a black T-shirt. He'd cut his hair since Claire had seen him last and was now sporting a Marine-style buzz cut.

"Detective," he said, extending his hand. "Nice to see you again."

"Where's your boss?" Claire asked.

"Not here."

"I didn't ask if he was here, I asked his whereabouts. There's a difference."

"I couldn't say where he is."

Claire indicated the receptionist. "You and Chatty Cathy here ought to go on the road with this act. Ronnie's got his finger on every pulse in this place and you're trying to tell me you don't know how to get in touch with him?"

Marvin sighed and shook his head, as if committing himself to an unsavory task. "Let me buy you a coffee."

Claire didn't particularly want a coffee but it seemed as if Marvin Nightingale was willing to talk if she accepted, so she did. They went down to the restaurant off the lobby on the main floor. There were two restaurants there and Marvin chose the less fancy of the two, more of a diner than anything. They sat in a corner booth and waited until a waitress brought coffee for them both.

"What's this about?" Marvin asked, spooning a large quantity of sugar into his cup.

"It's about a woman dying in your hotel," Claire said.

"The overdose."

"Yeah. Except it wasn't an overdose. The heroin was bad."

Marvin frowned. "That's unfortunate. What does it have to do with Ronnie?"

"That's what I'd love to ask him, Marvin. Since I can't do that, then I'm going to have to let my imagination run wild here. For instance, I could imagine that Ronnie had a huge crush on Kari Karson, and I could imagine that Ronnie considered Nicole Huntsman's presence to be a determent in his courtship of Ms. Karson. Then I could further imagine that Ronnie found a way to remove Nicole from the equation."

"That's ridiculous."

"Is it? There are people in the Watertown area who tell me Ronnie's pulled this before. It was poison meth last time."

"Ronnie had nothing to do with this," Marvin said. "I'll admit there's a drug problem here. We struggle to stay on top of it but we fail more than we succeed. It comes with the territory. That woman could have bought the dope anywhere. For instance, we have busloads of Chinese tourists coming here every day."

"Ah, the Chinese," Claire said, smiling. "Well, if it's true that some outside influence has been peddling bad heroin on the premises, why is it that only one dead body has turned up? Not only that, but this drug problem must be brand spanking new, Marvin, because when I spoke to you a few days ago you assured me there were *no* drugs here. Which is it, Marvin?"

Marvin sighed. "That was public relations."

"Save the PR bullshit for *Entertainment Tonight*," Claire told him. "When you're talking to a cop, tell the truth. Now, where's Red Hawk?"

Marvin took a moment to put more sugar in his coffee, although Claire suspected it was already as thick as molasses. He took a sip, watching her over the brim of the cup, then set it aside.

"She broke his heart."

"What?"

"Kari Karson broke Ronnie's heart," Marvin said. "I know it sounds ludicrous but it's absolutely true. He really thought the woman was going to fall for him."

"You're right," Claire said. "That is ludicrous."

"I know. But it's also true. You have to realize that Ronnie is . . . well, he considers himself above the crowd. Trust me, there are a lot of women who would love to be with him. He's rich, he has power. But those women don't appeal to Ronnie. He needs a woman who he feels is on his level."

"Someone like a starlet with a criminal record?"

"He doesn't see that. He sees someone like him—someone who's misunderstood. And he thought he found her. He got her the role in the movie, for Chrissakes. I'd call that a full-court press. And then she brushed him off like he was a bug. And she was callous about it. She's trash, you know."

"I don't know, and I don't care," Claire said. "All I know is that there are two dead women, and Ronnie was in very close proximity to both of them when they died. And by that I don't just mean physically close, I mean close in terms of motive. So I need to talk to him. Where is he?"

"You won't find him."

"Why not?"

"He's gone on retreat. I told you the last time you were here. He does that—like the great chiefs of old. He fasts and seeks a vision for his future."

"I could lock you up for obstruction," Claire suggested.

"Go ahead. I can't help you because I don't know where he is."

"Maybe a few days in county jail would help jog your memory."

"I can't tell you what I don't know," Marvin said.

"You know where he is," Claire began and then she hesitated as she realized that she knew it as well. The property near Watertown. What had Bill Sully called it—Ronnie's retreat?

Marvin took a sip of coffee. "He'll come back when he's ready. Not before."

Claire wasn't about to tell Marvin what she suspected. She didn't need him tipping Ronnie off. She got to her feet and put five dollars on the table. "Maybe when he does, I can help him out."

"How can you help him?" Marvin demanded. "I told you—he has a broken heart."

"Didn't you say he was looking to see his future?"

Marvin nodded, watching her warily.

"I have some ideas about that," Claire said.

Virgil hooked the Massey tractor to the four-furrow plow and pulled it out of the machine shed into the yard, where he went about greasing the fittings and checking the shares and the coulters. One share needed replacing but he had a couple of extras in the shed. It was a little before noon when he drove the tractor onto the wheat field, scattering a flock of Canadian geese who were cleaning up the fallen heads of grain the combine had missed. Virgil dropped the hydraulics and the moldboards landed with a clunk. He had traveled maybe fifty yards when the plow, refusing to cut the baked clay, kicked up out of the ground, releasing the shares but a second too late. He broke a runner where the board met the frame.

Back in the yard, he removed the damaged runner and took it into the machine shed to weld it. Tom Stempler, who'd owned the farm before Virgil, had left a lot of tools behind, and one of the things Virgil had inherited was an ancient 110-volt welder. He'd taught himself to weld, and although he wasn't particularly accomplished at it, he could usually do a serviceable job if he took his time, and time was something he had today, as it was obvious he would not be doing any plowing until the ground softened.

It was hot in the shed and as he worked his mind kept returning to Olivia Burns. There had been something rattling around in the back of his brain for some time now, a piece of information that for some reason remained just beyond his reach. As he worked at the runner, grinding the damaged area into a *V* that would hold the weld, he was reminded of his playing days, his last couple of years with the Mud Hens. As catcher, one of his jobs every night was to go over the charts of the hitters they would face the next day. It was a solitary and thankless task, but Virgil took pride in it. Being prepared was a part of his job, and it could prove the difference between a win and a loss. But every now and then, he would feel like he missed something, and leading up to game time he would have a nagging feeling that there was something in front of his eyes that hadn't registered in his brain. Sometimes nothing would come of the feeling but there were occasions when it would come back to haunt him. Some kid, just up from Single-A ball and hitting a buck eighty, would step up to the plate and rip the first fastball he saw over the fence to win the game. And Virgil, in hindsight, would look at the kid's scouting report from the minors and see that he was known as a dead-red fastball hitter. They should have thrown him nothing but junk.

After welding the runner and bolting it back onto the plow, he drove the tractor into the shed. He wouldn't be plowing the wheat field until rain came, and who knew when that would be. It wasn't a big concern; as a rule he would have waited for fall to plow the field anyway but this year he thought he would get a jump on things. The weather intervened, as it usually did.

He had the remainder of the previous night's pizza for lunch. When he was finished, he was heading out the door, thinking he would service his hay mower, when the phone rang. He went back inside to pick up the receiver and heard Tommy Alamosa's voice.

"What are you doing?" he asked.

"I'm about to grease my mower," Virgil said. "Getting ready for my second cut."

"Speaking of second cuts," Tommy said, "they've decided they need a shot of the two gals racing away from the cabin in the buckboard. You know, before we film them heading into the fort later on."

"They want to shoot it today?"

"They do," Tommy said. "They need to film something because there was a scheduling screwup and the Indians never showed. Hard to shoot an Indian attack with no Indians. This should only take a couple hours. I'll make sure you get paid for a full day. What do you think?"

"I think my mower can wait."

"Talk it over with Bob and Nelly," Tommy said.

Virgil told him he'd be there in an hour and hung up. As he drove into the hills, with the Percherons in the trailer behind him, the nagging feeling he'd been experiencing, the feeling he was missing something, grew stronger, and it was coupled with his growing concern about Claire. Virgil didn't like the thought of her bracing Ronnie Red Hawk, even though she had another officer with her. Virgil had even thought of volunteering to tag along, but he knew she would never go for that. The only time she'd involved Virgil in one of her investigations was when she'd been investigating *him*.

When he arrived on set, the crew had already pulled the buckboard from the barn and had it in place in front of the cabin. Tommy Alamosa walked over as Virgil was hitching up the team.

"I want to run them first," Virgil said. "Get them used to it."

"Sure," Tommy said. "They'll head up that rise and disappear over the hill. We're only talking a couple hundred yards or so."

"Who's going to be in the buckboard for the actual shot? It'll cost you a lot of money to get me in a dress."

"Nobody wants to see that. We got a stuntwoman says she can handle a team. And Georgia's stand-in is going to ride with her."

"All right," Virgil said, tugging on the traces. "Let's do it."

He took Bob and Nelly around the field a couple times, urging them first into a trot, then a lope. By the time he pulled back into the yard, the crew was set up and ready to shoot. It took the better part of two hours, moving the cameras to shoot from different angles, but the horses were fine, even breaking into a gallop occasionally when called upon.

The director was nowhere to be seen; they called it second unit stuff with Tommy running the show. Between takes, Virgil carried water to the horses and fed them a little grain. As they finished the final shot, he heard footsteps and turned to see Kari Karson approaching, dressed in her frontier dress but without the wig or bonnet.

"Hey cowboy," she said.

"Hello."

"They about done?"

"I think so," Virgil said. "What's up?"

Kari pointed her chin toward the two horses. "They want a shot of me and the kid running from the cabin to the buckboard."

"Through a hail of arrows?"

"Something like that. I wanted to drive your horses but they wouldn't let me." She smiled. "Guess I'll have to wait until you invite me to your farm."

Virgil smiled.

"You've got a good smile, cowboy."

Virgil shifted topics. "Did you hear anything about your friend?"

"No."

"It wasn't an OD. The heroin was bad."

Kari stared at the ground for a moment before looking up at him. "Who told you that?"

"I got it from a good source. Red Hawk allegedly has a history with this. I thought you should know. You're probably doing the smart thing, staying away from him."

Kari ran her hand across her forehead, her eyes darting back and forth. "Fuck."

"What?"

"Nicole didn't get the heroin from Red Hawk."

"I thought you didn't know where she got it."

"I knew," Kari said. "She brought it from LA. She was supposed to bring Ecstasy but she couldn't score. So she bought a gram of smack from some sketchy dude on the Strip. I wouldn't touch the shit, but she said she always wanted to try it."

"You said she never did needles," Virgil reminded her.

"She never did. She said she was going to smoke it. But she must have changed her mind. That was Nicole."

"And why didn't you tell the police this?"

Kari looked at the ground again, as if not knowing where else to cast her eyes. She sighed before looking back at Virgil. "I told you before. I need to be on my best behavior here. This is my comeback movie, and I don't need any scandal. Telling the cops wouldn't have helped Nicole any at that point. So I pretended I didn't know anything about any heroin."

Virgil heard Tommy yell cut, and he turned to watch as the team came trotting back across the field, the stuntwoman handling the reins with one hand while lighting a cigarette with the other. Virgil turned to Kari.

"You're saying it was accidental?"

"I guess it was," Kari said. She looked earnestly at Virgil a moment, as if trying to convince him that this time she really was telling the truth. "I have to go get ready. This is so fucked up, man."

Virgil watched her walk away and then stepped through the fence and went over to the team. Both horses were sweating heavily in the thick humidity. He took them by the harness and led them toward the open gate. Tommy met him as he passed through.

"I'll rub them down," Virgil said. "I hear you want them for another shot."

"Stationary," Tommy said. "Standing outside the cabin. But yeah—they'll have to be dried off. Take your time. We have to set up."

Virgil led the team into the shade of the barn and unhitched them. He needed to rub them down and brush them.

And he needed to get in touch with Claire. He knew her home number but he also knew she wasn't there. Her cell phone was a work number and the department had changed it a couple of weeks ago. He had it written down back at the farmhouse. It would have to wait.

Once he had the horses cooled off, he gave them more water and hitched them to the buckboard again. After positioning them in the yard, he stood and waited impatiently for the crew to set up the shot. He wanted to be out of there. As they were getting near, a transport van pulled up and Georgia, in costume, got out, looking at a pink cell phone in her hand. Seeing Virgil, she put the phone away and headed straight for him.

"Hello, Virgil."

"Hi."

"I'm doing a scene with Bob and Nelly. So cool."

"That's all they've been talking about."

"I just bet."

A few minutes later Kari appeared, in wig and bonnet now, walking toward the cabin, and then Tommy called for Georgia. She started over, then stopped and held out her cell phone to Virgil. "Can you hold this for me?"

Virgil took it and he watched as they blocked the scene they were about to shoot, the two actresses breaking from the cabin, running across the yard, and jumping into the buckboard. The scene was simple enough but Virgil knew it would take an hour or more to shoot and reset and shoot again. And again. He was anxious to be on the road. The nagging feeling was growing stronger.

Then he looked down at the little girl's cell phone in his hand and the feeling went away.

# TWENTY

Virgil watched as the two actresses ran out of the cabin and down the steps to the buckboard a total of a dozen times, the action shot from three different angles, before Tommy Alamosa was happy with the footage. When they were finished, Virgil moved over at once to unhitch the horses, keeping his eye on Georgia, who was standing on the front porch of the cabin, talking to one of the crew. Kari had headed off toward her trailer the moment they had the shot, apparently done for the day. Virgil pulled the martingales from the team and waited for the crew member to leave.

"Georgia," he said when the man stepped away. "You want to help with the horses?"

The little girl looked over. "Sure!"

Virgil slipped halters on both the Percherons and clipped a nylon lead on each. He let Georgia walk Bob over to the trailer and he followed with the mare. After they'd loaded both horses, he shut the tailgate before reaching into his shirt pocket for the pink cell phone and handing it over.

"I almost forgot," Georgia said.

"Do you remember the day you first rode Bob?" Virgil asked.

"Of course."

"We talked about Olivia," Virgil said. "And you told me how much you liked her."

"I remember."

"You told me she gave you her cell number, and that she asked you not to give it to anybody else."

"And I didn't," Georgia assured him.

"I know you didn't," Virgil said and he paused. "You didn't by chance write that number down, did you?"

"No."

Virgil exhaled heavily and turned to check the safety chains on the trailer. It had been worth a try.

"Why would I write it down?" the little girl asked. "I put it in my phone."

Virgil turned back to her. "And you still have it in your phone?"

"Yeah. I never thought to delete it."

"I know you made a promise but if you could give it to me, it might help the people who are investigating the case," Virgil said.

Georgia grew quiet for a long moment while she considered what to do. Virgil could see it was a moral dilemma for the kid. No wonder he liked her so much. "I think you're somebody she would give her number to anyway," she decided.

"Why, thank you, Georgia."

"You are welcome, Virgil."

When he got back to the farm, Virgil pulled the truck and trailer up to the house and went inside to call Claire's cell. It rang a half-dozen times and went to voice mail. Virgil hated those damn things but for once he left a message, asking her to call him.

He went out into the yard and unloaded Bob and Nelly, moving quickly, not wanting to be away from the phone when she called. He turned the horses out to pasture, then went back to the house, where he sat on the front porch drinking a beer and waiting for the phone to ring, all the while thinking there was nothing in the world so futile as waiting for a goddamn phone call. But in this, he had no choice. After an hour, he called her cell again and left another message. Then he opened a second beer.

He sipped at the cold Budweiser and considered what to do while wondering why Claire hadn't called back. She was never without her cell phone and not hearing back from her was making Virgil nervous. He hadn't been comfortable with her going after Ronnie Red Hawk in the first place. Now Virgil had two key pieces of information that she needed. The first was that Red Hawk was, in all likelihood, not responsible for Nicole Huntsman's death. The second was a phone number that could, conversely, tie Red Hawk to the murder of Olivia Burns.

Of course, that was just speculation on Virgil's part. The phone number might reveal nothing. Maybe Olivia *had* been talking to her mother that night. Or her doctor or her accountant or her acting coach. But would she be talking to any of those people around midnight, and moments before she was killed?

After downing the second beer, he'd had enough of waiting and he got into his truck and drove to Claire's house in Kingston. Maybe she wasn't feeling well and was home, with her phone turned off. She wasn't there, and Virgil wasn't surprised. It had been a long shot. Sitting in his truck in front of her house, he wondered what to do next. Tracking down cell phones and servers wasn't exactly in Virgil's skill set. Claire could do it but Claire wasn't around and Virgil was becoming more worried by the moment about her. He couldn't wait. He needed someone who knew what to do, and he needed them now. He started the truck and headed north.

Buddy Townes wasn't home, but his Cadillac was in the driveway with a flat tire on the right rear, and his aluminum boat was tied to the creaky dock along the riverbank. On his previous visits to Buddy's place, Virgil had noticed a road-house a few hundred yards farther along the river road. Virgil knew Buddy well enough by now that tracking him down didn't require a whole lot of deductive reasoning.

He was sitting at a table with four other men, drinking a pitcher of draft beer and playing bullshit poker with one-dollar bills. By the stack of singles in front of Buddy, Virgil guessed he was doing all right. The place was typical, more of a sports bar than a restaurant, with lots of TV screens and two pool tables at the back. The special of the day, scrawled on a blackboard just inside the front door, was a cheeseburger and fries.

Virgil nodded to Buddy when he entered and sat at the bar to order a beer. He didn't want to join Buddy and his friends, where he wouldn't be able to speak freely. Buddy stayed at the table until the pitcher there was empty, making sure he got his fair share, then he wandered over to Virgil, tucking the wad of bills in his shirt pocket as he sat down.

"Here you are again," he said. "You're not in love with me, are you?"

"Nope, but I'll buy you a beer," Virgil said.

"Buy me a beer and tell me what you're up to, because it looks like you're about to bust a gut."

So Virgil did both, the buying and the telling. When he was done he produced a receipt from Woodstock Saddlery, on the back of which he'd written the cell number Olivia Burns had given Georgia. Virgil smoothed the wrinkles from the paper and laid it on the bar.

Buddy looked from the receipt to Virgil. "And what is it you intend to do with that?"

"Well," Virgil said uncertainly. "Apparently there's a way you can find out who called that number. And what day and what time. So how do I do that?"

"How do *you* do it?" Buddy asked. "You don't do it."

"Then who does?"

Buddy laughed and took a drink of beer. "Look at you, going toe-to-toe with modern technology. You're like Dan Quayle at a spelling bee."

"Well, maybe I need a sophisticated guy like you to enlighten me," Virgil said. "A sophisticated guy who's holding his pants up with a piece of rope."

Buddy looked down at his waist, at the frayed length of twine tied with a reef knot around his dirty khaki trousers. "My belt broke," he explained.

"I don't care," Virgil told him.

Buddy picked up the scrap of paper. "First thing you need to do is find out the server for this number. Then you request the usage records for whatever date you want. When you find an incoming number you want to identify, then you go to *that* server and request that info." Buddy had another drink. "The problem is—you need a warrant to do all of this. Which is why *you* can't do it, Virgil. You do realize you're not a police officer."

"Yeah."

"Claire could find it," Buddy said, putting the slip of paper back on the bar.

"Yeah, but I can't find her," Virgil said. "She took off this morning after Ronnie Red Hawk and she hasn't returned my messages. Which is odd."

"You two aren't scrapping, are you?"

269

"No."

"Maybe she's someplace where she can't get a signal," Buddy said. "You could call the state police, ask them to send her a message."

"I did think of that. They're going to ask a lot of questions, though."

"They probably are."

"With my luck, I'd get Joe Brady and I've had enough of Joe Brady to last me," Virgil said. He tapped the paper. "So the only way I can get the phone records is to go through the cops."

"That's the only way *you* can do it," Buddy said. Pulling his cell phone from his pocket, he reached for the paper on the bar. "I need the date and time of day in question."

"Are you saying you know somebody?"

"Come on, Virgil. Of course I know somebody."

After Buddy made a couple of calls, he said they would have to wait to hear back, and they might as well wait at his place. He bought a twelve-pack to go and when they got to his cottage he opened two beers and proceeded to fry up a dozen perch he'd caught that morning in the little cove out front. Virgil sat at a wooden table that was covered with textbooks and papers and watched Buddy at the stove. He picked up one of the books. It was a volume of New York State Supreme Court decisions.

"What is this?" he asked.

Buddy, slicing potatoes and onions into a skillet, glanced over. "My homework."

"No, seriously."

"I can't have homework?"

"You can have homework," Virgil said. "You could have a belt too, but you don't."

"Up yours," Buddy said. "I'm going to write for the bar. I'm sick of living hand to mouth. I got a degree in law thirty years ago, before I joined the force, so I'm going to try to pass the bar."

"Well, well."

"I'd be a good lawyer, Virgil," Buddy said. "I've seen all the shit and heard all the shit and even caused my fair share of it. And I'm a lot smarter than I look."

"I'd hire you," Virgil said.

"The way you find trouble, you'll probably have me on a retainer."

They ate on the back deck, sitting on wobbly lawn chairs, plates balanced on their laps. Virgil nursed his beer; he had no idea how much more driving he would have to do before the day was done. Buddy kept pounding them back, with little apparent effect.

The sun was setting behind them as they finished the perch and potatoes, the last rays reflecting in a broad orange corridor across the surface of the river. The Hudson became noisy with the approaching dusk, with the constant croaking of frogs and the sporadic calling of loons. A pair of mergansers splashed down not fifty feet from Buddy's dock and began diving for their supper.

Buddy ate the last piece of fish and put his plate on the low wooden table between them. He lit a cigarette and had a long look at Virgil, as if analyzing him. Of course, Buddy, for all his excesses and faults, was nothing if not an analytical guy. They'd been pretty quiet while they were eating. Now, with his belly full and beer in hand, he was apparently ready for some conversation, although not necessarily serious discourse.

"How long you owned that hat?" he asked.

Virgil couldn't remember which cap he'd plopped on his head when leaving the house, so he took it off to have a look.

"A while," he said, putting it back on.

"Since you played for them?"

"Yeah."

"How long were you a Mud Hen?"

"Three years."

"What did you hit?"

"Overall? Only .226. But I was hitting .260 when they let me go."

"So why'd they let you go?"

Virgil shrugged. "Injuries mostly. That, and the off-speed stuff killed me. Especially the changeup. Word got around, I guess, and pretty soon that's all I saw. But I was starting to wait on it. And .260 isn't bad."

Buddy took a pull on the smoke. "How was your arm?"

"Pretty good. I threw out thirty-one percent of base runners my last year. League average was twenty-three."

Buddy smiled. "Tell me—what was your grade average your last year of high school?"

Virgil frowned. "I got no idea."

The phone rang inside and Buddy got to his feet. "Ballplayers," he said. "You know your stats from Little League on, but you don't have a clue how much money you've got in your pocket right this minute, do you?"

"How much money I've got in my pocket doesn't matter," Virgil told him. "By the way, my on-base percentage was over three hundred."

Buddy laughed and went inside and Virgil could hear him talking on the phone for several minutes. When he came out, he was carrying two unopened cans of beer in one hand and his cell phone and a sheet of foolscap in the other. Tossing a beer to Virgil, he sat down in the lawn chair and put his phone on the table.

"The phone number the kid gave you is with Verizon," he said, looking at the paper. "And it's registered to a woman named Martha Jones."

Virgil smiled.

"You know her?" Buddy asked.

"Nope," Virgil said. "She doesn't exist."

"What the hell does that mean?"

"She's the character Olivia Burns was playing in the movie."

"All right," Buddy said. "So she bought a phone plan under a bogus name so the paparazzi and other assorted riff-raff couldn't track her down. Probably standard procedure for actors." He glanced at the paper again. "You're looking for the night of the fifteenth, from ten o'clock on, right? She made two calls, one to a landline in LA listed to a guy named Curnew, the other to a cell phone in Chicago, under the name Burns. A relative, I assume."

Whoever Olivia Burns had been calling, Virgil doubted that those people had any involvement in her death. There was too much geography in the way. "What about incoming calls?"

"Sixteen," Buddy said.

"Sixteen?" Virgil said, leaning forward to look at the fools-cap. "Are you sure about that?"

"The records don't lie," Buddy said. "Sixteen calls."

"You got the numbers?"

"I got one number," Buddy said. He offered the paper forward so that Virgil could see. "The same person called her sixteen times in—well, roughly an hour and a half. The last call was made just after midnight. The phone has not been used since."

Virgil opened the beer Buddy had tossed him and took a long drink before asking the obvious question. "So who made the calls? You have a name?"

"No name," Buddy said. "Well, not a person's name anyway. The phone plan is registered to a company out of New York City." At this point he handed the paper to Virgil. "The company's called Big Deal Productions. Gee, that sounds like somebody in the film business, Virgil."

Virgil took the foolscap and read what Buddy had jotted down there in a nearly illegible scrawl. Two calls going out and sixteen coming in, all of the incoming from the same number. All from somebody employed by the company shooting *Frontier Woman*.

"I suppose," he said slowly, his eyes still on the numbers in front of him, "I suppose there's a chance that the person who called her sixteen times in an hour and a half had nothing to do with her death."

"Yeah—about the same chance as me not finishing this beer," Buddy said, and he took a long slug from the can to drive home his point.

Virgil nodded as he got to his feet. He carefully folded the foolscap in half, then quarters.

"Where you going now?"

"Find Claire," Virgil said. "And tell her this. Or find out who has the phone that matches this number, and tell her that."

"How you figure to do that?" Buddy asked. "You got a plan?"

"I got about half a plan." Virgil indicated Buddy's cell phone on the table. "Can I borrow that?"

Buddy thought about it for a couple of seconds and then handed the phone over.

"Watch yourself," he said.

"Hey, I know what I'm doing," Virgil said. He turned to go but then stopped, looking at the phone in his hand. "Um . . . you'd better show me how to use this thing."

It was nearly six o'clock when Claire drove into Watertown from the south, parked in the city police department lot, and went inside. Chief Heisman was still in her office, despite the hour, hunched over her desk and inexpertly typing something into her computer.

"You're back," the chief said, glancing up briefly before returning to the laptop. "Looking for more information on Ronnie Red Hawk?"

"No," Claire said. "This time I'm looking *for* Ronnie Red Hawk."

Heisman cocked an eyebrow but continued her search-and-peck at the keyboard. "And you have reason to think he's in the Watertown area?"

"Not a good reason, no," Claire said. "But he's gone on a walkabout and I hear he owns property east of here. Some sort of retreat where he goes to—I don't know—talk to the bears and the birds and the frogs and the turtles."

"And you're thinking he might talk to you too, when he's done with the turtles and whatever."

Claire looked around and saw a chair against the wall, just inside the door. She went over to sit in it. "Actually, I'm thinking he may have gone there to chill out after he killed a couple of women down in the Kingston area."

That was enough for Heisman to abandon whatever she'd been typing. She hit a couple of keys and then shut the laptop. "If you have a warrant for his arrest, why doesn't my department know about it?"

"I haven't gotten to the warrant stage yet," Claire said. "Right now I just want to have a conversation with the man."

Heisman leaned back in her chair and rested a pair of heavy brogue shoes on the desktop. She had huge feet. "But you suspect him of killing two people?"

"At the very least," Claire said. "That's just down in my neck of the woods. Bill Sully tells me there's a theory that Ronnie spiked some crystal meth that took out a character named Syracuse Sid a few years ago."

"We were never able to prove that," Heisman said.

"If something is true, it's true whether you can prove it or not."

Heisman nodded, regarding Claire cautiously for a moment, as if there was something not right about the equation. "So you're here to beard the lion in his den."

Claire shrugged.

"Tell me something, Detective," Heisman said then. "Is the state police department overwhelmingly shorthanded at this time?"

"I wouldn't say that."

"Then why in the name of Jesus would you even consider going after a murder suspect holed up in the wilderness all by yourself?"

"Like I said, I just want to talk to him," Claire said. "The man loves to babble and you and I both know the more a suspect talks, the better the chance he'll say something to incriminate himself. And that's even more true when the suspect in question considers himself to be the chosen one. This guy is delusional."

"Which is a pretty good argument for backup right there," Heisman said.

"No," Claire said. "He's not going to talk if I go in there

with a team of officers. First he'll clam up and then he'll law-yer up."

"I wasn't suggesting a team," Heisman said. "I'll go with you."

Claire got to her feet. "I appreciate the offer. Let me sleep on it. I'm going to get a room and go looking for him in the morning."

Heisman stood now as well. "Up to you," she said. "Just so you know, I'll never forgive you if you get yourself shot in my bailiwick. I hate it when I have explaining to do."

Claire smiled. "I'll bear that in mind. Now I need you to show me where this little retreat is."

"Ronnie's retreat is anything but little," Heisman said, indicating a large area map, maybe six feet square, on the far wall. "Come have a look," she said.

Claire got a room at the Comfort Inn a few blocks from the interstate. She ate an early dinner at a diner alongside a ball field a couple of blocks from the hotel, then bought a copy of the local paper at a corner store and went back to her room.

The paper didn't have much to offer. The city council was squabbling over the same things that Claire imagined every city council in the country was fighting over—crime, zon-ing issues, budgets, who insulted whom in the course of the previous day's squabble. Those quoted in print were vari-ously outraged, insulted, or mortified, depending upon their respective roles in the dealings in question. One woman claimed to be "gobsmacked," a word Claire had always admired but never thought to use. She glanced at the sports section to see that the Mets were a depressing twelve games under five hundred. Claire despaired of them ever winning again. She did the word jumble in the classified section in less than a minute and tossed the paper aside, got an outside line, and dialed Virgil's number. No answer. It was a quarter past eight; he was probably fixing a tractor or feeding calves or wandering about the property as he sometimes did in the evenings, seemingly without purpose, although Claire knew that his mind was always on what needed to be done the following day or week or month. There was a lot more going on in that head of his than he'd like her—or anybody else—to believe.

She picked up the remote and flipped through the channels until she found a black-and-white movie, with Myrna Loy and William Powell swilling gin and cracking wise while a young Jimmy Stewart lurked in the background. She settled in to watch for a while, thinking that William was a little too old for Myrna. She tried Virgil again at nine and then once more at ten, but there was still no reply. She wondered where he could be. Maybe he'd come home and gone to sleep and she'd missed him. He didn't have a phone upstairs. Claire was a little surprised he had one at all.

By the time she dozed off, she'd decided to go after Ronnie Red Hawk by herself in the morning. For some strange reason, she'd determined that he was hers to take down. It had nothing to do with sharing the credit with Chief Heisman or anybody else, it was just that she felt he was her responsibility. Not only that, but she was reluctant to put anybody else in the man's path.

She would go it on her own.

# TWENTY-ONE

The cabin had been built against the rock face of a low-running cliff and looked east to the rising sun. The exterior was constructed of logs of white pine, which Ronnie had paid a considerable cost to ship from northern Ontario. A couple hundred feet from the main cabin was a smaller building, which housed the generator. The shed was heavily insulated; from the front porch of the cabin one could barely hear the steady rumble of the diesel engine.

Ronnie sat in the front room eating Cap'n Crunch from a bowl and watching television, flipping from one morning show to another. He was on his second bowl of cereal. He'd come to the cabin three days earlier, after his last conversation with Kari Karson, intending to fast for a week and clear his head. So far, he'd been unable to deliver himself to the fasting part of his plan. In fact, he'd been eating prodigiously since Billy had dropped him off in the limo. Steaks and lobster and chicken and pizza. A lot of pizza; Billy had found some frozen ones, new on the market, that really did taste like they came from a pizzeria.

Ronnie wasn't exactly roughing it. The cabin was every bit as nice as his penthouse suite back at the Red Hawk Hotel. He'd had it built two years earlier at a cost of just under a million dollars. Of course, the price had been high because the place was set back two miles from the nearest road and all of the building materials had to be hauled in over a rough lane that had been bulldozed through the center of the two-thousand–acre parcel. The place had three bathrooms, central air, satellite television, and a walk-in freezer that would hold enough food for a bivouacking army.

Only Billy knew what the retreat was like and Billy wouldn't tell tales about it, not if he wanted to have a future on the planet. The other Indians back at Running Dog were under the impression that Ronnie came here to live in a traditional tepee and to fast on a rocky crag for days on end. Those Indians didn't need to know the truth. Ronnie had given them virtually everything they had. He wasn't under any obligation to give them truth as well. What the hell would they do with it?

Maybe he would begin his fast tomorrow. He'd told Billy to pick him up on Monday, which meant he could still go three days without food, three days to try to figure out where his head was at after this latest assault on his heart.

If nothing else, he knew he was finished with actresses. Kari had been nothing like he'd imagined. She was neurotic and self-centered. Strangely enough, Ronnie had expected that of her, and he could have handled it. However, she was also ordinary, and that he hadn't counted on. He'd fallen in love with her, admittedly from afar, because he'd been convinced that she was a special person—that she was, in fact, like Ronnie himself. Nothing could be further from the truth. First of all, if she were anything like Ronnie, she would have loved him from the start. Secondly, if they had truly been soul mates, she wouldn't have proved to be so pedestrian. In the end, she had turned out to be no different than the dozens of cocktail waitresses working at the casino. Not only that, but—up close—her skin was not that great.

But none of that changed the fact that Ronnie had, right

up until he had met her, loved her, and unconditionally. A broken heart takes time to heal.

After finishing the second bowl, he decided he needed to go for a walk. If he stayed in the cabin he would keep eating until Billy had to haul him out of there on a travois. He got out of his robe and pulled on pants and a T-shirt. He tucked a short-barreled Smith & Wesson .38 in his belt—in case of snakes or a rogue bear—and started down the narrow road out front. Fearful of the copperheads he'd seen occasionally sunning themselves on the rock outcroppings near the cabin, he stayed on the gravel lane. It was still cool in the forest, and he descended toward the south in mottled shade, thinking he would walk to the paved county road two miles away, and then back.

Maybe he wouldn't fast at all. Getting over Kari was something that only time would provide and fasting wasn't going to make any difference one way or the other. He could remain there until Monday when Billy came for him, and then go back to the business of running the casino and all its complements. He reminded himself he had a golf course to complete. He could always provide details of his fast, and accompanying visions, to anybody who wanted to hear.

What he wouldn't do was involve himself any further with the filming of the movie. He would stay on as producer, and continue to funnel cash to the project, as he'd agreed. It was a good way to hide income. Not only that, but he wanted to stay in the mix in case the movie turned out to be a winner. Ronnie would love to go to the Oscars. If he won, he assumed he would be allowed to make a speech. It occurred to him that it wasn't too early to begin working on it. Oscars or not, he was now officially a player in the film world. He would choose his next project more carefully, of course, and he wouldn't be taking on partners. If he found a script he liked, he might even direct the thing himself. After all, he'd been calling the shots at Running Dog since its conception, and what was it if not a high-concept fantasy film?

After descending for twenty minutes or so, he began to hear the occasional sounds of vehicles passing on the road below. The property was remote and the nearest neighbors were miles away; as such, there was very little traffic on that stretch of road.

When he was five hundred yards from the highway, Ronnie grew winded and stopped to rest, leaning against a dead birch tree that was tilted at a forty-five-degree angle to the ground, its fall interrupted by a massive oak beside it. It took him several minutes to catch his breath. It wasn't a good sign, he knew, getting tired walking *down* a slope. He might have to start working out. Maybe some time in the gym would help him forget Kari Karson.

Now he heard another car approaching but this one seemed to be slowing down. He thought he heard tires pulling onto the gravel road. His road. Ronnie pushed himself away from the birch and began to angle through the brush to the entrance. From a couple hundred yards away, he could see a blue sedan parked on the lane, just off the main road. After a moment the door opened and Claire Marchand got out, a paper coffee cup in her hand. She stood there looking at the gravel road before her, winding its way upward through the trees.

Ronnie pulled the revolver from his belt and opened it to check the cylinder. He'd brought it along in case he encountered a snake, and in that his instincts had, as always, been on the money. But the snake that had just gotten out of the unmarked cruiser was bigger game than he'd expected. It was obvious to Ronnie now that the woman was going to keep poking around until she found something. The snub-nosed .38 was efficient enough for a copperhead up close, but not for a nosy cop, not at any distance anyway. He needed more firepower, so he turned around and headed back to the cabin for his rifle.

Virgil called Claire before he went to bed and then again when he got up in the morning. By this point, he was past expecting her to answer. Something was up, and he hoped that whatever it was turned out to be simply the fault of failed technology. She should have been back by now, with or without Ronnie. After he did the chores he got into his truck and drove to Kingston again to check once more on her house. Seeing that her car still wasn't there, he finally gave in and drove to the state police station outside of town.

Claire's CR-V was there in the parking lot, as it would be when she was working. Occasionally she used the Honda when on duty but she usually took one of the unmarked cruisers. Virgil parked alongside and had a look in the passenger window. Claire's jacket was on the front seat and peeking out the side pocket was her cell phone. One mystery solved.

Virgil turned and looked at the front door of the station. The last time he was there, he'd just been arrested for murder, fingerprinted, photographed, and interrogated. It wasn't the first time he'd been in handcuffs but he'd been hoping it would be the last. He didn't feel like walking in today, but he really had no choice. He needed to talk to Claire. More than that, he needed to know she was all right.

His luck was running okay at first. A young woman in a tan skirt and crisp blue blouse saw him approaching the front desk and walked over to ask if she could help him. But before Virgil could open his mouth, a door at the rear of the station opened and Joe Brady entered. He was talking over his shoulder to a man in a suit who trailed along behind him.

"I could've told them exactly what was going to happen," Joe was saying. "I knew it from the moment—" He stopped in midsentence when he saw Virgil. The man in the suit took the opportunity to escape down a corridor; presumably he'd heard enough of Joe holding forth about how right he'd been about something. Joe, his focus squarely on Virgil, made no note of the man's leaving. Instead he headed for the front desk.

"What's going on here?" he asked.

Virgil didn't look at him. "I want to leave a message for Claire Marchand," he told the young woman.

"I'll take care of this, Marina," Joe said. When the woman looked as if she might protest, he turned to her. "You can go."

The woman named Marina arched her eyebrows as if in apology toward Virgil before walking back to a desk across the room to sit down. Joe regarded Virgil as if he were a possum caught sneaking into a henhouse.

"What are you up to, pal?"

"I'm not up to anything," Virgil said. "I want to leave a message for Claire Marchand."

"Is it a matter for the police?" Joe asked.

Virgil hesitated. If he said yes, then Joe was going to insist that he be given the information. Which, in Virgil's opinion, was pretty much the same as writing it down on a piece of paper and tossing it out the window. Or it could be even worse; Joe might want to act on it. And the only thing worse than Joe Brady ignoring a situation was Joe Brady taking charge of a situation.

"Personal," Virgil said.

"Personal," Joe repeated, nodding his head. "Are you under the impression that we're here to provide some sort of messaging service for the general public, Cain?"

"No, I'm not," Virgil said. "I'm here to ask if you would forward her a phone number and ask that she call me at her convenience." As he finished talking he noticed a notepad on the counter, with a pen alongside. He reached for it and jotted down Buddy's cell number.

"Maybe Marchand has no interest in calling you," Joe said. "Maybe you're bothering her."

"That's for her to decide," Virgil said. "You can tell her it's . . . um . . . urgent." He was hesitant to use the word, fearing it might encourage more idiotic questions from Brady. He slid the number across the counter.

Joe took a while to think it over before finally reaching for the slip of paper, taking it between his thumb and forefinger as if it were tainted. "I'm a senior investigator with the New York State Police," he said. "My duties don't include being a messenger boy for you. There's a Western Union in town, pal. Give them a try." He crumpled the paper, tossed it into a wastebasket at the end of the counter, and walked away.

"Nice talking to you, Joe," Virgil said.

Joe gave him the finger without turning. Virgil walked back outside to the parking lot. He wrote down the number and a short message on a scrap of paper he tore from a hardware flyer in his truck and slid it under the windshield wiper on Claire's Honda. Then he headed for the hills.

The Indians were there when he arrived on set. There had to be forty or fifty of them, dressed in buckskin and breechcloths, their faces painted and oiled, feathers dangling from lances, bows and arrows at the ready. When Virgil pulled onto the property, they were gathered around the food tent, smoking cigarettes and talking on cell phones.

Virgil parked and shut the engine off, then sat in the truck for a few moments, looking around. Will, the firearms guy, stood in the entranceway to the barn. There were maybe two dozen muskets lined up there, leaning against the open door. A wooden table with folding legs was set up alongside; on top of the table were boxes of musket balls and percussion caps, as well as a number of brass powder flasks.

The cinematographer and the rest of the crew were setting up in the clearing between the cabin and the forest to the south. The director was standing on the front porch of the cabin, talking to Tommy Alamosa.

Virgil got out of the truck, slipping Buddy's phone in his pocket. Leaning against his front fender, he watched the proceedings in the clearing. It appeared that Tommy was explaining to the director what they were doing. It seemed to Virgil that Tommy did that a lot.

At one point, the director shook his head in apparent frustration at whatever he was hearing and then turned to notice Virgil's presence.

"What the fuck is he doing here?" the director demanded.

"We could always ask him," Tommy said. "Hello, Virgil."

"Why are you here?" the director asked.

"Just came to watch," Virgil said, shrugging.

"You're not getting paid to be here. You weren't on the call sheet."

"I just want to watch," Virgil said again. "I wouldn't pass up a chance to see an artist at work."

The director paused, as if trying to decide whether Virgil was being sarcastic. In the end, he evidently decided to let it pass. "Just keep out of the way," he advised.

"Ten four."

The director turned to Tommy. "I'm still not getting this. I need to look at the storyboards."

After they walked away Virgil climbed onto the porch and sat down on the wooden chair there, propping his boots on the railing as he'd done before, Henry Fonda style. The crew was laying dolly tracks now across the clearing, securing the rails with sand bags before shimming them to level.

After a time, the black Audi pulled onto the set and rolled to a stop next to the trailers. Levi Brown and the producer named Sam got out, both carrying Starbucks cups, and went into the trailer where Tommy and the director had disappeared. A few minutes later a production van arrived and Kari Karson and Georgia emerged and headed for their respective trailers.

Virgil sat on the porch and watched the comings and goings for another fifteen minutes or so, and then he pulled Buddy's phone from his pocket and flipped it open and closed a couple of times. Looking from the phone to the trailers, where all the unusual suspects were gathered, he went into his pocket again and produced the phone number Buddy had given him.

He was about to dial the number when the phone rang in his hand.

Claire stood leaning against the hood of the cruiser, sipping the bad coffee she'd bought at a place that quaintly called itself a trading post, about five miles back along the winding country road. If the place actually were in the business of trading goods, she'd go back there this minute and swap the coffee for damn near anything, as long as it contained a little caffeine and didn't taste like turpentine.

She was debating whether to walk in to Ronnie Red Hawk's retreat, or to drive up. If she drove, he would in all likelihood hear her coming. Walking, she might surprise him, at his fasting or his convening with nature, or whatever the hell he did there. Catching him off guard might be the preferable route.

She knew now that Ronnie's retreat was in reality a luxury vacation home. Chief Heisman had told her that. Ronnie wasn't fooling any of the locals. It was a remote part of the state, but it wasn't that remote. It was pretty much impossible to build a million-dollar log home on a parcel of land bigger than a small town and expect nobody to notice. Apparently Ronnie thought he'd pulled it off. Like Claire had told Heisman—delusional.

She decided she would walk in. She dumped the toxic brew out onto the ground and took her Glock from its holster to check the clip. She walked back around to lock the car and as she did, she heard Marina trying to raise her on the radio. She slid behind the wheel and replied.

"Where the hell are you?" Marina asked.

"Up north. What's going on?"

"Sal's been calling your cell. He's got something for you on the Olivia Burns thing."

"I left my phone in my car," Claire said. "Is he there? Put him on."

"No, but he's on his way. I can patch him through when he gets here."

"I'll be away from the radio for a bit. I'll check back."

"Wait a minute," Marina said.

"What?"

"Virgil Cain was here," Marina said.

Claire was more than surprised. "At the station?"

"Yeah. He wanted to get in touch with you. He left a cell number for you to call."

"A cell number," Claire said. "Then it wasn't Virgil Cain. What did the guy look like?"

"Like that good-looking farmer you've been screwing the past two years, Claire. I know Virgil Cain. He and Joe had words and Joe tossed the number in the trash. I dug it out after he left."

"I'm gobsmacked," Claire said.

"You're what?"

"Nothing. What's the number?" Claire waited and then wrote it down on her pad. "All right. I'll give him a shout later."

"He mentioned it was urgent."

"He used that word?"

"He did."

"Okay, Marina. Thanks."

Claire sat in the car for a time after signing off. She was inclined to go after Ronnie Red Hawk and then find a phone and call Virgil afterward. But something was definitely out of sync in what Marina had told her. That Virgil had allegedly acquired a cell phone was one thing. That he had used the word "urgent" when requesting that she call him was another. One of those developments was enough to make her think that something was seriously amiss. Both made her decide to go looking for a pay phone.

If nothing else, she would find out what type of situation Virgil Cain might consider to be urgent. Maybe the Toledo Mud Hens had hauled him out of retirement for the stretch run; that might possibly get him excited. But excited enough to buy a cell phone? Claire doubted it.

Ronnie put the crosshairs on the cop's face, then dropped them to a spot between her breasts. After a moment, he moved the sights to the coffee cup she held. He smiled to himself. Wouldn't she shit herself if her take-out coffee suddenly exploded in her hand? Her surprise would be fleeting, of course, because then Ronnie would be obligated to put the next bullet between her beautiful brown eyes.

She'd been standing there, the lady cop with the insolent mouth, for ten minutes, looking up at the gravel road that led to Ronnie's retreat. Looking up, not even drinking her coffee, as if coming to a decision of some kind. Ronnie, hidden in the trees, was in the same boat, trying to decide whether or not to blow her fucking head off. She obviously had stumbled across something in her investigation. Maybe that something was Syracuse Sid and maybe it was something else. Ronnie couldn't imagine that she'd uncovered anything resembling hard evidence, but she might have figured she had enough to make an arrest. Ronnie's reputation didn't need that, even if it ended in acquittal. Not only that, he had things to accomplish, goals to meet. The golf course itself was a huge undertaking. He didn't have time for judges and lawyers and preliminary hearings and all the rest. Ronnie had seen enough courtrooms in his youth.

The question, as he saw it right this moment, was whether the woman was working alone. She had a bit of a lone wolf quality to her, and if that were the case—if she hadn't shared whatever she'd found with anyone else—then Ronnie would feel much more comfortable putting a .30–06 slug in her. He'd have no trouble getting rid of the body, and the car, afterward. There were lakes in the area that were a couple hundred feet deep. Ronnie had dumped cars there before, after wild midnight joyrides when he was a kid. However, if the department knew what she was up to, and where she was, it was a different situation. Ronnie didn't need that either.

He moved the sights to her face again. She was a beautiful

woman, he had to admit. Maybe he wouldn't shoot her in the face after all. He could put a round precisely between those nice breasts. Ronnie had never dated a cop before. Maybe he should consider it in the future. It might be exciting, with the guns and the handcuffs and all. Of course, it wouldn't be this cop, he knew, as he dropped the crosshairs to her chest.

Too late for that.

Then she moved, and with purpose, as if she'd arrived at her decision. She walked around to the door of the cruiser and opened it to toss the cup inside. But when she closed the door, she hesitated a moment before opening it again and sliding in behind the wheel. Ronnie put the sights on the windshield but the sun struck it at such an angle that the glare prevented him from seeing inside the car. He should have taken the shot when he had the chance. Now he would have to wait again and Ronnie didn't like to wait. On top of everything else, he was getting hungry.

After a few moments, the woman reached out, closed the car door, and put it in reverse. She drove off, heading west.

Ronnie was left standing in the woods, holding his rifle and trying to figure out what had just happened.

# TWENTY-TWO

The phone didn't actually ring. It played the *William Tell* Overture, although Virgil was pretty sure that Buddy would identify it as the theme from *The Lone Ranger*. He opened it and pressed the little green button, as Buddy had instructed, and then held it to his ear.

"Hello."

"Wow," Claire said. "It is you."

"Yup."

"I declare."

"Where have you been?" Virgil demanded. "I've been trying to get you for two days."

"I left my phone in my car."

"I know that now."

"I'm up north, Watertown area," Claire said. "You worried about me, Virgil Cain? So worried you went off and bought yourself a cell phone?"

"I didn't buy a cell phone. I have some information for you. What are you doing up there?"

"We'll get back to the part about you being worried about me later," Claire said. "I'm following Ronnie Red Hawk, that's what I'm doing. But a little while ago I got a call on the radio from Marina at the station, and she gives me a cell phone number she dug out of the trash, and tells me that the number belongs to *you*. And that it's urgent that you talk to me.

So now I'm convinced that I have arrived in an alternate universe. What's going on?"

"You're on the wrong trail," Virgil told her, and he gave her a quick recounting of what he'd learned the past couple of days.

"Sixteen times," Claire repeated when he'd finished.

"Yeah."

"I would have to call that suspicious."

"I thought you might. What do we do now?"

"The first thing we do is get rid of that particular pronoun," Claire replied. "There is no 'we' in this. You done good, Virgil. Now step back and leave the rest to the professionals."

"I just heard the professionals are on a wild-goose chase somewhere up around the St. Lawrence River," Virgil reminded her.

"I'm heading home as soon as I get off the phone. Where are you anyway?"

"On the movie set."

"You're working, then?"

"Not really," Virgil said. "Just hanging around."

She paused. He could imagine her coming to her own conclusions as to why he was there. "Goddamn it, Virgil. Stay out of it. When I get back, I'll get a warrant and find out who the number belongs to. And take it from there. There's a right way and a wrong way to do things, Virgil."

"Okay."

"I really don't like the way you say 'okay.' I know you."

"I'm glad you're safe," Virgil said. "See you when you get back."

He closed the phone. Leaning back in his chair, he looked again toward the trailers before glancing down at the number he'd gotten from Buddy. He opened the phone again and closed it. He put the paper back in his pocket.

People continued to mill about, readying for the big Indian attack. Virgil watched for a few minutes, then pulled the paper from his pocket again and punched in the number of the person who had called Olivia Burns sixteen times. The phone rang and at that moment Tommy Alamosa walked around the corner of one of the trailers.

He had his cell phone to his ear.

Virgil closed the phone at once. "Sonofabitch," he said out loud. He'd been worried all along that it might be Tommy, but he'd been hoping it wasn't.

He kept watching, though, and to his surprise Tommy didn't lower his phone. In fact, he kept walking and appeared to be talking into it. He must have gotten a call—or made a call—at the same time Virgil had dialed the number.

So Virgil dialed it again.

And this time Levi Brown came out of one of the trailers, phone in hand, looking somewhat perturbed, like a guy who'd received two calls in quick succession with nobody on the other end. Virgil hung up again and saw Levi shouting into his phone, holding the screen up in front of him, looking at the display, no doubt wondering who the hell Buddy Townes was.

Virgil sat in the chair, tapping the phone lightly against his chin. So that was it. When Levi turned to go back inside, Virgil called again and watched as Levi jerked the phone to his ear.

"Who the fuck is this?" he demanded.

"It's the hired hand, Levi."

"What?"

"It's Virgil."

"What do you want?"

"Come on, Levi. Aren't you just a little curious as to how I got your phone number?"

"No," Levi said. But Virgil saw him looking around now, as if he sensed that Virgil was near. "Everybody on set has it."

"I'm over at the cabin." Virgil waited for Levi to glance over and then he waved to him, as if he were riding a float in a parade. "And I didn't get your number from anyone on the set, Levi. I got it off Olivia Burns's cell phone."

Virgil could hear the man's breathing grow quicker.

"I believe I've rendered you speechless, Levi."

"I have no idea what you're talking about."

"Then I'll help you out," Virgil said. "I came across Olivia's phone down by Rondout Creek. You called her sixteen times the night she died. Now, I realize, Levi, that you're not the sharpest tool in the shed, and so you might have called her by accident once. You know, the wrong number. Maybe even twice. But even a dipshit like you wouldn't call the wrong number sixteen times. Would you, Levi?"

"Go to hell," Levi said, and he hung up. Glaring over in Virgil's direction, he turned and went back into the trailer.

Virgil placed Buddy's cell phone on the railing and leaned back. There you go, Claire. No need for your warrants and all that paperwork. Levi Brown was the man. What was behind it wasn't something Virgil could even speculate on. But Levi appeared to be a man who was easily offended, and he obviously had a temper. With his golden locks and weight-room muscles, he was also someone in desperate search of an image. Of course, that didn't make him a killer and Virgil had no idea what did.

Claire would find out, though. It was the type of thing she was good at. Virgil was lucky she was; otherwise he might have gone down on the murder charge a few years back. Claire had been the only one willing to entertain the notion that he might be innocent.

Virgil knew he should contact her and tell her what he knew. He considered calling the station and asking for the woman—was Marina the name?—that Claire had mentioned. He picked up the phone, wondering how to do that. He could call 911, he guessed, but he wasn't sure if that would put him in touch with the state police or the local authorities. He could always drive back to the station, but that might mean another encounter with Joe Brady. He sat looking at Buddy's phone, trying to decide and thinking how unlikely it was that he was the one with a cell phone while Claire was roaming the state without.

He glanced over to see that Levi had emerged from the trailer again. He walked behind the units and stood there, looking across the open field at Virgil. Staring at him. As Virgil watched, Georgia came out of her trailer and moved toward Levi, her body language hesitant, suggesting she'd been summoned. Levi leaned over the little girl, telling her something, then they both walked toward Levi's car, parked a few yards away. Georgia got in the passenger's side and Levi moved around to the driver's door. He stopped there and looked defiantly back at Virgil again.

He got into the car and drove off.

Virgil, his heart in his throat, was on his feet and off the porch. But the Audi had already reached the road out front, turning left there to head west up into the hills. Virgil, cursing, sprinted for his pickup, jerking open the door and climbing inside. As he put the truck in gear, though, he flashed back to the day in the clearing, when Levi had pulled the handgun and shot up the forest.

Virgil looked desperately around and his eyes settled immediately on the muskets, leaning in a row against the barn door. He got out and ran over, grabbed the first one in line, then stuffed some lead balls and percussion caps in his shirt pocket. Picking up a powder flask, he headed back to the truck, and as he ran he could hear Will, the weapons man, yelling at him.

He hit the road out front and turned left, wondering how much of a lead they had on him. Up ahead there was nothing but forest, with any number of narrow roadways and lanes leading off into the brush, to hunting camps or trout streams or picnic areas.

Virgil floored the old Ford and kept to the main road, which curved and dipped through the forested hills, making it impossible to spot a vehicle up ahead. Virgil had no choice but to hope that Levi kept to the highway. He wondered what the sonofabitch had told Georgia to get her into his car. Maybe he'd invented a family emergency, or told her she was needed at another location. Whatever it was, it was Virgil's fault. Claire had told him to keep out of it.

He had no idea if he was even on the trail of the Audi; Levi could have turned off miles back. After a while, though, he began to notice cardboard signs posted at every intersection, signs with the production company's logo and arrows pointing west beneath the words FORT HOWARD. Virgil knew they were scheduled to begin filming at the old fort the following week. Is that where Levi was headed? Maybe that's what he'd told Georgia, that she was needed on set at the old fort.

Virgil's mind went back to the look Levi had given him before taking the little girl, as if daring him. It suddenly occurred to him that Levi wasn't trying to get away from Virgil after all. Maybe he wanted him to follow.

But he had no idea what it meant if he did.

Cresting a hill, he came upon a straight stretch of road that ran down into a broad valley and up again on the far side.

And there in the distance was the Audi, climbing out of the shadow of the hollow and starting up the incline. Levi wasn't driving particularly fast, not for a man on the run.

If Virgil's memory was correct, Fort Howard was ten miles or so past the top of the rise. As he descended into the valley, he found himself a little calmer, knowing he hadn't lost them. It was apparent now that Levi very much wanted Virgil to catch them. It seemed as if he was spoiling for a showdown.

Just like in the movies.

# TWENTY-THREE

Virgil turned off the gravel lane and drove the truck into the overgrown brush. He guessed he was a quarter mile or so from old Fort Howard, and he had no intention of driving up to the building, with Levi ready and waiting, presumably armed. Virgil didn't know for certain that Levi had taken the turn for the fort. But it seemed to be the play.

He parked and got out, the heavy musket in his hand. Walking around to the rear of the truck, he opened the tailgate and sat there while he loaded the antique weapon. He wasn't sure how much powder Will had used, so he did it by guesswork, reasoning that a little too much was better than a lot too little. He took a lead ball from his shirt pocket and drove it into the barrel with the ramrod, then slipped one of the little percussion caps on the nipple beneath the hammer.

When he was finished, he regarded the weapon unhappily. He was woefully under-armed; Levi was carrying a semiautomatic handgun that probably held a dozen rounds or more.

There was nothing to do about that. He'd brought this on himself—and on Georgia—and there was no point in dwelling on what he had, or wished he had. Being outgunned by Levi Brown made no difference at this point. There were no decisions to be made. Virgil had put the little girl in danger and now he needed to get her out.

With the musket in his right hand, he slipped the powder

flask into his hip pocket and started through the brush. The forest was mostly hardwood, second growth he would guess, smaller trees that were a foot or less in diameter. They were spaced fairly well apart and walking was easy. Above him sparrows and finches flitted from tree to tree, keeping ahead of him like riders on the point. When he was close enough to see the walls of the fort in the near distance, he moved through a stand of blue spruce, the smell of the evergreens strong and sharp to his nose. Through the heavy branches he saw the black Audi parked in the gravel lot by the fort's entrance. Plain sight. Levi was making no effort to hide its presence, or his own.

Virgil stopped by the edge of the clearing. The huge front gates of the fort were swung wide open and Virgil assumed that some of the crew had been there, getting things ready for filming. There were no other vehicles in sight now, though. The open gates were like an invitation that he had no intention of accepting. He walked around the edge of the clearing to the rear of the wooden garrison, toward the door that he and Tommy had used earlier. He stood there in the trees for a time, listening. There was no sound from inside the fort. As he waited he heard a distant thunderclap and looked up to see dark clouds moving in from the west. Finally, it was about to rain. Ordinarily that realization would have made Virgil happy.

But right this minute he had other things on his mind.

He moved quietly to the wooden door and pushed it open halfway, enough for a look inside. There was no one in his line of vision. He stepped through the opening, his eyes going at once to the ramparts up above. Still there was nothing to be seen, nothing to be heard. The place was eerily quiet, like the ghost town that it was. Staying close to the outer wall, he walked toward the buildings to his right—the remnants of the general store, the old courthouse, the jail. Glancing in the dirty windows, he saw nothing but cobwebs and dust. As Virgil moved cautiously forward, something caught his eye in one of the windows of the stable, some faint movement. Crouching down, he trotted to the wall, then straightened for a look inside. Georgia was there, standing unsteadily on an ancient two-wheeled cart.

She had a rope around her neck.

Virgil recoiled, flattening himself against the rough plank wall. Urging his mind to work, he recalled a back door to the stable, where the horses would have been led in and out in bygone days. He quickly moved around the building. The door was closed, secured by a rusty iron latch. He reached forward cautiously and tried the latch. It was locked. The image of the little girl with the rope around her neck was imprinted on his brain. Cocking the musket, he moved backward and with his heavy work boot kicked the door off its hinges and stepped inside.

"Virgil!" Georgia screamed.

"Don't move!" he yelled, his hand reaching toward her, even though she was fifty feet away. The cart beneath her teetered. Virgil saw now that her hands were tied behind her.

He felt the gun on him before he saw it.

"Good advice," Levi told him. "Don't you move, asshole."

He was standing inside the front door of the building, where he'd presumably been watching for Virgil's arrival. He was maybe forty feet from where Virgil stood at the back of the building, with the two rows of horse stalls between them. The wood planking immediately in front of him gave Levi cover, and he held the big semiautomatic handgun in both hands, the barrel pointed at Virgil's head. Virgil forced himself to look away, back to the little girl.

"Don't move," he told her softly. "It's going to be okay."

She was trying hard not to cry. "I'm scared."

"I know," Virgil said, and he turned to Levi. "Let her go."

"You don't tell me what to do," Levi said, then, realizing what Virgil had in his hand, he smiled. "You brought a musket? You really are a fucking moron, aren't you?"

"Let her go. Please."

"I would, since you're asking so nicely," Levi said. "But that would ruin my little plan."

"Your plan doesn't have to include her. You've got me. Think about what you're doing. She's a child."

"She's a fucking child *actress*. They're all the same."

Virgil gauged the distance between himself and Georgia, trying to decide if he could cross the dirt floor quickly enough to get the rope off her. The cart was moving beneath her, back and forth every time she breathed it seemed. She was too far away, especially with Levi's finger on the trigger.

"What's this plan?" Virgil asked, trying to stay calm.

Levi smiled. "It's a beauty. And I came up with it like *that*." He took one hand off the gun, snapped his fingers. "I've always been good under pressure, man."

"Let Georgia go and you can tell me about it."

"Oh, no," Levi said. "She's a part of it. And so are you. In fact, you're the star. Without you, there is no plan. I guess I can tell you, since you're not going to be around later to hear about it. By the way, I'm giving you a bigger role, from dumb farmer to troubled drifter. Here's the pitch—you fell in love with Olivia Burns at first sight and became obsessed with her. You stalked her to the hotel and lured her outside with a cell phone you stole from the production company. You like it so far?"

Virgil was thinking that if he dropped to a crouch, under

cover of the stalls, he could reach Georgia. Maybe he could get the rope from her neck and push her out the window there. She could run for the gates, escape into the woods.

"It's a cropper," he told Levi. "But why did you kill Olivia?"

"Because she fucking deserved it," Levi snapped. "She slept with me and a week later she wouldn't even *speak* to me! Who does that? We made a connection, and she treated me like I was trash." He laughed. "Like I was *you*."

Virgil realized that he couldn't make any kind of move toward Georgia. If Levi started shooting at Virgil, and that seemed inevitable, it would put her in the line of fire. He needed to think of something else.

"But what about this situation?" Virgil asked.

"This? This is simple. You were a godsend. Part two—after Olivia, you then became obsessed with our little girl here and kidnapped her."

"But people saw you leave the set with her," Virgil pointed out.

"I don't think so," Levi said. "I was watching. Everybody's attention was on setting up the Indian attack. And let's face it—it's going to be pretty easy for me to make a guy like you into a serial killer. A sick hillbilly with a star fixation. I chased you down—but got here too late. You killed two people. I had no choice but to take you out. You see?"

"Yeah," Virgil said. "I see."

Georgia was sobbing now.

"It's okay, kid," Virgil said. "He's just talking. But it's like a movie, he won't really hurt you. He's not that kind of guy."

"I'm exactly that kind of guy," Levi said, and he started shooting.

Virgil hit the floor and rolled on his side into the nearest horse stall, landing awkwardly on the musket. He could hear the wood ripping into splinters above his head. Georgia was screaming. Virgil got his feet under him and keeping to a crouch he scuttled along the row of stalls, moving away from the little girl on the cart. Levi kept shooting, following Virgil as he moved, the slugs tearing into the rear wall of the stable.

The firing stopped as Virgil reached the end of the building. He heard a metallic click and then something hit the floor. Levi was changing clips. Virgil stood at once, saw Levi behind the top boards of the stall, his face partially concealed by a post that ran to the ceiling. Virgil raised the musket and fired; the roar of the shot was deafening in the confined building. The musket ball hit the post inches from Levi's face, driving splinters into his cheek. He screamed, then hammered the fresh clip home and began firing again.

Virgil had run himself out of room, and Levi, knowing that he'd fired his one shot, got brave and came for him. Virgil could hear Georgia yelling, telling him to run. The open granary was behind him, a few feet away, across an open space.

Crouching low, he could hear Levi moving across the floor, stalking now, holding his fire. Virgil took a breath and ran for the granary. Levi opened up again with the .45; Virgil could hear the slugs thudding into the planking behind him as he ran. He threw himself onto the floor of the granary, smelled the musty odor of grain from decades past. Rolling over, his back to the wall and the musket in his hands, he fumbled with a percussion cap and slipped it in place, then pulled the powder flask from his pocket and dumped a heaping amount of gunpowder down the barrel. Levi had stopped firing again. Virgil could sense him, stealthily approaching the granary door, knowing that Virgil was trapped.

Hands shaking, Virgil reached into his shirt pocket for a

musket ball. And came up empty. They must have spilled out when he'd hit the floor earlier.

Now he heard Levi's footsteps a few feet from the granary door. Virgil shoved the ramrod into the barrel of the musket and scrambled to one knee. Levi stepped into the opening, both hands on the .45, like a gangster on film. His cheek was bleeding where the splinters had struck him earlier but he was smiling behind the barrel of the semiautomatic, his eyes bright.

Virgil swung the musket up, pulled the trigger, and drove the ramrod clean through Levi's body.

Virgil and Georgia sat on the tailgate of his truck in the overgrown parking lot of old Fort Howard. It had been three hours since Virgil called 911 on Buddy's cell phone. Police from various departments were still arriving. There were two forensic units on the scene—one from the state police, the other from the county. A sheriff and his constable, both from the little town of Butlersville, ten miles away, were roaming around like tourists, on the scene but out of the loop.

Virgil and Georgia had been interrogated separately by the county cops. Virgil had mentioned that Levi Brown had confessed to killing Olivia Burns, but he got the sense that his words hadn't carried much weight. He also got the sense that he was about to be arrested for killing Levi Brown. It seemed that the different departments were trying to decide who should do the deed. It was apparent that there was some confusion among the cops and he could understand that.

Claire arrived before anybody actually put the cuffs on Virgil, pulling up in a blue sedan to park beside his truck. She got out and, after regarding all the law enforcement vehicles on hand, walked over to Virgil. She gave him a look he couldn't read, then turned to the little girl.

"Hi," she said. "I'm Claire."

"I'm Georgia. This is my friend Virgil."

"I know your friend Virgil," Claire said.

"He saved my life," Georgia said. Her tone was rather conversational; she might have been saying that Virgil bought her an ice cream cone.

"So I hear." Claire looked at Virgil again. "I got the bare bones of it on the radio. So it was Levi Brown."

"Yeah," Virgil said. "She kicked him to the curb. Or so he said."

"He told you that?" Claire asked.

"Yeah."

Claire glanced at the little girl, not wanting to delve into things too deeply with her there. "Maybe she did but there was more to it than that. Sal Delano turned up an insurance policy on Olivia Burns for half a million dollars. Taken out by the production company but the signee was Levi Brown. And Sal's been hearing about a large loan Levi floated from some gangster last year, something to do with a movie that never got made. Apparently Levi had a habit of raising pocket money that way. This time it backfired. Sal doesn't have all the details yet but there's a giant Samoan with visa problems who's about to get talkative."

Virgil nodded.

"Are you a cop?" Georgia asked, noticing Claire's badge clipped to her belt.

"I am."

"Virgil's like a super cop."

"No," Claire said. "He's not."

Virgil looked away from her, to the crew of plainclothes

officers standing by the gates of the old fort. "I have a feeling they're about to take me into custody," he said. "Can you make sure Georgia gets back?"

"You can drive her back," Claire said after a moment. "I'll straighten things out with the gang over there, at least for now. I'll tell them you're not a flight risk, your past history notwithstanding. I'm sure they'll have more questions for you at some point." She paused. "And you and I are going to have a long discussion later."

"I kinda figured that." Virgil waited until she walked away, then turned to Georgia. "I guess we can go."

They walked around to get into the truck. Virgil started the engine and then, aware that the little girl was watching him, glanced over.

"Are you in trouble?" she asked.

"Maybe a little."

"Are you always in trouble, Virgil?"

"Comes and goes," he said. He put the truck in gear and the two of them drove off, heading into the heart of the Catskills in the fading light of the day.

# ACKNOWLEDGMENTS

They say that writing is a solitary game but if the truth be known, there are a lot of fingerprints on a manuscript by the time it hits the bookshelf. In that regard, *Shoot the Dog* is no different. So I would like to thank the following:

My editor, Daniel Burgess, and the terrific bullpen at Scribner.

Linda Muir, for delivering both advice and movie minutiae.

My wonderful agent, Victoria Skurnick, who always has my back.

And my friend, the lovely Jen Barclay, who still puts up with me even though she has been transformed from a quiet English lass to a Greek Goddess.

Printed in the United States
By Bookmasters